The Sin-Eater's Confession

ILSA J. BICK

carolrhoda LAB
MINNEAPOLIS

Text copyright © 2013 by Ilsa J. Bick

Carolrhoda Lab™ is a trademark of Lerner Publishing Group, Inc.

Carolrhoda Lab™
An imprint of Carolrhoda Books
A division of Lerner Publishing Group, Inc.
241 First Avenue North
Minneapolis, MN 55401 U.S.A.

Website address: www.lernerbooks.com

Cover photographs © iStockphoto.com/Nic Taylor (envelope);
© iStockphoto.com/Renee Keith (blood); © iStockphoto.com
/t_kimura (stamp).
Interior photographs © Julian Ward/Flickr/Getty Images (face);
© iStockphoto.com/Nic Taylor (envelope); © iStockphoto.com/
Renee Keith (blood).

Main body text set in Janson Text LT Std 10/14.
Typeface provided by Linotype AG.

Library of Congress Cataloging-in-Publication Data

Bick, Ilsa J.
        The sin-eater's confession / by Ilsa J. Bick.
          p.   cm.
        Summary: While serving in Afghanistan, Ben writes about incidents
    from his senior year in a small-town Wisconsin high school, when a
    neighbor he was trying to help out becomes the victim of an apparent hate
    crime and Ben falls under suspicion.
        ISBN 978-0-7613-5687-5 (trade hard cover : alk. paper)
        [1. Conduct of life—Fiction. 2. Murder—Fiction. 3. Hate crimes—
    Fiction. 4. Farm life—Wisconsin—Fiction. 5. Homosexuality—Fiction.
    6. Photography—Fiction. 7. Wisconsin—Fiction.] I. Title.
    PZ7.B47234Sin 2013
    [Fic]—dc23   2012015291

Manufactured in the United States of America
1 – BP – 12/31/12

**For those who think this can't happen:
this book's for you**

Look...to go through life and call it yours—your life—you first have to get your own pain. Pain that's unique to you.

—Peter Shaffer

OCTOBER 27

0223 (WHICH IS MILITARY TIME

FOR TOO DAMN EARLY)

TO ALL WHOM THIS MIGHT CONCERN:

Call me Ben. Okay, it's not Ishmael or anything, but the idea's the same. Wicked and repentant, that's me.

But here's the truth: I could be anyone from my town, or any soldier. People make assumptions on the basis of what they see all the time. In the airport, total strangers wander up and thank me for my service. Old guys want to shake my hand. Little kids want to know if I've killed anyone. And girls give me that . . . look. Come on, you know the one I'm talking about. And honestly? It's a little creepy. It's like I'm Batman. What everyone sees and imagines . . . it's not about *me*. It's the uniform.

Yet here's what they forget: the face in the mirror is the

mask. Way better not to peek or ask because that way, you never have to tell and they don't have to know. They see what they want. The mask doesn't slip. Everybody's happy you haven't rocked the boat.

So I'm Ben.

Right now it's dark, but I'm writing this by hand—yeah, a real, live, hi-tech ballpoint—because a computer's so bright you might as well wear a sign: SHOOT ME. I've got night vision, though, and a red penlight, and the moon is this glowing thumbnail sliver. Without NV, the snow shimmers silvery-white and the night's milky with stars. Cold, too, because we're in the mountains, and my fingers are stiff. So if this is messy, you understand. I've got a thermos of mint tea, but that stuff runs right through you and then you pee neon green in the NV. I know a marine who does piss angels. Which you'd think is sick, but isn't. I mean, this is Afghanistan—and just about as far away from Wisconsin as I could run.

––––––––––––

Anyway.

Reason I've started this now is because this lance corporal ate his gun about two hours ago. His buddy started bawling for a medic. (Actually, he screamed, "*Doc, Doc*," because that's what all marines call their medics. See? Not even *they* really know my name. It's all about the mask.) Anyway, there wasn't anything *I* could do except cover the mess with a blanket. The buddy was pretty freaked out. Not screaming-hysterical. These are marines, after all. But he was shook. Crying, moaning. Had a bad case of the *shoulda-coulda-wouldas*: how he *shoulda* seen this coming, and then maybe he *coulda* done something for his buddy, and then the dead dude *woulda* gotten help. Guilt—like God—is real big over here because life is so frigging random.

Things went downhill when the senior NCO arrived on scene about thirty minutes later. He's like a cartoon, a bull-necked jarhead, the kind of guy who probably picks his teeth with his KA-BAR. Not five seconds after he got there, but he started in on the oorah-marine-speak: how they were tough and had to stick to the mission and blah, blah, blah. Went on about how the dead guy didn't deserve a real marine send-off, seeing as how he's burning in hellfire for deserting his unit because he ended his life in a way that wasn't God's will. Whatever *that* is. Guy's a real maniac.

Only he kind of has a point. I'm saying *sort of*, okay? With all the crap you go through here, when someone checks out like this, you're upset, you're sorry the guy's dead, but you're also kind of like: *Dude, fail on* so *many levels.*

Then you kind of freak out, because that same exit? No matter what that senior NCO says about brimstone and ever-lasting hellfire? Eating a bullet's occurred to you more than once. Because what's waiting on the other side can't be worse than the second that IED's triggered: that monstrous orange plume towering so high and bright and terrible your eyes melt if you stare too long.

Only, the hell of it is . . . you can't help but look. That tower of fire might be all that's left of the Humvee your buddy was riding. Looking away from his death would be wrong.

Because someone should remember how he died. Someone should get it right.

Someone.

Now, this is a true fact: everything can always get worse. In this case, it's our captain who's coming back from Kabul sometime tomorrow or the next day. Scuttlebutt is he'll ask for—insert air-quotes—*volunteers* for a mission into a village where we know the Taliban are strong. The *volunteers* will infiltrate, figure out where the bad guys are and, oh, try not to get shot. And did I mention that one squad already got its butt kicked, lost two guys last week? That's how bad this village is. Call me a pessimist, but I figure a *volunteer*'s got about a one in a bazillion chance of getting out alive. Trust me: this is a megabucks lottery you'd be better off skipping.

Except I don't think that I will.

Which is okay. It's time I got all this down and as fast as I can, without too many breaks. It's when you step away from something that you can change your mind or just flat-out not finish.

And then . . . we'll see. It might be like a friend once said: sometimes writing things out helps you see your path. Now I don't know if that's true. I'm not sold that writing or talking does diddly. But I'd like to believe that it might.

Because—trust me—I need all the help I can get.

I don't have all the answers to what happened back home, or why people did what they did, or, more to the point, why I didn't do what I should've. All I know is that I can't stand the secrets anymore. There's blood on my hands, which is ironic considering

I spend my days breathing in the stink of overcooked gore and flash-fried guts. Considering that, some days, I don't have time to wash the blood from my boots before the next dust-off.

Anyway, I need to tell someone what happened back in Wisconsin. Because I've been looking over my shoulder these past few years, and I guess I'm getting tired. It's the weight of it, all that horror and guilt and doubt I've swallowed back, bottled up. Kept deep down in the dark.

Everything happened almost three years ago. I was just a kid, a senior in high school. I've kept the secret all this time for a lot of different reasons. Mostly, I was afraid. That may sound stupid coming from someone who spends his days with bullets whipcracking around his head as he tries to keep soldiers from bleeding to death or figures out which ones are going to die no matter what. But I was seventeen and scared out of my mind. There wasn't anyone I could tell, not my mom or my friends or my little sister, and no way I could tell my dad, because he'd have put me in jail. I was just a kid.

The other thing is, even now, I'm not exactly sure *what* happened. That is, I think I know what I saw, but I was far away; it was night, and I wear glasses only they got knocked off . . . and, honestly, everything happened so *fast*.

The thing is, every story has a beginning that sometimes doesn't become clear until you've made it nearly to the end. Your life's story doesn't necessarily start when you're born, but maybe when you're five or ten, and your mother dies, or your dad runs off, or a tornado tears your house apart while you're cowering down cellar.

Or maybe your story starts when you're seventeen, and the life you thought you were destined to lead gets derailed.

Like the train you've taken to work for a million years suddenly slams another head-on.

I think: *Dude, that's me.*

So, I just broke my own rule. I stepped away. Mentally, and just for a sec. Put down the paper and my pen and took a couple minutes to look at the stars. This may sound stupid to you, but I never looked up much when I was home. I was always head-down, staring at my own feet, thinking about what had to get done before it was time to move on to the next assignment or essay or test. Now, I sometimes wonder if maybe the stars weren't put there on purpose so we'd *have* to stop walking and tip our heads and let the mask slip so you can really *see* all those lights of far-off places you've decided to forget but which have always been there. Come to think of it, I guess the stars are like memories. Just waiting for you to find them again.

Anyway, clock's ticking. So, the beginning.

Well, that'd be where I'm from: a little town named Merit, about three hundred miles northwest of Milwaukee and an hour north of Wausau. Farm and timber country, mostly. The town's about two thousand people, so the school is pretty small, about five hundred kids altogether, and no more than forty kids to a grade. I was pretty normal. My parents weren't divorced; they still loved each other; no one had cancer; I wasn't abused; and my little sister was a pest. I was a good student, top of my class. I worked two jobs: one to look good for college and the other because it was the right thing to do. Which I'll tell you about in a sec.

So, yeah, normal. Maybe a little boring. Which I didn't have a lot of time to worry about because when you're normal, it's like the refrigerator's always full and you never have to put gas in the car. Bad things happened only to other people who deserved it.

I was way too busy to think about girlfriends. I mean, I had *friends*—three guys I'd hung with until we were about fourteen or so. Then I started to bear down on my studies, and they got girlfriends. We still saw each other in school, and they'd invite me to hang out, but I really didn't have time. I was busy. Anyway, there just wasn't anyone I was all that into.

The summer before my senior year, my mom was all over me about getting my Common App essays done before school started. My mom is a surgical nurse and was really hot that I should get into someplace like Yale, Cornell, Harvard. She'd lug home books from interlibrary loan: how to write killer essays, what colleges look for, the ten most frequent mistakes people make on their application, what *not* to say if you get an interview, and blah, blah, blah. Crap like that. She was a real maniac about it.

I tried not to think about *not* getting into Yale—my first choice from *her* list—although I had backup schools. How I was going to pay for school . . . I hoped that would sort itself out. My dad just didn't make that much as a chief deputy. There were scholarships, and I could take out loans. I just didn't want to. Starting out life after Merit with a mountain of debt wasn't appealing.

The real irony? I got a ton of calls from military recruiters, who fell all over themselves wanting to help me put together the money in exchange for a little quid pro quo. Only my mom always ran interference. Soon as she saw *US Govt* flash on that caller ID, she'd give that recruiter an earful about how no son of hers was going to fight an unjust war, blah, blah, blah.

So, yeah. I guess the last laugh is on her.

Anyway. That summer, I hunkered down at the computer, trying to think of all the exciting, amazing things I'd ever done and coming up with a big fat zero. I hadn't composed a symphony, written a novel, discovered a comet, or gotten mauled by a grizzly and then stitched myself up before racing through the forest—at night, in a snowstorm, with no shoes—to save the grizzly from getting shot by a squad of sharpshooters. About the most exotic thing about me was being from Wisconsin.

"What about the emergency room?" asked my mom. This was in August, about a week before school started. She pestered me at breakfast because coffee was one of my main food groups and she was into extortion. She held the pot over my mug but didn't pour. "Don't tell me *that's* not interesting."

If only. Volunteering in the ER, which I'd been doing for almost two years by then, meant I wheeled people to X-ray, cleaned treatment rooms, and mopped up blood. Sure, I got to *see* a lot of things: heart attacks, drunks, MVAs, moms who brought in their whiny little kids at midnight because the ER seemed like a fun place to hang out. I was even thinking that maybe being a doctor would be pretty cool. But I hadn't actually *done* anything because of liability and all that, though a surgeon let me put in a couple staples once.

Well, and then there was Del. But there was no way I'd write about him.

"There's really nothing." I held up my mug, hoping she'd get the hint. "Honest."

Mom kept the pot out of reach. "That's ridiculous. What about Del?"

"Absolutely not," said my dad, who was into his second cup already. He'd just switched from third to first shift, which he wasn't happy about at all. Normal people like being awake when the rest of the world is, but my dad really loved being chief deputy, and he especially loved third shift, when all the good stuff happened. Well, I don't know if he *loved* accidents, which he said were bad because, like as not, he knew the people involved. Sometimes kids my age got killed.

Like Del Lange.

That past May, Del had been on his way back from prom. His whole life ahead of him and then, boom! A head-on collision with some jerk so drunk he rolled right out of his car, not a scratch on him.

I was in the ER when the EMTs came crashing through, doing CPR on something that looked more like bloody hamburger than a person. The nurses and docs swarmed all over Del, and then my dad was there, his khaki uniform soaked purple with blood because he'd been first on the scene and done CPR.

After the Langes—Del's parents and his younger brother,

Jimmy—got to the ER, the doc and my dad kind of herded them into the back. A few seconds later Mrs. Lange started screaming, and they had to give her a couple shots and put her in a room.

Dad drove me home. I was pretty shell-shocked. I didn't know Del all that well as a person, but he was our star quarterback, good enough that he got a full ride to Minnesota. So, a big deal. Anyway, on the way home, Dad mentioned that the Langes ran that dairy farm, fifty head of cattle and about thirty goats, and those animals would need milking come morning.

Now, I'd never milked a cow. Or a goat. But every time I blinked, I saw the EMT straddling Del's body as the gurney clattered into the trauma room. I knew what the doctor had said that started Mrs. Lange screaming, and I couldn't shake the image of Del's brother, Jimmy: this skinny, sad kid standing by himself, face streaming with tears. So I told my dad, sure, I'd help with the milking.

And that's what we did, my dad and me and three other farmers who'd heard the news and came at dawn to help out. Sure, it was hard work. I had no idea how to attach the milk cups, and I wasn't in love with filling the manure spreader, which was just about the most spectacular fun I'd ever had in my entire life. But helping out was the right thing to do. The look on Mr. Lange's face when he came out to the barn later that day told you that.

You might think things like that don't happen except in movies, but they did in Merit.

Along with a lot of other things.

Anyway. Helping out at the Langes was how I got to know Jimmy.

Jimmy wasn't like Del, who'd been big and handsome and athletic and popular. Jimmy was rail-thin, shy, and very clumsy, as apt to get all tangled up by his own feet as anything. He was a sophomore when Del died, but I really didn't know him. The school let Jimmy finish out the year at home on account of school would've been up in two weeks anyway. I'm sure the school thought this was a kind thing to do, but if I'd been Jimmy and stuck on that farm during all that sadness? I'd have had a nervous breakdown. Mrs. Lange wasn't in any kind of shape to do much. After the funeral—where pretty much the whole town showed—she retreated to her bedroom and hardly ever came down for the first month or so after Del died.

Other people tried to help. The Langes were big into this new evangelical church in Hopkins, which was about twenty-five miles west of town. The first week or so, people from their church came by with casseroles and groceries and things like that. Only the flow of people out to the farm gradually slowed to a trickle, then stopped. After the first two weeks, I and one other farmer were the only people still coming by every morning and evening to help with the milking.

Anyway. One morning, I'm biking up the Langes' drive and suddenly catch a whiff of something burning. Then I spotted black smoke churning out of a kitchen window. At the sight, my heart jammed into the back of my throat, and I thought, *Oh crap.* I didn't have a cell phone, which I know sounds unbelievable, but phones cost money and my parents couldn't "see the need." I knew that biking to a neighbor's would take too long. So I did the only thing I could think of. I pedaled up that hill fast, thinking, *Got to get everyone out of the house* . . . My bike skidded, but I was already hopping off, slip-sliding on gravel. *And the cows, got to get to the cows, turn 'em loose in the heifer pasture up the hill, drive out the goats* . . .

Just then, the screen door *fwap-banged* and Mr. Lange plunged out, hollering bloody murder, clutching this big cast iron frying pan—which was on fire. Yes, it was; I swear to God. Mr. Lange darted to the hand pump and dumped the flaming pan into the cattle trough. The water hissed and boiled as steam sizzled into the air.

"Mr. Lange!" I huffed up. My lungs felt like they were going to burst. "Mr. Lange, you okay?"

He didn't say anything but just stood, looking down into the fizzing water, his chest going like a bellows. His hair was wild, and crumbs of sleep crusted the corners of his eyes. Then he swung around, fists bunched, face about as purple as a plum. "Jimmy!" he bellowed. "JIMMY!"

That's when I spotted Jimmy, still as a statue, on the kitchen stoop, this humongous red fire extinguisher in his hands. I remember how big and dark his eyes looked, like they were almost too large for his face.

"You *idiot!*" Mr. Lange bawled at Jimmy. Screaming, veins bulging, spit flying: "You *stupid* . . . aren't things bad enough without you trying to burn down the goddamned *house* . . . what the *hell*— "

You get the idea. I thought Mr. Lange was going to have a stroke. Me, I just stood there, completely paralyzed. I mean, I was only a kid; what was I supposed to do? After another minute of Mr. Lange yelling, I heard a truck crunching up the drive and knew that the other farmer was there to help with the milking, and I was never so relieved. The farmer eventually got Mr. Lange calmed down and walked him out to the barn.

Now, that whole time, Jimmy hadn't twitched so much as a muscle. Something about Jimmy standing there really tugged at me, the way movies about animals can get you all choked up. So I said, real casually, "So, you tried cooking breakfast, or what?"

Lips trembling, Jimmy nodded, his flop of brown hair fanning over his eyes. Even though he was only two years younger than me, he looked about ten years old. "I wanted to let Dad sleep, so I tried making bacon and eggs, only I got too much grease and it caught fire."

"Hey, at least you knew where the extinguisher was, right? Not many people can think that fast." I don't know why, but I reached out and smoothed his hair back. You know. Like he was my little kid brother.

Now, the cows were probably standing there with their legs crossed they needed milking so bad, but I fished the frying pan out of the trough instead. The pan wasn't a total loss, but it would need a good scrub and seasoning. I said, "Let's go check out the damage and maybe get you all some breakfast, okay?"

The smoke in the kitchen cleared up once we opened a couple more windows and Jimmy lugged down a fan from his room. I pawed around the cupboards for another skillet, and then I showed him how to scramble eggs, how to pour off bacon grease so you didn't get a fire, and how to use the coffeemaker. After about fifteen minutes, Jimmy really got into it, and then the kitchen started to smell pretty good.

Maybe ten minutes later, Mr. Lange and the farmer headed down from the barn, pushed into the kitchen, and washed up as Jimmy plunked down plates of bacon and eggs and toast and poured coffee. Then we all had breakfast. No one said much, though I caught Jimmy sneaking peeks at his dad from under his flop of brown hair, which just didn't seem to want to stay put.

Finally, Mr. Lange wiped his mouth on a napkin and said, "Jimmy, you think your mom might want a tray?"

Poor Jimmy, I wish you could've seen how his face brightened, all the fear and anxiety draining away. Maybe that was the closest Mr. Lange could come right then to saying he was sorry, I don't know, but Jimmy had that tray ready in no time. The other farmer said he was going back to the barn to keep on with the cows, and Mr. Lange went with him and only nodded at me on his way out.

When Jimmy came back downstairs, he was grinning so much I thought his cheeks would split. We finished the dishes, and then I showed him how to scrub out the char with salt and then oil up the skillet with Crisco and set it in the oven to season so that skillet would come out good as new.

Which it did.

I guess you could say that I took Jimmy under my wing. The summer passed, and I spent a lot of time at the Langes', not only with the milking but helping out with barn repairs and haying and working the forklift to move the really huge bales to the barn. All jobs Del would've done, I guess, although Mr. Lange started paying me after about a month. When I think back on it, I think he and Mrs. Lange were relieved to have someone

older for Jimmy to hang with, like Jimmy needed s
role model. Which I kind of wondered about.

Because I started to notice that things there we
strange.

At first I thought Mr. Lange was so hard on Jimmy because
of Del, who'd been everything Jimmy wasn't. But when you get
right down to it, Mr. Lange knew how to be mean. Like, if I was
lifting something really heavy—hay bales or sacks of feed—
Mr. Lange would bawl for Jimmy to do it. It wasn't like I could
argue. I was just a kid. So we'd stand there, the tiny muscles
in Mr. Lange's jaw working while he watched Jimmy struggle.
The more Jimmy sweated, his knotty little biceps balling under
his skin, the more Mr. Lange's face got this disgusted look,
like he'd stepped in a cow pie and tracked it all over the house.
Watching all this made me embarrassed and ashamed, like I
was standing by while Mr. Lange kicked a dog, and especially
because something always went wrong. A sack would break, or
the manure spreader would uncouple and dump cow poop all
over. Then Mr. Lange would swoop down and chew Jimmy
out: *What are you, some kind of baby needs his ass wiped?* Or: *You
keep this up, you are never going to be any kind of man to be proud of.*
Then Mr. Lange would yell at Jimmy to clean up whatever the
mess was and stomp off.

Of course, I'd help Jimmy after the fact—like some kind of
terrific big brother.

One blazing-hot August afternoon about three weeks before
school, we did the haying. Now, each square bale weighed

about fifty, sixty pounds, give or take, and had to be loaded into a wagon by hand. I did the lion's share because Jimmy just wasn't strong enough.

Loading the first batch took the whole morning, though Jimmy and I worked out this system where I'd hump ten or twelve bales onto the wagon and then Jimmy would put the tractor in neutral, hop down, and climb onto the wagon to help me straighten the bales to make that first base layer. Then he'd get back into the driver's seat, creep along the field until I'd hoisted another ten or fifteen bales onto the wagon, and then stop the tractor and do the whole thing all over again. Did that until we had four rows, and then Jimmy would chug over to the barn and back into the loft where, oh joy, we got to stack those bales again. Then it was back out to the field to wash, rinse, repeat.

We started at eight. By noon I'd sweated to a grease-spot. My clothes were sticky, my hands were swimming in the heavy leather gloves I had to wear so they wouldn't get all torn up by the baling twine, and my throat was as dry as the Sahara. There was so much hay stuck to my shirt I felt like a human pincushion, and my glasses kept sliding down my nose until I tied them around my head with some twine.

We'd finished hauling and stacking one load and had backed up the wagon to offload the second batch when we decided to take a break. I'd taken to bringing over a cooler so we could keep sandwiches and bottles of pop and Gatorade cold and not have to go into the house. To be honest, I just didn't want to give Mr. Lange a chance to get in any kind of dig.

Jimmy fished out a couple bottles of orange pop and some sandwiches while I peeled off my shirt and draped it over a rafter to dry. After guzzling our Orange Crush, we tore into the sandwiches: thick turkey with lettuce and tomato and mayonnaise. By the second bottle, I was feeling almost human and kind of dozy. So I took off my glasses and sprawled on some bales. The hay stuck and itched against the bare skin of my back and shoulders, but I was too tired to care and already dreading the rest of the afternoon. High above, a paper wasp droned in a heavy curtain of dusty sunlight.

I pretty much passed out, which you'd think would be next to impossible lying on itchy hay, but both doors were open and a northwest breeze lifted cool air from the lake and I was dog-tired. I dreamed, too: something confusing that involved the lazy hum of wasps and the chatter of machines whirring and clicking, like in the ER. My mind turned liquid, my consciousness rising and then sinking . . . and then Jimmy's voice cut through: "I'm really sorry."

"What?" I peeled back one gluey eyelid. Without my glasses, I saw a blurry Jimmy hunched on blurry bales with a blurry half-bottle of pop dangling from fuzzy fingers. "Sorry for what?"

"For all this. Not just the work, but my dad. Me."

"It's okay." It was just something to say. To be honest, talking about Jimmy's dad made me uneasy, like I'd accidentally opened the door to the bathroom while there was somebody on the can. "Uhm . . . you know," I floundered, still a little sleep-addled, "he's probably upset." I know: Mr. Eloquent. Give me a break; I was exhausted. "Was he, you know, so hard on you before Del . . ."

"Oh yeah," said Jimmy, "though not as often, because Del was always around. I never realized before how much he protected me. As long as my dad had Del, he pretty much left me alone. Now it's like my parents haven't got anything or anyone else to focus on. Like at supper? I'll look up and they're both staring."

"They'll get over it."

He shook his head. "I know they never have liked me the way they did Del. Del, they worshipped. If I left tomorrow, they'd be relieved."

If I'd only been half-awake before, now I was completely there. I knew these were secrets, things Jimmy hadn't told anyone else and maybe had barely acknowledged to himself. Knowing he trusted me gave me this funny feeling. It was kind of a rush that Jimmy saw me as the good guy, and I was proud that he could confide in me, knew I'd keep my mouth shut. At the same time, I couldn't escape this niggling sense that with secrets came responsibility: that Jimmy was laying his burden at my feet. As bad as I felt for Jimmy, I didn't need that, didn't want it. I had a life. In another year I would be out of this town, shaking the dirt from my shoes. I couldn't afford to get bogged down.

"Come on. It can't be that bad." I fumbled on my glasses, and Jimmy firmed up until there was just one kid with bits of hay poking from his hair and grass seed clinging to his shirt and yellow dust ringing the neck of his tee. "Just give it time. I mean . . . is it that you don't play football, or what?"

"Oh, Dad wants me to. They'd probably let me on the team out of pity, but I'd spend the entire season on the bench. What would be the point? Although, you know, if I got a little bloodied up, Dad would be thrilled. He'd think I was a man, you know? That I could take it on the chin."

Part of me wanted to ask Jimmy why he didn't stand up to his dad. I'd like to think that, if our roles had been reversed, *I* would've. Then I thought about college and those stupid essays and how my mom wasn't so different from Jimmy's dad. I loved my mom, but I was kind of burned out with her picking at me all the time. I mean, all *summer*. Sure, no question, I wanted to get out of state and be a doctor . . . Only *was* that my idea? It felt like it was, but at what point did what *I* want get all mixed up with what my parents, and especially my mom, thought? Like, does any kid have an original idea? Think about it. What's the point of school, really? No, not to see your friends, not in the beginning anyway. When you're little, it's to tell the teacher what you know. Right? Watch a bunch of little kids sometime, the way their hands shoot up and they're squirming all over their seats and wiggling their hands and going, *Pick me, oh, pick me.* You can see the pride when they've got the right answer, this big honking grin that just gets bigger when the teacher tells them what good kids they are.

But none of that is the kid's idea, not at first. It's a way of getting an adult to tell him he's a good person. Eventually, that morphs into getting good grades and even then you're performing for your parents, right? You want to make them happy, and their pride becomes yours. Like a dog doing tricks.

I didn't like where my thoughts were going. They felt . . . well, not dangerous but upsetting, like thinking this way was the first step to really throwing a monkey wrench into the machinery of my life and gumming up the works.

So I said, as much for Jimmy as me, "Look, things will get better. Just give it some time. Once school starts, I'll only be here on weekends and you'll have homework and stuff, so your dad will have to hire someone on to help out. You'll be off the farm most of the day, and then your dad can worry about something else." Then I added: "Besides, you ever get into trouble, you can count on me."

Okay, that was stupid. It was impulsive. But I said it anyway, like an idiot.

The worry lines in Jimmy's face melted. "Yeah?"

"Yeah. What are friends for?" And then I mussed up his hair, releasing a puff of hay dust that made us both sneeze.

Man. Would I live to regret all that.

———————

As we got ready to start hauling again, Jimmy said, out of the blue, "You know, Dad got me this job I've been doing for the past couple months, almost as soon as the funeral was past. Down at the Cuppa Joy."

Ugh. I knew about the Cuppa Joy, a Christian coffeehouse west of town run by the same pastor that preached at Jimmy's church, but you wouldn't catch me dead in that place. There were stories about how after they'd gotten a crowd to listen to a Christian band—usually local talent and most of them pretty terrible—they'd lock the doors. This kid I knew said it was kind of creepy because the pastor would tell you how you were this miserable sinner and going to hell and needed saving. Then the pastor would ask who wanted to accept Jesus in his heart. The kid said they wouldn't unlock Cuppa Joy's doors unless they saved a couple souls.

Personally, I didn't believe the locking the door part because that's illegal and I can't imagine the management would be thrilled about having to explain how a bunch of kids got crisped in a fire or something. I also wondered if coercion counted when it came to salvation. Sort of like the Salem witch trials. Confess, or we'll crush you to death with these stones. Oh, and if you're a witch, then we're going to hang you. Like that's some kind of choice.

"What's the job?" I asked Jimmy.

"Dishwasher. Bussing tables. It's not too bad. At least I got a cell phone, so I can call for rides and stuff on the days they don't let me take the truck." Now, Jimmy was only fifteen, but when you grow up on a farm, driving a truck is something you learn. "I think my parents figure this way I'll come around."

"Come around?"

"Yeah. You know, to being . . ." He faltered, got quiet.

I waited a sec. Jimmy had this very weird look, and there was more than one emotion warring . . . no, *begging*, for its place.

And I got to tell you: this was one of those moments I still wonder about because of everything that happened later. Looking back, I now realize that Jimmy's expression was both excited and . . . well . . . *scared*-excited. There's a big difference, you know. Like, there's *wow, I've got this really, really cool thing all bottled up that I'm just busting to tell*.

But there's also *I have this secret. It's terrible and huge and awesome all at the same time that I am dying to let out—and only to you. Because only you will understand. Only you matter. But I am also so scared because I don't really know what this means or what might happen next. If I tell, maybe everything changes—and not for the good. And I don't know if I can bear that.*

"Being what?" I asked.

It was a mistake, that question. I didn't know it at the time, of course—how could I?—and now it's too late. So I'll *never* know what he might have said, what he *wished* might come next, because I realize only now that, maybe, he'd hoped *I* would find the words for him. That maybe *I* was the other half of a story that neither of us truly understood had begun the day I slipped into his life: when I brushed hair from his eyes and showed him that not everything was ruined beyond repair.

If I close my eyes now, Jimmy floats there in the dark, and I can see at this very moment what I saw then, in the barn, on the hay: how his face smoothed, his expression not so much clearing as rearranging itself, the jigsaw pieces of a mask snapping into place as he caught the moment, snatched it back, and shoved it down deep into his gut where no one could see.

If that makes sense.

"Nothing." His eyes slipped away, and then he sighed, swirled the last of his pop and tossed it back. "It's nothing."

We worked the rest of that day. We didn't talk, mostly because the work was hard and it was hot—but also because I knew that whatever Jimmy had wanted to say *wasn't* nothing. There was more to this story. But I didn't ask.

The truth is . . . I really didn't want to know. Jimmy had his life. Whatever was going on had nothing to do with me. No way I needed to take on anyone else's problems. I had plenty, thanks.

By four my back was stiff, my legs all noodly from the heat, and then, oh joy, it was time to milk. My job was to clean the cow udders with an iodine solution and then wipe them with paper towels while Jimmy attached the milk cups. We had a system worked out by then that would keep me about ten cows ahead of Jimmy, and then while he finished with the cows already in the parlor, I returned the milked cows to their stalls and led in the next batch. Maybe halfway through milking, Jimmy said, again out of the blue, "Do your parents . . . I dunno, are they after you? Like, do they want to know what you want to do after graduation?"

"Sort of," I said. Maybe if I kept my responses brief, we'd just get past this.

Jimmy was quiet a sec, then said, "Like how?"

"Oh . . ." I dipped a cow's teats in iodine. "You know . . ." I mentioned my mom and medical school and then said, "Only sometimes I'm not sure if medical school's really my idea." Just as soon as the words tumbled from my mouth, I wanted to scoop them back. *Why* I went that far—admitted that out loud to somebody else—I don't know. In a way, it was like I was picking up where Jimmy left off. Only now it was me daring *me* to lay all my secrets in the sun where everyone could see—and me, most of all. Because once said, it couldn't be unsaid. I'd hear and I'd know—and so would someone else.

"So," Jimmy said, naturally enough, "what would you be if there was no one around to tell you what to want?"

Now I'd put my boot into it. "Well . . . maybe . . . I'd like to write."

"Seriously?"

"Yeah, you know . . ." The cow I was working on had a little stamping fit and it took me a second to calm her down. But that gave me time. This was real-life *don't ask, don't tell*. I'd never breathed a word to anyone about my writing. By then I'd done a couple long-winded, tortured, frankly embarrassing poems and taken several stabs at short stories, which I actually thought might not be half-bad. I'd gotten this idea of taking out an anthology of Stephen King shorts and then taking the theme of each one and seeing what kind of story came to me. One story—about a kid who couldn't decide if maybe his parents' spirits had gotten swapped out for aliens—I was kind of proud of. The rest of my stories were crap, though, and I knew it. But why was I telling Jimmy any of this? Bad idea.

"I'm honestly not sure," I said and turned it around. "What about you? I mean, you're doing college, right?"

"I hope so. Maybe. It's not just the money. I don't think my dad will fill out any of the financial aid forms."

"Why not?"

"Cuz." Jimmy was suddenly very intent on fitting cups. "He doesn't approve."

"What do you want to be? A terrorist?"

"No," said Jimmy, "an artist."

I did a double take. "Really? Like . . . painting?"

"Photography."

"Shut up. You mean, like a real photographer? Like *National Geographic*?"

Jimmy looked both embarrassed and kind of like he was about to bust a gut, he wanted to let out this secret so much—and, all of a sudden, this huge wash of relief swept through me, too: this sense of *so that's it; phew, no big deal; dodged that bullet.*

"Kind of," he said. "There's magazine work, and then there's portraiture and art photography. Del got me a pretty nice little digital camera for my birthday, and I figure on saving up for a better one and some decent lenses. If I can put together a good-enough portfolio, I might even win a prize or get scholarships so it won't matter what my parents do. There's this summer program at Rhode Island School of Design, and they give out a lot of money. So, yeah, maybe."

"Wow." I didn't know anyone the least bit *artistic*-artistic. "So what's the problem? Photographers make money. Some of them are pretty famous."

"I know. Like Annie Leibovitz. She did this awesome photo of Daniel Radcliffe. You know, Harry Potter? Only he's completely naked and crouched on this black horse—and together, they make something beautiful." Maybe it was the heat, but his face was flushed, a line of sweat standing on his upper lip. "There's also this old guy in the photograph, except he's got all his clothes on and so Radcliffe looks even *more* naked. But you also feel that there's no connection between Radcliffe and the old man." His voice got a little dreamy, his eyes fixing on something distant only he could see. "It's the horse Radcliffe's in love with. For him, people aren't really there."

I didn't know what to say. For a second, it was as if Jimmy had gone somewhere else where real people, like me, weren't invited. After a small silence, Jimmy blinked, his eyes sharpening on the here and now.

"Anyway," he said. "It's really amazing."

"So your folks don't want you to take pictures of naked movie stars?" I said it lightly enough, but all this talk was making me a little uncomfortable. I mean, it wasn't like I'd never been in a locker room before. Guys are always commenting, and some like to strut. But I don't think too many would admit if they stared.

"They just...don't approve. Of the photographers, I guess. Some of their reputations." Jimmy rinsed pails, so I really couldn't see his face. "They think those kind of people are a bad influence."

Those kind of people? "What do you take pictures of now?"

"Landscapes, mostly." He did a one-shouldered shrug. "A couple candids here and there. I like candids, because it's when they don't think you're looking that you catch people being themselves. Anyway, I'll probably do the yearbook and school newspaper. Some of the bands that play down at Cuppa Joy want me to do them, too. You know, publicity shots. I even get paid. I do them between sets, or before the band gets started. I figure this way my dad will see that it's not what he thinks."

"So your dad doesn't know?"

"That I'm doing this?" He shook his head. "He'd take away my camera."

Now, this sounded like a recipe for disaster. Whatever was going on had to be about more than just a kid wanting to be a photographer, and if his folks found out, things would end very badly. I could feel it.

Knowing what I do now, I wish I'd pushed Jimmy harder. Then all the bad stuff that came later might not have happened. But I didn't, and a few minutes later Mr. Lange came to bawl out Jimmy about how it was time to wash up and get ready for church, and that pretty much rescued me. I got out of there—which, you'll see, is kind of a recurring theme in my life.

I regret that to this day. If only I could've gotten out of my own way and really *talked* to Jimmy, those pictures wouldn't have come out and Jimmy never, ever would have gotten into that car.

Oh, the things you realize in retrospect: Coulda. Woulda. Shoulda.

School started. After a couple days, I didn't have time to worry much about what was going on with Jimmy. Besides all my regular classes, I was enrolled in calculus and advanced chemistry at the university extension. My mom's idea, of course. Between all that and my regular work and the college applications that I was still finishing up, I was pretty squeezed. Jimmy and I would occasionally pass one another in the halls, but I felt like I had to make an appointment just to take a leak. So I really wasn't paying attention, know what I'm saying? I had my life going.

One thing I did notice, though: he was always toting a camera around, snapping pictures for the yearbook and school newspaper. That, his parents must've approved. He also had to be earning plenty at the Cuppa Joy, because he had at least two cameras, one you could slip into your pocket and another, larger Nikon for which he had a couple lenses. We still saw one another on weekends, when I'd come do the milking twice a day, although his dad always seemed to be around. Jimmy didn't bring up his photography again, and it kept slipping my mind to ask. Or maybe I decided I just didn't need more responsibilities than I already had.

So I kept my mouth shut and steered clear. I was getting pretty good at that.

The third Saturday in September we held a college fair. This is where different places come to convince you they're the greatest schools on Earth. We do it every year, only I never saw a point to going because I already knew the only Wisconsin school I'd be applying to was Madison, as a safety school, and all the schools that came to the fair were either from Wisconsin or Minnesota, with the odd Michigan school thrown in for variety. I had to go that year, though, because I was president of the student council.

We got there early to help the schools set up in the gym and lug in the boxes of pamphlets and junk they gave away to try to get you interested: T-shirts, key chains, chocolate-chip cookies, bottled water with the school logo. Pizza. One school even had a raffle going for an iPad, which I thought was cool. I even listened to the sales pitch just to get my name entered. Mostly, though, I went around to the different tables to make sure things were running smoothly and to see if the reps needed anything.

The only guys who got no traffic at all were the military recruiters, which was a little strange because this was farm country. Like me, not every kid could afford college without a lot of help. Then, too, not everyone went to college—and no shame in that, by the way; where do you think your food comes from? Anyway, the military was always another option for some kids, but not that year. Maybe the uniforms put people off or, more likely, Iraq—where we still had boots on the ground, despite the beginnings of a withdrawal—and Afghanistan seemed endless.

On the other hand, the Marines' guy came in this amazing Hummer, painted red, white, and blue, with the Marines' logo and sword and things like that. A lot of parents didn't see any problem with taking pictures of their kids standing next to the Hummer. They just didn't want their kids signing up to get killed.

The fair lasted from ten until five, and the gym was packed with students from as far away as Wausau. People didn't finish trickling out until almost six, and then it was another hour helping the reps break everything down. The military guys took a while because they had to lug back out pretty much everything they'd brought in. I was helping the marine put away pamphlets when he peered at my name tag and then grinned. "I was wondering if you'd be around," he said.

I was puzzled. "Sir?"

"I called your house a couple times this summer." He stuck out his hand, one of the largest I'd ever seen, like a garden spade. But then again, he was also very tall, easily six-five: a giant with a buzz cut in a navy blue pullover sweater and khaki shirt. You wouldn't think the military would want such tall guys. They'd be easy targets, know what I'm saying? "Staff Sergeant Bruce Pfeiffer. Your mom's good at minding the gates."

"Oh. Yeah," I said as we shook. "Sorry about that."

"Don't be. Your mom's polite compared to a lot of other parents. At least she says good-bye before she hangs up. So . . . what are your plans?" He listened as I told him about Yale and a couple of the other schools I was looking at. "Wow, you've really set that bar pretty high."

I was embarrassed. "I don't expect to get in. To Yale, I mean. The others, I maybe have a shot."

"More than a shot, if your record's any indication." He must've read the surprise on my face because he added, "Because this school district gets federal funding, military personnel have access to your name, address, phone number."

"You're kidding. Isn't that spying?"

"I guess that's one way of looking at it. I prefer to think of it as the government gives and sometimes it asks for information in return."

"That doesn't tell you my grades, though."

"No, but I'm not stupid. Honor rolls are reported in the town newspaper. You're always on the high honor roll. So I know what your grade point average has to be, approximately." He flashed another grin. "The rest I gathered after your mom gave me an earful. So how are you going to pay for all that schooling?"

"Scholarships. Loans, if I have to."

"Fair enough. I don't suppose it would be worthwhile my telling you about ROTC?"

"I want to be a doctor. The Marines don't have a dedicated medical service."

"True, but the Marines get their doctors and combat medics from the Navy. What about the Naval Academy?" When I shook my head, he dug underneath his blue sweater and fished out a business card from a breast pocket. "Well, if you ever change your mind, or want to discuss some ideas of how we might be able to help you put the money together, give me a call."

"Thanks." I had no desire for the card but didn't want to be impolite. Plus, like I said, I felt sorry for him. It must've been hard, knowing that these days, virtually every mother in town believed that you were out to kill her little boy. I wondered if maybe he had combat stress and that's why they'd put him behind a recruiter's desk, but he didn't seem like the kind of guy who slept on the floor and ducked every time he came to an overpass.

The card was much nicer than I expected: a cream beige

with Pfeiffer's name embossed in blue and the Marine Corps symbol in gold. Tucking the card into my hip pocket, I hefted a carton of fliers and, as we started for the door, I said, "Mind if I ask you a question?"

"What I'm here for." Pfeiffer hip-butted the front door, and we passed under the breezeway just as the lights in the parking lot came on with an audible pop and buzz. Our vehicles, his Hummer and my truck, were the only ones still there. "Shoot."

"What's it like being a recruiter? I mean, it's not like you're a soldier-soldier, if you know what I mean."

"Yeah, I do, and it's a fair question." He looked thoughtful as he thumbed the Hummer's remote and popped the back hatch. "But, some days, it's not too different from being a soldier-soldier. Like this time a couple years ago, I saw this woman pulled over in the breakdown lane about five miles out of Quantico. Her hazard lights were on, but no one was stopping. Rush hour, you know how it is. I guess everyone figured she had a cell, she'd call for help. Anyway, I pulled over, jogged back to see what was going on. Well, that woman had a belly out to here and was in hard labor. Her cell was dead, and she just couldn't drive herself anymore. So I'm pulling out my phone when this other Jeep slots in front of mine, and out jumps this marine commander. *He* stopped because he saw *me*. That was the best of the Corps right there: a marine helping someone in distress, and a brother marine by his side." He paused. "I guess that doesn't really answer your question."

But I thought it did. "Do you miss combat?"

"I miss my brother marines. They're my family. When my time's up here, I'll request a deployment." He slammed the hatch down with an emphatic bang. "Killing people gives me no joy. Keeping my two nephews safe to enjoy their freedom does. But, mostly, it's knowing where I belong that matters the most. Anyway, if you ever want to belong in that world, you let me know, okay?"

We shook, and then he swung into his Hummer as I walked to my truck. What I noticed was he didn't pull out until I had. At first I thought he was following me. But at the exit, I signaled my left; he waved and chugged right in that big Hummer—and I realized he'd wanted to be sure I made it out okay.

Which felt . . . good. Warm. And a little upsetting, too. Like, I didn't want to have that kind of feeling. I couldn't afford it. I was going to Yale and then medical school.

So, no, I didn't tell my mom about the conversation. It would only have upset her.

But I remember all of it, even now, and especially the expression on Pfeiffer's face: proud, but also wistful and lonely, the faraway look of a caged animal remembering what it was like to run free.

At the time, though, the only thing I did was to slip Pfeiffer's card into my desk drawer, where I forgot about it.

Fall was early that year. Night started coming on fast, by 4:30, and the air got that knife-edged chill that cuts to the bone. By the second Saturday in October the leaves were mostly gone; the bare branches clawed the sky like gnarly fingers, and a small patch of pumpkins the Langes had grown glowed neon orange in a swath of setting sun.

I remember that Saturday in October really well. Mr. Lange was in town, I forget why, so only Jimmy and I did the afternoon milking. I don't recall trying to start much in the way of conversation with Jimmy. I was preoccupied, I know that. The deadline for Yale was a couple weeks away, and I still hadn't the courage to press <send>. I couldn't figure that. Wasn't Yale what I wanted?

Jimmy wasn't too talkative either. In fact, looking back on it now, I should've realized how anxious he was. He kept going to the door of the milking parlor and glancing down the driveway, then checking his watch.

We were just finishing up when I heard a squall of brakes and then a furious crunch of gravel as someone took the corner onto the Langes' property too fast. Startled, I cranked my head around and saw Mr. Lange's truck tearing up the drive, slipping and slewing on all that loose stone. There was just enough light so I could see there were two people in the truck.

Which wasn't right. Mr. Lange had gone into town alone.

I glanced over at Jimmy. From the look on his face, I could tell: he knew what this was about.

"What is it?" I asked.

Jimmy didn't respond. The truck roared up the drive past the house. Mrs. Lange rushed out of the kitchen, her apron still on, a towel in her hand. "Harlan?" she called. "Harlan, what is it? What's wrong? Harlan?"

But that truck kept coming, the grill grinning so big and shiny, it was a maw with bared teeth. Maybe fifty feet from the barn, Mr. Lange braked hard enough that the truck rocked on its suspension. Then the driver's-side door popped, and Mr. Lange came rocketing out, his eyes all buggy and his face as thunderous and twisted as a gargoyle's, like something out of a nightmare.

By now the passenger door was also open, and this lanky guy in jeans and black zip-hoodie unfolded from the seat. "Harlan," he said, wheeling fast around the grill, trying to head Mr. Lange off. I recognized him from Del's funeral: Pastor John, from their church. "Take it easy, Harlan, take it easy."

All this time, Jimmy hadn't said a word. Hadn't moved. He watched his dad come. There was something in Mr. Lange's hand that I thought was maybe a stick until he got closer, and then I saw that it was a rolled-up magazine. Mr. Lange's rage had made him bigger, more menacing, a hulk, and he loomed, blowing like a horse.

For a second, it was like we were all in this frozen instant of time. Like they talk about in physics class, where timelines go off in all sorts of directions. That point of decision when a different Mr. Lange spun on his heel before it was too late and went into his house. Or another Pastor John grabbed Mr. Lange from behind. Or a braver Mrs. Lange ran to shield her son. Or another *me* let go of the stupid cow I was holding and stepped between Mr. Lange and Jimmy, the way hero-kids always did in movies.

But there was only this timeline, and I did nothing. I said nothing. The moment came, then slipped past, and the river of time quickened.

Without a word, Mr. Lange clubbed Jimmy across the face. The sound the magazine made when it connected was like a jam jar exploding on concrete. Jimmy's head snapped around, and he staggered.

"*Liar.*" The word struggled up from some animal deep in Mr. Lange's chest. Mr. Lange hit Jimmy again, and this time Jimmy went down on his hands and knees. Mr. Lange clubbed him again and then again and kept going: "You *liar*, you *think* I wouldn't find *out*, you think I'm *stupid*, you think I'll let this *go*?"

My mouth dropped open, and my chest went tight like someone had cinched down a rubber band. The milk cow I held stamped her hooves and snorted and jerked her head. My mind was screaming: *Do something, somebody do something, somebody stop him! I'm just a kid, but you guys are adults! How can you let him do this?*

But they let Mr. Lange keep on. The adults did nothing. Mrs. Lange stood on the stoop. The pastor's face was unreadable. In the silence, there was only the grumble of the truck's engine and the scattered bleats of goats and the sickening slap of that magazine on Jimmy's back and head, across his face.

"Mr. Lange." My voice came out as a croak, barely audible. "Mr. Lange . . . Mr. Lange . . ."

At the sound of my voice, the pastor stirred and glanced at me, like he was coming awake. Or maybe it finally dawned on him that having a witness wasn't such a hot idea. "Harlan." His hands closed around Mr. Lange's forearm. "Harlan, that's enough."

At his touch, a tremor shuddered through Mr. Lange. He jerked around, and for a second I thought he might hit the pastor. But then his shoulders slumped and he was making these raw, grunting sounds that I recognized, belatedly, as sobs.

"Come on, Harlan," said the pastor. "That's enough now. You've corrected the boy. Let's all go in the house and sort this out."

"There's nothing to sort out," Mr. Lange said, his voice so ragged and raw it sounded like it must be cutting his throat. Sweat and tears glistened on his cheeks. "He's a *liar*, he's not my son, he's *filth*."

Hunched on hands and knees, Jimmy finally looked up. Blood snaked from one nostril. His chin was smeary, and his teeth were orange. He made a feeble gesture with one hand, reaching for his father's leg. Mr. Lange moved back with a little kick and left Jimmy grabbing air.

"Dad," Jimmy said.

"Get in the house," Mr. Lange rasped. He pulled out of the pastor's grip, stirring gravel that squealed and popped under his boots. He hurled the magazine, which flew across the yard, its pages fluttering like the broken wings of a bird, before it smacked into the barn. "Pick yourself out of the dirt and get out of my sight."

Without another word, Jimmy did just that. The knees of his jeans were torn, and the heels of his hands were raw. Incredibly, he looked at me. "I'm sorry," he said, palming blood from his upper lip. "I didn't mean . . ."

"I said, get in the house!"—and then Mr. Lange grabbed Jimmy's shirt and whipped him around. There was a ripping sound as Jimmy's shirt tore. Mr. Lange gave his son a mighty shove. Jimmy's legs tangled and as he went down, I had this awful moment when I thought Mr. Lange's foot would flash out and kick Jimmy like a dog.

"Get up." Mr. Lange's fists clenched, relaxed, clenched again. "Get up. Go on, get *up* and get out of my sight."

Jimmy did, but slowly, like an old man. When he reached the kitchen stoop, I think Mrs. Lange said something to him, but I wasn't sure and Jimmy never stopped. Shuffling past, he pulled open the screen door on a squall of hinges and disappeared into the house.

"And *you*." Mr. Lange rounded, his mouth working as if the words tasted bad. "Put that cow in her stall and don't come back here, *ever*."

I wasn't sure I heard right. "Sir?"

"You heard me. You are not welcome here. Don't ever show your face on my farm again, you understand me?"

Well, I *heard* the words, but it was like Mr. Lange was suddenly speaking Swahili. Confused, I looked at the pastor, who returned my look with an expressionless gaze—and you know what's weird? I remember that there was a word printed on the front of that black hoodie. *Fallen*, it said. Funny, how I remember that.

I wet my lips. "Mr. Lange, what's wrong? What about the . . ."

"Don't." Mr. Lange cocked his finger, like a kid with an imaginary gun. "Don't play innocent with me. Get. Out. Don't show your face here again. And don't ever, *ever* let me catch you with my son." Then he stalked over to the barn, swiped up the magazine, and followed Jimmy. The pastor trailed behind. Mrs. Lange was nowhere to be seen.

So I did what Mr. Lange said. I put that cow away in her stall and then I hopped on my bicycle and pedaled as fast as I could for home.

Where things only got worse.

It was dark by the time I made it home, but in the glow of an outdoor spot I saw my sister, Mallory, waiting at the head of the driveway. She was so revved she was bouncing on her toes, like she couldn't hold it one more second. "Oh my God, Ben," she cried. "Oh my God, have you *seen* it yet?"

I leaned my bike against the far wall of the garage. My shirt was clammy with sweat and stuck to my back. "Seen what?"

"In the kitchen. Mom's got it. This is so *cool*."

"I don't know what you're talking about." Sometimes Mal made, like, no sense. "What's so cool?"

"Oh my God, you don't *know*?" Mal's hand clapped her hand over her mouth. Her eyes were wide as saucers. She dogged my heels as I pushed into the kitchen. "Just wait until you see."

"See what?" I asked.

"Oh, *Ben*." Mom was still in her scrubs, and she sat at the kitchen table, a magazine spread before her. "Oh, honey, I'm so *proud*."

"He doesn't know," Mallory blurted before I could get word one out of my mouth. "He doesn't have any *idea*."

"Know what?" I was pretty irritated by now. "What are you guys talking about?"

"This." Beaming, Mom turned the magazine so I could see. "Isn't it *wonderful*?"

I will remember that moment—in that kitchen, by her chair— for as long as I live. It was then that I saw, for the very first time, what had so infuriated Mr. Lange that he would beat his son bloody and banish me. And yet this very same thing pleased my mother no end and so tickled my sister that she was fit to bust a gut.

It was the moment—the instant—that everything changed.

––––––––––

First, there was the headline, or whatever you call it in a magazine, all black caps: EMERGING ARTISTS: TEN PHOTOGRAPHERS OF THE FUTURE. My gaze scraped over the rest of the page, enough to figure out that some famous New York museum had run a youth photography contest and was announcing the winners.

Jimmy Lange's entries were on the third and fourth pages. That was because he hadn't won first place. But he *had* come in second, and that should've been cool and *was* . . .

Until I got a good, long look at the pictures Jimmy had seen fit to put right out there, in the open.

You know how you read about all the blood draining out of people's faces? I felt that happen, all the feeling and warmth flowing from my head and pooling in my toes. The room wavered.

Mal, sudden concern in her voice: "Wow, you don't look so good."

"Honey, are you all right? Come here." Mom pulled out a chair. "Sit down."

I did what she said. My hand shook as I dragged off my glasses, closed my eyes. My head had gone airy and my stomach fisted. In another moment, I thought I just might be sick all over those beautiful pictures in that stupid magazine.

I like candids. That's what Jimmy had said. *Because it's when they don't think you're looking that you catch people being themselves.*

Well.

Jimmy had caught me.

OCTOBER 27

0533

TO ALL WHOM THIS MIGHT CONCERN:

Nothing in life prepares you for something like that, nothing you've heard in church or school. Try finding hints for this in a cereal box, like one of those decoder rings: how a kid is supposed to feel about another kid taking pictures of him half-naked and then splashing them up for everyone to see and get ideas about.

You think I'm kidding?

———————

Even now, I see them so clearly. The pictures were black-and-whites featured on facing pages. The one on the left was of Jimmy's father. The picture was very simple and had been taken in the Langes' kitchen. I recognized the frilly curtains framing the window above their porcelain farmer's sink, and I could see a silvery gush of water suspended in midstream from the tap, which probably explains why Mr. Lange never heard that little snick-snap of the shutter. If he had, he'd never have let Jimmy put this picture out in the open.

Mr. Lange was naked from the waist up. His back was to the viewer. The hallway was dark, and the only illumination was a spray of light from a fixture above the sink. Mr. Lange's muscles were chiseled, like deep fissures in stone. His work-hardened hands rested on the lip of the sink, and his head was bowed, his face only a silvery blurred reflection in the window. The picture was . . . beautiful. Sad, too. Weary. Quiet.

The second portrait, on the facing page, was of a young man. A boy, really: asleep on a mound of hay, his shirt off, his right arm flung over his head and his face half-obscured in shadow as a bolt of sun, bright and luminous, broke over his lean, taut body. Beads of sweat on his chest and face gleamed like pearls. If you looked closely, you could see a pair of glasses cupped in one relaxed hand.

If that first picture of Jimmy's dad was of tender despair, *this* one spoke of . . . desire. A fierce kind of need and want . . . and love. Don't ask me how I knew that. It was all just *there*.

And it was me.

That shimmery young man—that boy—was me.

————————

As near as I can figure it, Jimmy must've thought that no one in town would ever know or find out. The contest was huge, open to any kid in the U.S. brave enough to send in a portfolio. Jimmy probably reasoned he wouldn't come close to placing. His was a Hail Mary, a chance in a trillion.

And when he *did* place? Made it first to the quarterfinals, then the semis? He couldn't share it with anyone, or even be happy. It was like that afternoon in the barn: an exhilarating secret that filled him with dread. Each time he advanced to the next level in that contest must've felt like the tick of a horrible countdown to a point of no return: him sweating bullets for weeks; thinking that this really *couldn't* be happening; worrying about what to do, how to break it to his folks. Hell, his winning might still have flown under the radar, because who, in our village, would ever bother with a glossy photography magazine? Right: no one. Except he *did* win, and someone must've tipped off the local village rag—we're talking a slim eight-pager—which picked up the story. Then everything unraveled for Jimmy.

And me.

"Ben?" Mom said. She put a hand on my balled fist. Swear to God, I was *this* close to cratering that table. "You really didn't know? Jimmy didn't ask your permission?"

"No." My voice came out all strangled, and that scared me because Mr. Lange's contorted face suddenly bloomed in my vision. I didn't know what I felt more: betrayal, shock. Rage. Confusion?

"Maybe you can sue him," Mal said.

"Mallory." Mom's voice was firm. "That's not helpful.

No one's going to sue anyone." To me: "I can understand you being a little upset. But you *do* have to admit: the pictures *are* beautiful."

Beautiful, my ass. I couldn't think with my mom and Mal around, so I grabbed that magazine and got the hell out of there before I . . . before I . . . well, I don't know. Before I did something. Don't ask me what. But *something*.

In my room, I scanned the rest of the article, which mainly consisted of gushing art critics. Of course, it just goes without saying, doesn't it, that they grooved on that one of me. *Reminiscent of a young Robert Mapplethorpe*, one said. *Filled with lush imagery, a sensuous and undeniably erotic lyricism*, another wrote.

So that was just really freaking great.

Mom knocked as I was googling Robert Mapplethorpe. "Do you want to talk about it?" she asked.

"Mapplethorpe was gay. He was *gay*. He died of *AIDS*, for God's sake," I said, blanking the screen, too embarrassed to let her see some of the pictures I'd pulled up. I mean, his pictures of nude women were just pictures: posed, but without much emotion and nothing truly beautiful. But his men—especially his portraits of black men—were a different story. I could imagine Mapplethorpe spending time trying to get the lights just right to emphasize their muscles, the angularity of their bodies—and other things that I didn't think you were supposed to stare at, much less *dwell* on, but which Mapplethorpe made sure were right there, front and center. Right in your face. Out in the open, daring you to look away.

Now, to be fair, Mapplethorpe had done a lot of celebrities, too. I really liked a black-and-white of Donald Sutherland in a trench coat and fedora; the curve of his eyebrow was just amazing.

But the male nudes kind of freaked me out, to tell the truth.

Because the thing was . . . I could see the echoes of Jimmy's photograph of *me* in *them*.

"I'm not gay," I said. Downstairs, the phone started ringing, and I waited while my mom shouted down at Mallory to answer it and then continued, "But now everyone's going to look at that picture and *that's* what they're going to think."

"Now why would anyone believe that?" Mom asked. "Granted, it's a very beautiful, sensual composition—"

"See, *see*?" I threw up my hands. "You just said it yourself."

Mom tipped me a look. "Sensual and *sexual* are not the same thing. Honestly, Ben, you're getting worked up over nothing."

"Then Mr. Lange is getting all worked up over a lot of the same *nothing*. He sure acted like it was *something*. He probably thinks Jimmy and I were . . ." I let that die. Just *thinking* it totally creeped me out. I didn't know any gay people. There weren't any in our school. Everyone knows there are no gay people in Wisconsin . . . well, except maybe Madison.

Then I thought, *Was Jimmy . . . ?* No, it couldn't be. He was just a kid, after all. Sure, I'd never heard of him having any girlfriends, but I didn't have any either. Didn't mean a thing. I was busy. I had stuff to do.

"Oh, honey." Shoving aside a stack of school crap, Mom perched on the edge of my bed. "I can understand that you're angry. Jimmy should've told you before he entered those pictures in that contest. But he probably thought he didn't stand a chance and, well . . ."

"What?"

"That picture isn't necessarily a bad thing. It might be very good."

"How you figure?" Then I got it. "Oh, great. You think Yale . . . ? "

"Why not?" Mom got this defiant look. "The Metropolitan is a very prestigious museum. If you're careful and word it right, you can put this on your résumé. You'll have collaborated on a work of art. Tell me *that* won't distinguish you from the pack. After all, you know what they say: the only bad publicity is no publicity."

This was just so typical. I wanted to shout, *Mom, catch a clue already.* She was like this 24/7: always scheming, trying to figure an angle to give me a leg up. But all I said was, "Mom, right now I have to go to school *here*. People are going to talk. The news is probably all over town by now."

"So what?" She folded her arms over her chest. "If people ask, tell the truth. You didn't know about it, but you're happy for Jimmy and flattered—"

I threw up my hands again. "Mom, five seconds ago, I was supposed to brag about my big artsy collaboration. Now you're telling me I should say I didn't know about it?"

"Only for local consumption." She threw me a withering look, like she was just disgusted I was being so thick. "Your college application is intended for a different audience altogether. As for this other issue, all you have to say is that you're not . . . not one of those people. That is . . ." Her eyes bounced from me to the wall and then the floor. "Unless . . . well, unless there's something you need to . . . ah . . . tell us?"

My cheeks heated. "*Mom.*"

"Well, honey." She was using her reasonable-mom voice, the one she pulled out whenever she'd thought of one more new project guaranteed to get me into the dream school of her choice. But you should've seen that glitter of dread in her eyes. She couldn't have begged me more emphatically to tell her she was wrong if she'd screamed it. "You've never had a girlfriend, you don't go out . . ."

This was unbelievable. "Because I'm *busy*! Everything you've asked, I've done!"

"Lower your voice . . ."

"Jesus, Mom, I'm in clubs; I run track; I'm student council president; I drive a frigging extra hour every day to take classes at the university extension . . ."

"Hey!" Mallory called up the stairs. "You guys, quit fighting!"

"Mind your own business!" To my mom: "To top it all off, I've got *two* jobs . . . until this disaster, anyway, because Mr. Lange doesn't want me back because *he* sure thinks Jimmy and me, we . . ." I couldn't say it. "So just when do you think I have *time* for a girlfriend?"

"Of course." Mom was patting the air with both hands, like I was this balloon of dough that she had to knead back into shape before I overflowed all over the counter. "I'm sorry. I shouldn't have said that. Of course, you're not . . ." She pulled in a deep breath. "I know you're very busy. It's just that we just have to . . . *spin* this to our advantage, that's all. We need to be on the same page about this."

"Spin."

"Yes," she said, firmly. "Those pictures are art. They're prizewinners, and you should be proud. Who cares what everyone else thinks?"

I care. Man, if *I* ever had a kid, I would never, ever forget what it felt like to *be* one. "So what am I supposed to do?"

"Sweetheart." Mom reached to brush the hair from my eyes, the same way I'd once done with Jimmy, but I jerked out of reach. An arrow of hurt darted across her face, and for some reason that made me feel both bad and angrier than before. Like, *now* I had to worry about *her* feelings, too? When was someone going to get all worked up about *me*?

"Tell you what: do nothing for the time being," she said, then added, "*here*, in town, I mean. We stick to the plan in terms of your résumé—"

"You mean, *your* plan."

She didn't bother to argue. "But if people in town ask, you tell them what we agreed on. If no one says anything, so much the better. Don't bring it up. Even if they do, it doesn't matter. In a week this will be old news. Trust me." She smoothed her scrubs and stood. "Everything will work out just fine."

The next day was Sunday.

The one good thing was that my dad was on first shift that weekend, which meant he was gone all day. Mom didn't try talking to me, and Mallory was out with her friends, so it was quiet around the house. I tried studying, but that was a complete bust. I kept thinking about how I never wanted to see Jimmy again. Then I'd get this maniac urge to go over to the Langes and maybe smack him around myself. I mean, what was he *thinking*?

Weirdly, what I did instead was go back to those Mapplethorpes and then, from there, to other photographs by people like Annie Liebovitz, who was, I found out, a lesbian.

Which was just so perfect.

Except their art *was* beautiful, and so much of it *was...* sensual. Like this nude of Lance Armstrong, muscles taut, hunched over his bike, and that photograph of Leonardo DiCaprio with a swan's neck twined around his. I truly *felt* those cords of muscle bulging on Armstrong's arms and hips and thighs: they were real; they had substance. The drape of that swan over DiCaprio's shoulders was an embrace.

But the picture I returned to that Sunday and for days afterward was the one of Daniel Radcliffe and the smooth, defenseless bow of his back as he huddled on that jet-black horse—and I couldn't help but remember Jimmy, hunched on the dirt, and the meaty sound of that magazine connecting with his face. How the adults—Jimmy's own mom, the first person you'd think would protect her kid, and that pastor—stood there and let it happen.

Still, I didn't get all gooey. Let's face it: Jimmy was also one messed-up kid. He'd effectively *stolen* my face. He'd exploited our friendship. What he had done to me might just wreck everything if I didn't do some serious damage control.

And you want to know what *also* ticked me off? The moment my mother worried that maybe, just maybe, I was gay. I wasn't. I knew that. No, no, scratch that: I know it.

I *know* it.

Monday rolled around. The mornings were too cold now to bicycle to school, and we lived too far out for the bus, which had been kind of a pain when I was a kid and my dad drove me to school in his cruiser (which is only cool until you're about ten). Like all law enforcement, the sheriff's department had a warehouse of stuff seized on drug raids or otherwise confiscated as abandoned or whatever. A couple years back, my dad had got this '88 F-150 Lariat XLT short bed on auction that we fixed up together. The whole operation took eight months, but now that truck was sweet: bright metallic blue, whitewalls, a blacked-out grill, and diamond-plate bed rails. I loved that thing.

Only that Monday? I would gladly have driven anywhere else but school.

Mal came with me. She was pretty cool for about ten minutes, and then she said, "I can't believe you didn't know Jimmy's gay."

"I really don't want to talk about that," I said, getting pissed. We drove in silence a few seconds while I fumed. Then I asked, "How do you know he's gay?"

"I thought you didn't want to talk about it." She must've seen the murder on my face, because she said, real fast, "Look, it's not, like, official? Like, he hasn't come out or anything. But he used to go steady with Sherry Strauss. This was last year, a couple months before Del died?"

"Okay." Jimmy had never mentioned Sherry Strauss. Why did I care about this anyway? "So what happened?"

"Nothing. We always thought it was stupid; I mean, we wondered what they did together? Sherry never talked about it, though; her parents are really strict, and she's taken this vow of chastity. She's even got one of those purity rings?" Mal had this bad habit of ending a lot of her sentences with a question. "Like, she said she's not going to do it until she's married?"

"Jeez. You guys talk about these things?"

"Of course. Don't guys talk about girls?"

Well, yeah. Mainly about which girl was hot or who you could date where you'd stand a chance of getting laid. There were a couple guys who were completely focused on that. I didn't join in, and honestly, I did my best not to hang around once they got talking about who might put out. Just never appealed to me. The whole thing kind of creeped me out. Not that I was gay or anything. It's just that they talked about girls like they were pieces of meat. Know what I'm saying? I mean, sure, I knew how to look interested and laugh at the right places and say things like how cool it must be to get laid, or wow, you really got your hands under her bra? But I really wasn't all that interested, and until that second, the fact that I *wasn't* hadn't bothered me either.

Except now it did.

Because I started thinking, *Shit, what if that means I really am gay?* My palms got clammy. Maybe this made a horrible kind of sense. I was the only person I knew who was sweating so much over college applications. I didn't go out. I'd never had a girlfriend. I'd never *kissed* a girl. And I worked *all* the time. I wasn't like the others, the ones I used to hang with, my friends. They went to *parties*. They went hunting together every November and snagged beers from their parents' refrigerators and got drunk and did stupid stuff like jump over open fire pits and puke into kiddie pools.

But the truth also was . . . I *did* have work, some of which I actually enjoyed. Getting drunk was stupid. There was nothing remotely cool about vomiting your guts into your little brother's baby pool. Besides, my dad was chief deputy. With my luck, the one time I get drunk and drive, he'd be the guy to pull me over.

"... so, really, Jimmy was a perfect choice," Mallory was still chattering on. "Because Sherry wouldn't sleep with him anyway? Jimmy probably doesn't know what goes where with a girl."

"Jeez. Mal." This was coming out of the mouth of my thirteen-year-old sister? "Give it a rest. You guys shouldn't be spreading rumors. You don't know Jimmy's gay. Even if he *is*, it's nobody's business. It's discrimination."

"Oh puh-leez," Mallory said. I could just *hear* the eye-roll. "Do you see anyone in this school coming out and saying, yippee, look at me, I'm proud to be a homosexual? *Hellooo*... this is *Merit*."

Well. When she put it *that* way.

As I swung into the school lot, heads turned and the elbows got going. Great. At least Mal knew enough to keep her mouth shut until the front doors. Then she bailed, peeling off to go be with a gaggle of her girlfriends, and they all started chattering like geese.

No one spoke to me as I made my way down to my locker. There were a couple girls on this old striped couch the principal let us put in the senior hall, and they glanced my way. One girl, Brooke, I'd known since we were kids and sort of played together. Well, until we got to about sixth grade and she went with her crowd and I found mine. Anyway, she was pretty smart, and we'd been lab partners in bio and chemistry. Brooke smiled and said hi as I walked past, but the other girls only clamped their lips so tight their mouths seemed to disappear. You know the look. It's the one that says the universe is laughing behind your back.

I half-expected that someone would've plastered my locker with that stupid picture Jimmy had taken, but my locker was the way I'd left it on Friday, thank God. I stashed my junk and pulled out my first- and second-period notebooks.

"Hey," said someone at my elbow, and I looked around to see Parker. Right behind were Mark and Robert, the other guys I sometimes hung with, though . . . okay . . . not since before the summer.

"Hey," I said.

"So," Mark said, "those pictures were pretty cool. Were they posed?"

"Mine wasn't." I slammed my locker. "Knowing Mr. Lange, I doubt he posed either."

Parker grunted. "Well, you could be like the Calvin Klein dude, you know?"

"Which Calvin Klein dude?" Like I knew any. Who looked at guys in underwear?

"Yeah, come on, you know," Parker said. "The one with the really good six-pack. Whathisname. He makes movies now."

"Wahlberg?" Mark asked.

"Yeah." Parker bobbed his head like those dogs you see on car dashboards. "Him. That's a sweet deal."

"Soooo . . ." Robert, who was the most serious of the three, gave Parker a speculative look. "You look at guy models?"

"No." Parker was offended. "I'm just saying. You can make a lot of money modeling."

"No way. You're crazy," I said.

"No, man, I'm serious."

"So am I."

"Whatever." Parker did an all-purpose shrug. "Your parents upset?"

"Don't know about my dad. I kind of doubt it. Not much upsets him. Believe it or not, my mom thinks colleges might like it."

Mark brayed. "*My* mom would be shitting bricks."

"Thanks," I said.

Parker clapped a hand on my shoulder. "Look, this is going to blow over in, like, five minutes. Don't worry about it. And you got to admit, it *is* kind of cool. How many people get their pictures in a national magazine? And win a prize?"

"Yeah, but I didn't win a prize." As I said that, I realized I didn't know what, exactly, Jimmy *had* won. I'd been too upset to care. "How much was it anyway?"

"Man, first prize was, like, two thousand dollars. So I'll bet Jimmy made a grand. That's real money." While I was chewing on that, Parker went on: "How people react is going to be based on how *you* react. It's like my mom's always saying. Three-quarters of winning is mental." Parker's mom was a sports psychiatrist. I knew she'd been hired for the football team after Del died. "If *you* act like you did something wrong, then that's how everyone else will see it, too."

"Maybe. But I didn't do anything one way or the other," I said. *And I'm not gay.*

"Exactly." He punched my shoulder. "Be a winner. Just go to class and screw everybody else. Besides, this is all going to be old news in a couple days, you'll see."

Robert looked doubtful. "I don't know about that. My dad said about six, seven years ago? These two gay guys had a house east of town, only one of them's in jail now."

We all looked at each other and then back at Robert. "Come on," Mark said. "I never heard of any gay people in Merit."

"Me neither, until last night. Dad said it was like this open secret. Like, one was a bartender and the other guy worked second shift at the plastics factory over in Ely. No one talked about the gay stuff, though everyone knew. Only a couple older kids, seniors, kept going by the house and doing things: egging the front porch, knocking down the mailbox, driving by at night and blasting their horn, crap like that. Their parents didn't do anything to stop them, and Dad said the sheriff kind of looked the other way."

No one glanced at me, but I felt them doing it just the same. Ignoring stuff didn't sound like my dad. Was he chief deputy back then? Come to think of it, why hadn't Mom said anything about this on Saturday night? How come *I* hadn't heard any of this?

"What happened?" asked Parker.

"The gay guys had a couple cats, and one of them was black, I guess," said Robert. "On Halloween, the kids got drunk and went over and strung up the cat."

"Jesus," Parker said.

"Yeah. Left it hanging on the front porch. The bartender was out, and I guess the other guy found it when he came back after second shift. Dad said the guy freaked out, jumped in his car, went over to one of the kids' houses where I guess they were having this Halloween party in the backyard."

"Then what?"

"Gay guy torched the house."

"Holy shit," said Mark.

"Wait a sec," Parker said. "You mean the old Fletcher place on Grove?"

"Oh my God," I said. I remembered that fire. Every kid knew the Fletcher place. Grove was only two streets down from the school, and the Fletcher house had stood on the corner. The house had been nothing special: white clapboard with black shutters, a tar roof. But I remembered the stink of scorched wood and molten plastic that hung like smog for a couple days after the fire. The four of us went after school to gawk. I was about ten, and fires were still cool, right up there with haunted houses and sandlot baseball. The roof of the Fletcher place was gone, caved in, and the second story completely gutted. But all I'd heard was *there was a fire*. Period. No other explanation. Another house, this one made of sturdy red brick, had been built, and the family there now wasn't Fletcher, but everyone in town still called it by the old name. "If the kids were there, why didn't they stop him? Or call the police?"

"They were in back," Robert said. "The gay guy broke down the front door, went inside, sprayed gas everywhere, and touched it all off before they knew what was happening. When the fire department got there, the gay guy was standing across the street with the gas can in one hand, laughing his head off."

"What happened to the gay guys?" Mark said.

"The one who started the fire's still in jail. The other one moved away, I guess. All my dad knew was he wasn't in town anymore, and I guess the kids' family moved away, too."

"How come we never heard this?" Parker demanded.

"Because. Didn't you hear Mark?" I said, grimly. "There are no gay people in Merit."

The warning bell rang, and we four went down the hall as a pack for the first time in what felt like forever. Now, I know what you're thinking. But I still believe that they really *were* being my friends—and if a little notoriety rubbed off, that was okay too. Fame by association. Back then, though, it just felt good, like my friends were closing ranks to protect me. When the other kids looked at me, I didn't feel so strange. At the T, Parker and the other guys peeled off to the right for English while I went left toward my first-period Russian history class. I was maybe two steps along when someone said, "Hey."

I turned. Now, this wasn't the first time Brooke had ever talked to me during the year, but she'd never gone out of her way to hang out either. No, wait, that wasn't right. Last June, she'd called a couple days before end-of-the-year exams and asked if I wanted to watch a couple movies, maybe play some Halo or Portal. I don't remember why I didn't go. She'd invited me to a swim party out at her house this past summer, too, but I was scheduled for the ER that night.

"Uh, hi." I glanced at my watch. "Sorry, I got to get to class."

"Me, too. Economics. Okay if I walk with you?"

"If you want." I shrugged, like it was no big deal, but my stomach was churning and that ticked me off. Like, I didn't need charity. I wished Parker and the others were still with me.

She said, "Look, I sort of need your help. I called and talked to your sister Saturday night, but you never called back."

I remembered the phone ringing and my mom yelling at Mallory to pick up. "Jeez." I stopped walking. "Man, I'm really sorry. Mallory never told me."

She visibly relaxed. "Okay. Good. I mean, as long as you aren't mad at me or anything."

"Mad? Why should I be?"

"Well, you know, there's the picture, and I bet the phone was ringing off the hook."

"Actually, no. Unless it was before I got home. I don't think people outside of school are much interested in who's *in* the picture so much as who *took* it." For the first time, I realized how chaotic this past weekend must have been at the Langes': phone ringing off the hook, people calling to ask if the Langes had seen those pictures and if they *hadn't*, well, they really *ought* to know, and blah, blah, blah. I'll bet a lot of people picked up that phone and told themselves they were doing the Langes a favor. People love someone else's disaster, the same way they'll slow down and have a good long goggle at an accident, hoping to see some blood and guts. Maybe Mr. Lange had started in on poor Jimmy all over again. "So . . . what did you want?"

"Well, I'm TA'ing for bio, and we're doing the worms? And I have to do the demo worm?" She looked sheepish. "The truth is, I never liked doing the worm the first time around. They're just . . ." She wrinkled her nose. "Wormy."

I laughed, and that felt good. "You want me to do it for you?"

She let go of a relieved sigh. "Would you? Ms. Frank said you had the best hands."

"No problem." By then we'd made it to our respective classrooms—well, hers; mine was the next hall down—and she asked if I could stay late Friday afternoon. I said sure, and that was that. I ducked into Russian history a few minutes late, and heads turned, but the teacher didn't miss a beat and kept right on going. Pretty soon everybody was scribbling like crazy to catch up to her, which you had to think the teacher had done on purpose.

Which was a good thing.

Anyway, I held it together until after second period, when I left for the university. I'd just pushed out the front doors when Mr. Lange's truck swung into the lot. Like that, a jolt of panic made my heart do this weird stutter-step. There was no hope of avoiding the Langes, not unless I turned tail and ran like hell back into the school, maybe ducked into the library. I might have done that, too, except I was already halfway across the breezeway and I'd just look like an idiot. Worse, I'd look guilty, which I wasn't. I hadn't done anything wrong.

Mrs. Lange saw me first. Her eyes got this doe-in-the-headlights look. Then she darted a furtive glance at Mr. Lange, who was fumbling with the keys and hadn't seen me yet. Her lips wobbled into a nervous smile. "Oh, hello," she chirped. Color spotted her cheeks. "How are you today?"

"Fine, thank you, ma'am." At the sound of my voice, Mr. Lange's head snapped up, and then his mouth corkscrewed so tight, it was like he'd gotten a mouthful of something nasty he just had to spit out before it corroded his tongue.

But then my eyes settled on Jimmy. He looked awful, tired and broken, like a little kid a pack of bullies had backed into a corner after school. The left side of his face was swollen into an angry purple-blue bruise, and his lower lip was puffy and split.

The rest of his skin was bled of color, like glass.

Just like that, my anger boiled away. Somebody—a teacher, the principal, *someone*—would see what Mr. Lange had done and report him. This was child abuse and illegal as hell, and weren't people supposed to protect kids from their maniac parents?

"Jimmy," I said. "What happened to your face?" Daring Mr. Lange to say something, I guess. I also knew I was safe. We were in public. What was he going to do? "You look pretty beat up."

"Now, wait just a minute," Mr. Lange began.

"It's nothing." Jimmy's voice was toneless and so low I almost didn't catch it. "One of the milkers got me. I didn't move fast enough, and she kicked me."

You didn't need to be Einstein to figure that was a flat-out lie, but before I could respond, his dad broke in. "We have nothing to say to you," he rapped. "Jimmy. Mary. Let's go." Like a drill sergeant.

Pinking, Mrs. Lange passed by without another word. As Jimmy followed, I said, "Hey, Jimmy, I'll see you later, okay?"

Jimmy didn't answer, but his father looked back, his lips just a gash above his chin. "The two of you have seen enough of one another as it is," he said. "You come near my son again and I'll bring charges."

My stomach kind of bottomed out. Don't ask me why I answered at all, but I did. "Sir, I don't know what you think has hap—"

"Let me *tell* you something." Mr. Lange was so angry, the corners of his mouth bubbled with foamy spit. "There are *laws* to protect children from people like you."

"Sir?" Any idea of defying Mr. Lange whooshed out of me like air from a popped balloon.

"Don't play innocent with me. You abused our trust. You sat at our table. I allowed you to spend time with my son, a young *boy*, and all that time, all that *time* . . ." He choked off the rest.

"What?" The knot of a terrible premonition slowly unfurled in my brain the way a rosebud suddenly blooms at the least hint of sun. *Abused our trust*, Mr. Lange had said. *A young boy* . . . "What are you talking about?" My voice came out high and tight. Horrified, I looked to Jimmy, but he wouldn't meet my eyes. "Jimmy, what did you tell them? What did you *say*?"

"You leave him out of this," Mr. Lange said.

"B-but, sir," I stammered. "I d-don't . . . whatever Jimmy's *told* you . . ."

"Don't," said Mr. Lange, and his upper lip actually curled into a sneer. "Don't pretend you don't know. You may be able to lie to your parents and everyone else, but Jimmy's a good boy and you are *scum*." He made an abortive grab at my coat, but I stumbled back. He settled for shaking a fist in my face. "I will not give you the *satisfaction* of losing my temper. You will not goad me. You sicken me, you're *filth*. Don't think that just because your father's chief deputy, you're above the law." He put his hand around the back of Jimmy's neck the way parents do when they steer little kids through malls. "Let's go."

What the hell? Stunned, I just stood there like an idiot, an *idiot* . . . I might've gawked after the Langes for the rest of that day if the school bell hadn't shrilled. Great, now I would be late to class on top of everything else. I forced myself to get moving on legs that felt disconnected and unreal, but it was only when I actually had to fumble out my truck key that my mind jumped tracks and I could think.

What was going on? What had Jimmy said? Mr. Lange was acting like Jimmy and I had . . . *done* things. This was a nightmare. I hadn't *done* anything! Even if I *had*—no, no, what was I thinking; that was so *sick*—wasn't that supposed to be private? Other kids had sex. I might not have been into dating, but I wasn't a moron. People were always hooking up, and just because I hadn't didn't mean that I was some kind of closet *pervert* or *gay* or . . .

Stop. I twisted the key, listened to the truck grind, then catch. Jamming the stick into reverse, I managed to back up without ramming anyone, then threw the truck into first then second and then I was peeling out of the lot, my head ready to explode and my eyes stinging with angry tears.

"What's going *on*?" I hammered the wheel with a fist. "I haven't *done* anything, what the hell, what the *hell* . . ." Shouting until I was hoarse, all the way to the university.

Just like the maniac Mr. Lange thought I was.

———

Of course, it was just my luck that Brooke was TA'ing third period and in the main office doing about a million worm Xeroxes. So, naturally, she was there when the Langes stormed into the office. Apparently, the principal hustled the Langes into his office pretty darn quick, and she couldn't hear everything Mr. Lange shouted. Maybe ten minutes later, Mr. Badden, the art teacher, hurried in. More muffled yells and shouts.

Eventually, Brooke's TA period ended and she had to scoot to her next class. But the whole story came out anyway because the walls weren't *that* thick and this was more excitement than the secretaries got in six months.

It turned out that it was Mr. Badden who'd encouraged Jimmy to send in his pictures. The art teacher even let Jimmy tinker around with his school copy of Photoshop, which Jimmy didn't have at home. (And *when* had Jimmy done that? Where had he found the time?) Mr. Lange wanted Mr. Badden fired, but the principal stuck to his guns and said that the art teacher hadn't misused school property and teachers ought to encourage students to go above and beyond and blah, blah, blah. That got Mr. Lange even more pissed, and he started shouting about the school corrupting public morals and encouraging perversion . . . You get the idea.

Oh, and that *cow-kicked-me* whopper Jimmy told? The principal bought it. At least no one ever reported or investigated, far as I know.

The long and short of it was this: the Langes pulled Jimmy out of school. The art teacher didn't get fired, but the school board did meet with the school district's lawyer and teachers' union rep in some big-deal emergency session. The lawyer and the rep said Mr. Badden wasn't negligent and the Langes had no grounds for a lawsuit and blah, blah, blah. Like that.

As for me? Well, I braced for a call, but the Langes never sicced anyone on me either. So maybe Jimmy finally fessed up and told the truth? Or they realized how crazy their suspicions were? Everyone knew I was a good person. I never would've done such a thing. If anything, *I* was the one who'd been taken advantage of, right? Hadn't their son used me? Wasn't *he* the liar?

Yeah, yeah, I know what you're thinking, especially if you're a grown-up or maybe from San Francisco. You don't believe people still react like this. You're still shaking your head over that story about the gay guys and their cat. You all probably live someplace where there are gay and lesbian and bi- and transgender teenager support groups.

Or you *think* you live in that place.

Because this is the truth.

No matter what the experts say, it's not the same as someone being Hispanic or African American or Hmong. You may not hear it, but kids talk about *those* kinds of people. Mallory and her friends *laughed* about it. Most guys my age can barely figure out how to *talk* to a girl without getting sweaty palms or feeling completely stupid because we wore the wrong shirt or showed up in a dorky jacket. Reputation's everything. So you expect that something like me and Jimmy maybe . . . that something like *that* coming out—if anyone was brave enough to say word one, which they hadn't up to that point—you think there wouldn't be consequences? People wouldn't talk or gossip or laugh? Or think you're sick?

Hah. HAH.

Remember this: everyone made assumptions about Jimmy— about *me*—on the basis of a stupid picture and a reference to a dead photographer who just *happened* to be gay. Mallory and her friends gossiped on nothing more than a feeling. Hell, if I'd been around when other people were cracking jokes about Jimmy, say, before Del died? I'd have laughed, too. I'm not proud about admitting that, but I also know I'm not a saint.

In school, that's how reputations are made and lives destroyed. Because the way kids approach you and what they think is all based on what they've heard, not who you are. What they believe is based on rumors on top of hints and lies and other rumors that keep getting bigger and bigger and only build on one another. Look what the Langes believed. Look what my mother thought. Yeah, yeah, she said she believed me—but no matter what she said, I'd seen that flicker of doubt and fear in her eyes. She worried that, maybe, I was one of *them*.

And, well . . . I was kind of worried, too.

You think I'm kidding? I was going crazy, second-guessing every move I'd ever made with Jimmy, every conversation. Like taking off my shirt in the hayloft . . . why had I done that? Yeah, yeah, it was hot, but . . . had I *ever* taken off my shirt before, in front of him? Did I do that at home? I didn't know, couldn't remember, but I didn't think so.

More than that, a couple times, I *touched* Jimmy, smoothed back his hair. Given him a hug. A *hug*. And the way I wanted to protect him . . .

Jesus. *Jesus.*

Maybe there was more there than feeling sorry for him. Here I'd gone out of my way to be nice, teach him things, to try to make things right for him at home.

So did that mean I was in love with him? Could you be gay and not know it? I didn't even know anyone I could ask about that. The couple Google searches I did suggested that I should kind of just *know*, but reading down the checklists made me a little queasy. The one thing that kept popping up, though, was that if I hadn't had, like, a relationship with a guy the way I would a girl, then I wasn't a homosexual.

That didn't exactly make me feel better. I mean, what if I hadn't because I hadn't met the right guy yet? I didn't have a girlfriend either and for the same reason.

This is the kind of stuff that can drive you nuts.

One thing I *did* know, though: I *had* to see Jimmy again. Going to his house was out of the question. I wasn't suicidal. But then I remembered Cuppa Joy. I could meet him down there. Anyone could have a cup of coffee, right? It was a free country. So I would go to Cuppa Joy on Friday after I was done helping Brooke. Just go down there, get a coffee, sit down with Jimmy and hash things out. Clear the proverbial air. That's what adults did, right? Talk things out?

Worst idea of my life.

OCTOBER 27

0700

TO ALL WHOM THIS MIGHT CONCERN:

The rest of that week passed in a blur of classes and a calculus exam I'd forgotten to study for but passed anyway because it was still early in the year and most of what the professor taught was review.

Parker was right, too. On Wednesday, some idiot got caught with a bottle of Stoli in his locker, and everyone moved on. I was old news, which was just fine by me.

Friday finally rolled around. By that afternoon, my stomach was doing jumping jacks. Brooke had reminded me about the worm dissection that morning, though I hadn't forgotten. The worm, I figured, would be a snap, but I was grateful to have something else to think about and someone to be with, if even for a short time.

The smell of formaldehyde, greasy and too sweet, wafted down from the bio lab as I walked the empty hall. The clap of my footsteps echoed, rebounding off rows of silent lockers. Brooke looked up as I pushed through the door. "Hey." She waved a gloved hand. A pair of safety goggles was snugged around her head. "I just got them pinned."

"Great," I said, tying on an apron, then fitting on my own goggles and tweezing out a pair of latex gloves. A set of dissection instruments—scalpel, forceps, scissors, dissecting pins—was neatly arranged on a green cloth alongside two baby-blue dissection pads. On each a single dark-gray earthworm had been laid out, with surgical pins securing either end. "Mr. and Mrs. Earthworm, the lucky couple. You care which one we do first?"

"No. I'll pin as you go along." She frowned as I used the scalpel to make a small incision to the side of and just behind the mouth of the male worm before switching out the scalpel for the scissors and forceps. "You don't use a scalpel for the whole thing?"

"Too easy to cut through the esophagus and intestines. This way you're going with the tissues, pulling them apart instead of slicing. Like this." Using the point of the scissors, I gently teased intestines from the worm's connective tissue just under the skin. "Want to give it a try?"

"No, thanks. I may never look at spaghetti the same way either."

"Yeah. Just wait until you do a tapeworm."

"Eeeww." Brooke wrinkled her nose, but in a cute way. "It's weird that the worms bug me, but you know what didn't and never did? The fetal pig dissection, it was just . . . really interesting. I mean, I got totally jazzed about dissecting ours, I couldn't wait, which is kind of sad when you get right down to it, don't you think?"

"How?"

"Well, you know . . . Never mind. It's stupid." She looked suddenly uncomfortable, as if worried she'd said too much.

"No. What?" When she didn't say anything, I persisted. "I'm interested. Really. What?"

"The thing is, I realized something when I was maybe halfway through the dissection. I was so focused on cutting up the pig, it didn't hit me until later that those fetal pigs are born for just one purpose: for us to cut up. And that's it. That's all they're there for."

"Well, technically, they're not born at all."

"Okay, *made*. You know what I mean. They're tools, and that's all. We don't even think twice about using up a life like that. Its destiny is to die just so a bunch of high school kids can see what they already know is there."

"Brooke." I eyed her through my goggles. "It's a *pig*. You get right down to it, a fetal pig isn't even viable. I also doubt pigs stand around all day wondering about their destiny."

"Wittgenstein said that if lions could speak, we couldn't understand them. Same goes for pigs or any animal. We don't know how a pig thinks. Besides, I read that pigs are very intelligent, right up there with chimpanzees and maybe smarter. A pig is just as intelligent as a three-year-old kid. So it's not like a pig doesn't have a life and feelings. It's people who don't want to see that they do."

There would be no winning this, I could see that. "Whatever you say." I returned to peeling apart that earthworm. "The only pig I know is Wilbur."

"*Sommme* pig," she drawled, and giggled.

––––––––––––

We fell into a comfortable rhythm: me filleting the earthworm while Brooke pinned the body wall to the dissecting pad. Dissecting and labeling both worms took about an hour and a half. It was nearly six and full dark by the time we cleaned up the instruments and put the pads with the dissected worms in aluminum trays, which we then filled with formaldehyde and covered with plastic wrap. Brooke slipped the pans into a refrigerator, where they'd stay until bio lab on Monday morning.

As we walked toward her hulking Dodge Caravan, Brooke asked, "You doing anything tomorrow night? I'm having a couple people over for a bonfire after the football game."

"Game?" I didn't pay attention to football and never went to games. Our school was so small they'd actually dropped football a couple years back, when only eight kids tried out for the team. I guess someone got upset, because a year later our school teamed up with a private Lutheran school the next town over. Between the two schools they were able to come up with enough guys to field a team. So you can imagine how good we were.

"Yes. You know, football? Guys bashing other guys, parents yelling, and brats that have been boiling in the same water since September?" A smile flickered over her lips. "And that's not counting what's going on in the actual game. We'll probably do hot dogs and popcorn and marshmallows at my house after. Very wholesome. Cross my heart. Not a keg to be seen. My mom's chaperoning, but she's cool. So, you want to come?"

"Uhm . . ." I thought about it. I planned on stopping by Cuppa Joy tonight and then working the ER until two A.M. I was scheduled for the ER on Saturday, too, and I had a ton of work to do for my university courses. "I probably shouldn't. Thanks, though."

"Okay," Brooke said, but she gave me a funny look.

"What?"

"You never go anywhere." She said it right out, not in a confrontational way, but with the hint of a question. "I never see you at anything you don't have to be at? Like, you know, student council stuff you'll do, but that's it."

"I'm just busy. I have work. All the classes I take usually test on Monday or Tuesday, and the university ones, you never know when they'll pop a quiz. I run so I can stay in shape for track. And I've got my jobs."

"We all have work. Lots of us do sports, but most of us make the time to have a little fun, too. Or just relax and be with people."

"I relax. I'm with people all the time." Okay, I'm not a moron; I knew that wasn't what she'd meant. But it was like the hackles bristled along my neck. If I'd been a cat, the claws would've come out, too. "Look, it's . . . I have a schedule. I can't help it if I've got a lot of work and tests."

"Okay, okay," she said again and put a hand up like a traffic cop. "No offense taken. Just . . . think about it. Here." She scribbled her address and phone number on a piece of paper. "In case you change your mind. I hope you do. People can only offer so much, and then they stop offering."

I'd reached for the paper, but now I froze. Was that some

kind of threat? What, people wouldn't like me if I didn't go to a few parties? Who cared? Or maybe this was a test. Maybe I was supposed to show up, maybe hook up with some girl—Brooke, even—just to prove that I wasn't gay. Why invite me now, after all? What was Brooke trying to do?

A mean little voice in my head whispered: *What do you think? You're famous now. You come to her party, she looks good.*

I know. It was so crazy. That didn't sound like the Brooke I knew—well, *had* known. She meant well. Her tone was friendly, like she was giving a piece of advice. So I tried clamping down on all the nastiness simmering in my gut—and didn't succeed. To be honest, I probably didn't want to.

"You know," I said, carefully folding the paper and slipping it into my wallet, "if I were a different kind of person, I'd think you were trying to cash in on my notoriety. Or maybe this is a mercy invite. You know, show everybody how cool you are, being friends with the gay guy."

"What?" Her lips parted as her smile evaporated. She put a hand to one cheek as if I'd slapped her. "What's the matter with you?"

"Oh, I don't know." I was shaking now, all the rage and pent-up frustration threatening to erupt, even as I knew that Brooke hadn't done anything wrong. But part of me wanted to be cruel and mean and small. "I'm gay—or everyone thinks I am, right? Because of Jimmy? Because if *Jimmy* is gay—"

"Who said *anything*—"

"Then that means *I* must be, too. Doesn't that explain everything? Of course, I can't control my impulses. No one's little boy is safe. Now all I'm good for is a laugh and making you look tolerant."

"Stop," she said. Her eyes glittered in the glow of the parking lot lights, and I knew she was crying. "Just shut *up*. Why are you saying these things? I'm just trying to be nice."

She was. I knew that. I was suddenly ashamed, and that made me angrier still. "Yeah, well," I said as I peeled off for my truck. "Thanks for the invite, but I think I'll pass."

She shouted something after me, but she was crying hard by then and I didn't understand a word.

It's a miracle I didn't wrap my truck around a tree, I was shaking so badly. What was wrong with me? I wasn't that type of person. I got along with people. Brooke and I used to be friends. She was thoughtful and kind. Heck, she cared about fetal *pigs*, for chrissake. I should call her and apologize . . . but I'd ruined things.

I rammed the heel of one hand into my forehead, like when you bash a vending machine to make it cough up your can of pop. What the hell was going on? I used to be nice. No, no, I *was* a nice person. I just wasn't the kind of person everyone else now assumed, and all because of that stupid picture.

I called home from the pay phone of a Quik-Mart on the east end of town. I wasn't sure what I would say. My ER shift didn't start until nine, and even before Mr. Lange had kicked me off his property, I usually came home for supper. I didn't want my parents to know I was going to Cuppa Joy, because then they'd have asked why and I wasn't sure I could explain. No, that's a lie. I knew all right; I wanted to strangle Jimmy, wanted to figure out how he could ruin my reputation like this and how he figured he had the right.

To my relief, Mal answered. I told her I'd worked late at school (true) and would probably start early at the ER (false), so I'd grab a burger or something (maybe true, depending on what happened at Cuppa Joy). Mal started with the questions but got completely grossed out when I told her about the earthworms and hung up. Which was exactly what I wanted. You'd think I lied for a living.

Cuppa Joy was set off by itself on the left along the main road heading east out of town. The building's front was stone with an illuminated marquee and multicolored Christmas lights threaded along the gutters. That weekend, a band called the Penitents was playing. From the glut of vehicles nosed in the dirt parking lot out front, the Penitents were popular. A line of cars and motorcycles snaked along the shoulder in either direction. Most cars had those little metal fish or bumper stickers: *Got Jesus?* Or *My Boss is a Jewish Carpenter.* Or *God is my pilot. I'm just here for the ride!* Like that.

There was a postage stamp of a paved lot in back, taken up with other vehicles and two dirt-spattered panel vans wedged next to a trio of dumpsters. If the Langes' truck was there, I didn't see it. Hadn't Jimmy mentioned that he had a cell so he could call for a ride home on nights when he didn't have the truck? On the other hand, Jimmy said he'd driven himself to work plenty of times. So if the truck wasn't here, he might not be working tonight. I didn't know if I could live through another week, working myself up like this.

Weaving through the back lot, I hooked a left, drove nearly an eighth of a mile, slotted my truck behind a pair of Harleys, and slowly walked back along the shoulder toward the coffeehouse. After the warmth from the truck's heater, I was shivering from the cold and jammed my hands in my pockets. My breath plumed. All I had was a denim jacket I'd worn to school that day. Now I wished I'd brought a heavier coat or a sweatshirt.

The front door was heavy, dark wood with an oval of frosted glass. When I grabbed the handle, the metal vibrated with the heavy thump of bass. The warm aroma of coffee and cinnamon billowed out on a swell of music and voices. I let the door shut behind me. I stood a second, allowing my eyes to adjust, getting my bearings.

The place was much nicer than I'd imagined, clean and well lit. The main room was shaped like an L, with a wooden stage at the far end. Colored spots hung from an open ceiling, and electrical cords snaked to mikes and amplifiers. Three-quarters of the way up the wall was the Cuppa Joy logo: crosses and little musical notes rising from a coffee cup instead of steam. Below that hunkered a drum set. At that moment, a thin girl in black jeans, black tee, and black hoodie walked onstage with two guitars, which she propped against wooden stools. The music I'd heard seeped from speakers in the ceiling, so either the band was on break or the show hadn't started yet.

The main floor was packed with people seated at tables as well as in plush stuffed chairs and sofas. A bank of booths lined the wall just to the right of the front door. What surprised me were how many adults were there, mixed in with students with textbooks and open notebooks. A lot of people were poring over Bibles, but there were also chess boards and backgammon sets wedged between plates and bowls.

The sight and smell of the food reminded my stomach

that I hadn't eaten since lunch. To my left, along the L's short arm, was a steel counter behind which stood a ruddy-cheeked, round woman. Above the counter, the menu was chalked on blackboards. Along the near wall were shelves that held Bibles, T-shirts, and mugs with the Cuppa Joy logo and necklaces with crosses of every size and description for sale.

I ordered a latte and veggie burger, then asked, "Is Jimmy Lange working tonight?"

"In back," the counter woman said, pouring frothed milk and jiggling the jug from side to side. She slid the latte across the counter. "You a friend of his?"

"Yeah." I saw that she'd swirled a dove and cross on my latte. I fished out a ten-dollar bill. "When does he have a break?"

"Oh, whenever he wants," she said, making change. As she held out the coins, she searched my face, and then the smile dribbled from her lips. Her face hardened. "You're the boy in that picture."

"Uh . . ." Even though I'd expected this might happen, the moment was still a sucker punch to the gut. There was nothing I could think of that wouldn't sound dumb, so I kept my mouth shut.

"Don't you think you've made enough trouble? You should leave that poor child be." She actually shook her finger. "He's got enough problems without you influencing him in unhealthy ways. Does your mother know about what you do?"

"Thanks for the latte," I said—I know; completely sarcastic and just not like me at all. But I got this nasty little jolt of satisfaction at the way her head jerked back: I knew I'd landed a good one. For a second I thought she might kick me out. Maybe I even hoped she would so I could raise a fuss, let fly something else. But then she grudgingly shoved a numbered placard and said they'd bring out my burger when it was ready.

The good feeling I had lasted about five seconds, the time it took for me to realize I now had to walk a gauntlet of tables and faces. To tell the truth, my knees went a little wobbly, and a fine, sick sweat slicked my face and neck. No one else seemed to recognize me, though. I passed two tattooed guys in leather chaps sitting on a sofa and sipping from delicate, teeny-tiny espresso cups, which would've been funny if I hadn't been so shook. I kept expecting an announcement to blare from the speakers: *It's him! That boy with the glasses, he's the one!*

I made a beeline for a free table in a dark corner tucked behind the left edge of the stage. The table hadn't been cleared, but I didn't care. I maneuvered my chair so my back was against the wall. Didn't need any more surprises, thanks. I used my spoon to destroy the cross and dove froth, then took a sip and promptly burned the roof of my mouth. My hand shook so bad, milky coffee dribbled over my fingers.

Take it easy. I smeared my fingers on my jeans and studied a fan of pamphlets strewn over the table, just for something to do other than wait around and dare someone else to figure out who I was. One pamphlet invited me to take a quiz designed to gauge the state of my soul. Others had such scintillating titles: *How to Avoid Hell* and *Doubt: Satan's Secret Weapon*. After a few minutes, the counter lady brought my burger and seemed disappointed that a lightning bolt hadn't reduced me to soot. And she left the dirty dishes from whoever had been there before me. Subtle. I chewed on the veggie burger, not really tasting it. When I tried to swallow, my throat closed up and I kind of gagged. For a second I thought maybe I was going to be sick. But no way I was leaving. No way I was going to let someone like her win.

That's when I spotted Jimmy hip-butting his way out of the back with an empty tray. He wore one of those white kitchen aprons with big pockets, a white tee, and blue jeans. I wasn't prepared for how I felt. My chest got tight. I tried to suck in a breath and couldn't. My gut twisted and flipped, and what little of the veggie burger I'd choked down threatened to come back up. I gripped my shaking hands together and jammed them between my thighs because, suddenly, I really worried that all I'd do was wrap my fingers around Jimmy's neck and squeeze. Oh, and the counter lady had reappeared and was peering around the corner, a cell screwed in her ear.

Be cool. My legs wouldn't stop jiggling. *Just be cool. You can do this.*

"Hey," I said as Jimmy walked up. I tried for light and friendly and only came out sounding lame.

"Hi," he said, colorlessly, with absolutely no surprise. Someone must've told him that the gay pervert child molester was here. He began gathering soiled plates. "Sorry about the mess. We've been kind of busy."

"It's okay." Now that he was closer, I could see that his lip was back to its normal size and the bruise on his cheek had faded to a mottled yellow-green splotch. "Uh . . . How are you?"

"Okay, I guess." His eyes flickered to my face and then away. "I'll get out of your way in a sec."

I surprised myself. "Can you sit down a couple minutes? Or if this is a bad time, do you have a break coming up?" When he didn't respond, I said, "Look, you could've bussed this table after I left, but you didn't. You know we need to talk. So, come on, sit down a second."

Again his eyes clicked to mine before he craned a look over his shoulder. The lady with the cell phone had disappeared. "Okay." He scraped up a free chair, dropped into it, studied the pile of dirty dishes for a few seconds, and then said, "I should've told you. I'm sorry."

"Yeah, you should've." For some crazy reason, I felt suddenly paranoid, as if someone might be eavesdropping. Those guys in the chaps . . . could they hear us? Who had the lady called? I hunched over the table so Jimmy had to lean in, too, until we were shoulder to shoulder. "Why didn't you just ask?" I hissed. "Why didn't you tell me? We could've talked about it, Jimmy."

He gave a miserable shake of his head. "I don't know. I thought you wouldn't let me. You know . . . use the picture."

"You're right," I said. "I wouldn't have."

"I know. Honestly, I didn't think it would go this far."

"But it did, Jimmy. Saying you're sorry after the fact doesn't make things better. Do you realize what people are saying about me? About *you*? And what did you say to your parents? I thought your dad was going to punch me out. What did you tell them?"

Jimmy wouldn't meet my eyes. "I . . . I don't know. They kept picking at me and picking. Pastor John worked on me, too, trying to get me to confess and repent." He said this last with such bitterness I almost felt sorry for him. "But it would be a lie. Because I'm not sorry I took those pictures. I'm sorry for what happened, though. And the way I felt." His Adam's apple bobbed in a hard swallow. His voice dropped to a whisper. "The way I feel."

The way I feel. His words were a red scream in my head.

I did *not* want to know this—and, at the same time, I did. I wanted him to say it out loud, maybe so I could say to him that, yeah, it was *his* feeling but not mine. Whatever was going in his head was not the same as in mine. We were not together in this.

Jimmy said, "They're still talking about sending me away, to some Christian school out-of-state, or maybe one of those fundamentalist ex-gay camps? They're all over the place. There's this one in Tennessee where they keep you, like, in jail or boot camp or something, until you change from being... from feeling..." His eyes clicked to mine and then away. "You know."

"No," I said, and then my fingers closed around one of his wrists. "No, I *don't* know, Jimmy. I have no idea what you're talking about. What did you say to your parents?"

"I told them how I felt about..." His throat worked again. His gaze crawled to mine. "I told them about, you know, what I... what you... what we did."

"About..." The rest dried up in my mouth. I closed my eyes. The darkness spun. "Oh my God. Oh fuck, Jimmy. How could you..." My stomach curled. I was sick; I was going to be sick. "Jesus. Shit. *Shit.*"

"They got me all confused." Jimmy's voice was dim, as if he was broadcasting over an old radio channel from another planet. "I never meant for it to go this far."

"This *far*?" My eyes snapped open. I still had Jimmy's wrist, and for an instant I thought how easy it would be to snap the bones, to crush them. I gave his wrist a sudden, vicious twist and, yeah, all right, I confess: I liked his gasp of surprise and pain. I *wanted* him to hurt. "Like you didn't mean for the picture to go that far? Like you didn't mean for your lies to go that far? Jimmy, don't you *get* it? We didn't *do* anything. I don't *feel* that way about you!"

"Wait." Jimmy was whimpering. In the dim light, his eyes suddenly shimmered. "Just wait."

"For what? For you to tell more lies?" A sudden heat flooded through my face. Hate, bitter and vile, bolted up my throat. I do believe that, in another time and place, I would gladly have killed Jimmy there and then, and to hell with the consequences. Because—my God—he'd worked me into some twisted little fantasy; told everyone I'd been a willing participant; that I was *like* him when I wasn't, I *hadn't*! I jerked his arm so hard the table tottered and my latte sloshed in a muddy brown swirl. "What you need to do is tell the truth! You want to confess to something? Confess to this: I'm not part of whatever's going on in your sick—"

"Hey, hey," someone—a guy—said. "Take it easy."

Seething, I jerked my head round, ready for blood. "Mind your own fucking—" The words died in my mouth.

Pastor John was there. "Looks like this *is* my business," he said.

Shit. I'd been so furious I hadn't noticed him at all. How much had he heard? It was then that I also realized how quiet the coffeehouse was. Except for a tinny twang of a steel guitar seeping from the loudspeakers, it was completely silent. No hum of conversation. No clink of cutlery or dishes.

And everyone was looking. The two guys in chaps, their tattooed biceps bulging like melons. The counter lady poised at the corner. Even the scrawny band roadie onstage was staring from the depths of her black hoodie.

"I'm fine. It's nothing." Then I spoiled it by snatching my

hand away. I must've looked so guilty. My hands were trembling so hard, I sat on them. "We're just talking. Everything's fine."

"Oh, I don't think so," Pastor John said, his tone all calm and friendly, like we were buddies here. He dropped a hand on Jimmy's shoulder. "Time to get back to work, Jimmy. Lots of dishes back there."

Jimmy got up without another word. Pastor John stood back as Jimmy hefted his tray. Jimmy didn't meet my eyes once.

Pastor John waited until Jimmy had disappeared into the kitchen. Then, hooking Jimmy's chair with two fingers, Pastor John twirled it around and straddled the seat, cowpoke-style. He was in his usual uniform: black jeans and tee and plain black hoodie. A hefty silver cross on a beaded dog-tag chain dangled around his neck. "Let's talk," he said.

"I didn't do anything." My voice came out way too loud in the quiet. I swallowed, the sound harsh and liquid in my ears. "We were just talking."

Pastor John showed his teeth in a wide *we're-all-okay-here* grin. "Good, then you won't mind doing the same with me. Listen," and then he leaned in a little closer. The smile was still fixed to his lips, but his eyes stabbed a dark look. "It is clear to me and to that boy's parents that your friendship has been . . . unhealthy."

I dragged my voice up from my toes. "Unhealth—"

Pastor John shushed me with a raised hand. That smile hadn't slipped a millimeter. "Please. There's no need for a scene. I'm not making any accusations, but I think that picture shows exactly what the feelings have been between you two. Now, for the record, I have nothing against you people."

He paused, as if waiting for me to protest or parrot something back, but my brain was in a kind of total freeze. When I didn't reply, he nodded as if I had, or my inability to speak somehow confirmed something in his mind. "But there's a vast difference between feeling something and acting on that. Of harboring a carnal, bestial urge and then taking advantage of and leading a confused boy into sin."

This was a nightmare. I wanted to leave, but I was afraid that would make me look twice as guilty. I was too scared to look away, and too shocked to know what to say. Looking back on it, probably nothing I said would've made a whit of difference. Pastor John's mind was made up, same as the counter lady, same as the guys in their leather chaps. Same as everybody. No matter what the truth was, Pastor John would decide I was lying.

It was also right about then that I thought that sooner or later this—whatever this really was—would make its way back to my parents, if it hadn't already. For that matter, maybe the lady with the cell was calling the sheriff. Then my dad would show up, and I really didn't need that.

"Fine," I heard myself saying. "I'm going."

"I think that's best. In fact, I think it would be better for all concerned if you stayed away from Jimmy. I would be more than happy to speak with you in my office, though." Pastor John tweezed a business card out of the pocket of his hoodie and dealt it to me with two fingers. "Call me any time, day or night. We could address some of your . . . *issues*. There's nothing God can't heal."

"Issues? I don't have any issues." I wanted to shout, but my voice cracked like a kid's. I flushed, the heat prickling my scalp.

I couldn't believe what was happening. This wasn't right. It wasn't fair. It wasn't just. All I'd done was try to talk to some kid who'd started the whole mess in the first place. I wasn't a raving sex maniac; I'd never touched the kid, never felt that way.

Unless . . . Jesus, if Jimmy *was* . . . did that mean something about me?

Because I had liked him. I'd wanted to protect him. I *touched* him—and I didn't touch anybody. Did I?

Stop it. My eyes sprang hot. *You haven't done anything; you don't feel anything.* I held that close, recited it to myself in a mantra. "I don't need healing," I said.

"Yes. That's what they all say." Pastor John eyed me with undisguised pity. "That's the first problem we'll have to work on."

It took every ounce of my self-control not to run when I headed for the door.

The wind had picked up. Blades of cold hacked my cheeks. I could smell the aroma of coffee steaming from my hair and clothes. God, I wanted a shower. Jamming my hands in my pockets, I hurried out of the lot toward my truck.

Someone softly called my name. For a brief moment I thought it was Pastor John, come to try and save my soul before it was too late. Why I slowed, why I turned, I will never know.

Jimmy slid from the shadows. He still wore his dishwasher's apron and was hugging his thin, bare arms. He darted a quick look over his shoulder. "I'm so sorry," he said. His words tumbled in a rush. "I never thought any of this would happen."

"You keep saying that." Jimmy was the last person I wanted to see right then. Worse, I didn't want anyone to see us together. "Forget it, don't worry about it." I turned to go. "Just stay away from me, Jimmy."

"Wait!" He scurried after, his sneakers slipping on loose stone. "I need your help."

"You . . ." I couldn't believe my ears. "You have got to be kidding me."

"No, really. You're the only person who would understand, who I trust . . . You said I could count on you!"

"Go back, Jimmy." Jingling out my keys, I picked up the pace. I wished I hadn't parked so far away. "They're going to be looking for you. If they see you out here with me, we're both going to have way more trouble than we need."

"Please." Jimmy scuttled to keep up. "Five seconds, just give me five seconds."

"No." I broke into a jog. "Go away, Jimmy."

"Wait." Jimmy skidded and went down on one knee. I heard his quick gasp of pain. "Wait," he said. Now his voice was watery. "Please!"

"Jesus." My breath came in a cloud that a finger of wind tore apart. Jimmy wouldn't give it up until I gave in. So I stopped running and waited for him to struggle to his feet. "What?"

"You remember that I told you about how winning meant I got a shot at that special camp? For art and photography?"

"Yeah. So?"

"So, now my parents can't refuse, right? There's the magazine article. I could go to a newspaper or something."

His logic seemed seriously flawed to me. "You were just *in* a national magazine. That's what started this whole mess. I don't see how more publicity's going to help you. Besides, you're still a minor. Even if you'd won first prize, so what? If they want to stop you from going somewhere, they can."

"Yeah, but not if I raise a big stink. Not if I go to CNN. That would be harder for them to shut down."

Jimmy being interviewed by Anderson Cooper was the last thing either of us needed. "You just got done telling me how they watch you all the time."

"That's why I need you. I have to send in a portfolio."

"Portfolio? You mean, other pictures?"

"Yeah. Studio pictures."

"Studio?" I was astonished. "You mean, like, professional? How did you do that?"

"Some of the days I said I was coming here to work, I wasn't. I went to this studio near Wausau."

"What? That's . . . Jimmy, that's over an hour away. How did you get there?"

"Took the truck. Dad let me drive it here, and I got one of the guys at the studio to show me how to set back the odometer."

It was true: he lived in la-la land. No one sane need apply. The fact that he was also pretty single-minded was . . . I don't know what it was. Hell, I could see my mom just eating that up; she was as focused and crazy-obsessed as Jimmy. But Jimmy was a liar. "You're nuts, Jimmy. You're a maniac. If you get caught, your parents will send you away."

He pushed right past that. "So now they're watching me so closely, I can't get to a post office. They won't let me drive the truck anymore. Dad takes me everywhere now."

"Yeah, well, sounds like you earned that." I turned away.

"I'm sorry, but that's your thirty seconds, and the answer's still *no*. I'm not getting involved in this. Drive yourself to the post office. Do your little odometer trick. Get a bike. Or use your cell and call a cab. Whatever you do, just do it far away from me."

"Look, it'll be easy." Undaunted, he danced alongside, his words riding on little breath clouds. "All I need is for you to get the pictures put on a flash drive and then mail the application. I'd do it myself, but they watch my computer. My dad got some program installed that follows every keystroke, and I only know about that because he came down on me when I was moving some files I hadn't cleared with him. So I can't burn my own disk or move stuff onto another drive. He'll see. But if I bring in the memory card, which I don't have to do anything to, I could give you a list and you could copy out the ones I want. The card's so small, they'll never notice. I'll write it all down, and then you can mail the package. I just got paid Wednesday, so I can give you the money for postage. Please." He latched onto my elbow. "If *you* needed help, I'd do it."

You're not going to believe this. I can hardly believe myself, and I'm the one who thought it. But until that second, that last little bit, I'd almost considered helping him out. Again. What an idiot. "Believe me, Jimmy, your kind of help I really don't need. Don't you realize what you've done? I didn't do anything. *We* didn't. You took a stupid picture without my permission, sent it in without my permission, and that's all, you understand? There's nothing between us, don't you get it? There *is* no us."

"It would be easy," he persisted. Swear to God, it was like Jimmy's mind was screaming, out of control, down this one-way track: no curves, no turnouts, no way off this runaway train. Or maybe he was just so desperate, he couldn't see any other alternative. "I take out the garbage twice a night. I can be by the dumpsters at seven tomorrow night."

"No."

"Please." And then he was fading into the shadows, heading back for the coffeehouse. "I'll be waiting."

"Then bring a jacket," I called after. "Bring something to read. Pack a snack. Because you're going to be waiting a long damn time. I never want to see you again, Jimmy. Not ever."

———————

That was the last time Jimmy and I spoke.

TO ALL WHOM THIS MIGHT CONCERN:

So you'd think that would be it, right? I was smart enough to get in my truck and drive away from Jimmy forever?

Hah. HAH.

After Cuppa Joy, I worked the ER, which hopped until after three Saturday morning. Two MVAs came in right after the bars closed. One was really bad because some fool had swerved around a deer. (First rule: Don't swerve. Hit the stupid deer. Splatter its guts all over the damned road. Better you and your family walk away.) So then the fool lost control, zoomed across the median, and crashed head-on into a van. Of course, the fool was driving too fast because he and his wife were coming home from some party and they'd had a few drinks. And it goes without saying there were three little kids in the van. Of course, two died, the mom was probably paralyzed, and one kid got choppered down to the big hospital they got at Marshfield because her guts were all exploded.

I slept late the next day. Crawled out of bed at noon, took a shower, went downstairs still scrubbing my wet hair with a towel. The kitchen counters were lined with plastic tubs of ice water. Mom looked up from slicing celery sticks as I poured myself a mug of coffee.

"Bridge club tonight," she explained. "Your father has a hankering for curry dip, and I want to try a new recipe for key lime bars. You send in your Common App yet?"

"Not yet." I dumped milk, spooned sugar, and stirred.

"I see," she said, plucking a radish out of a bag. She ran it under the tap, then sliced off the top and root before expertly carving a flower. After years of surgical nursing, my mom was pretty handy with knives. "Well," she said, carefully, and dropped the radish into ice water, "when were you thinking of doing that, dear? Or have you decided not to go early action? Because, honestly, I've been reading that it's better to get your application in early, so—"

"I'll get it in," I snapped. "I have homework."

"Don't take that tone with me," she said.

"Sorry." I washed my face with one hand. "I'm just tired."

Like that, she went from freeze to warm and gushy. "Oh, honey, I know. I heard."

My whole body tensed. What had she heard? Had someone from the coffeehouse . . . Had Pastor John or Mr. Lange . . .

Mom went to work on a fresh radish. "Your father said the accident was horrible. That poor family. He called while you were asleep and said to tell you that the little girl they took to Marshfield is going to live."

"Oh." I gulped from my mug. The coffee had been on the burner too long and tasted like toxic sludge. "Well, that's good."

For the next hour, I tried to concentrate on calculus, but it was hopeless. Then I decided, okay, time to get off my ass. So I went online and called up my Common App. Mom was right. All I had to do was press <send>. So what was I waiting for? Early action at Yale wasn't binding. I could always change my mind, assuming I got in. Assuming they'd allow alleged sex maniacs into their school. Maybe it was better if I set my sights lower. Like, just do schools I was pretty much sure I'd get into and not try anything risky.

In the end, I did nothing other than close out the program and try to take a nap. Yet my mind wouldn't shut down. I kept replaying what had happened in the coffeehouse in my head, like a video on an endless loop. It all came back to this: no matter what I said, everyone assumed that I'd done something to Jimmy—that we'd done something to each other, *together*. I still didn't know, exactly, what Jimmy had told his parents. But I had a pretty good—pretty queasy, creepy-crawly—idea, even if all he admitted was that he'd told them how he felt.

And what did that mean, exactly? He'd never really said. An attraction? In love? Or just strange, funny, *queer* something he couldn't put into words? Maybe he had a crush or something, and so he'd imagined something happening that day in the hayloft when nothing did.

"God." I turned my face into my pillow. Thinking about that made me sick. Couldn't people see, wouldn't they know that *feeling* a certain way and *doing* something about the feeling were two completely different things? Why was I being treated like a criminal? I hadn't done anything. I hadn't *been* anything but nice and responsible, a good neighbor. A stand-up guy. The only thing I was guilty of was caring about what happened to Jimmy.

And you touched him. That damn little voice. *You touched him, you brushed his hair, you hugged him, you—*

"Shut up," I said, just to hear my own voice. So what was I supposed to do now? Jimmy sounded so desperate. I know you'll find this unbelievable, but as angry as I was, I *did* feel sorry for him. He was counting on me to be the big brother he didn't have anymore and I'd led him to believe he could. That I had to own, because I'd told him: *you can count on me.*

Yeah, but . . . I flopped onto my stomach and pulled the pillow down around my ears. There were limits. I was the one everyone ought to be apologizing to. Absolutely no way I was showing up at the coffeehouse tonight. With my luck, Pastor John would be waiting behind the dumpsters with a lynch mob. They were all in on it, watching Jimmy like a hawk, quick to assume that my appearance at the coffeehouse meant I was up to no good.

And even if I got away with it? If Jimmy and I made the hand-off, and then he got into this program? Was he really naïve enough to believe that his parents wouldn't know I'd been involved, somehow?

———————————

Two hours later, I jolted awake, my sheets moist with drool and the hair on my forehead matted with sweat. My bedside clock said it was after four. I was due in the ER at eight. Stumbling out of bed, I dragged on my running clothes and headed out for a quick four-miler to clear my head. Then another shower, turning the water as hot as I could stand, letting it needle my shoulders, neck, and back as steam filled the stall and made the wallpaper bubble.

In my room, I shrugged into my black-on-black scrubs. My Angel of Death outfit, the ER nurses said, but since the hospital didn't provide scrubs for volunteers, they couldn't get too torqued about what colors I chose. Hair still damp, I quietly padded to the top of the stairs. The air was thick with the intense, meaty aroma of chili. In between the clatter of dishes and silverware in the kitchen, I heard the rise and fall of voices: my mom and dad, still getting ready for their bridge club.

Now was as good a chance as any. Tiptoeing into my parents' room, I gently lifted the handset from the extension phone and dialed.

The ER manager was cool about the whole thing. "Of course you can take the night off. You've earned it. We were just talking about what kind of social life you could possibly have."

Okay, what did *that* mean? Why were even they talking about me? But the only thing I said was, "So I'll be in tomorrow."

"Enjoy yourself," the manager said. "See you Sunday."

Dad was grating cheese when I came downstairs. Mom looked up from spooning sour cream into a serving bowl and smiled. "Just in time," she said. "I need your opinion about the chili."

Dad grumped. "I told her it's not spicy enough. Only good chili's one that makes you break a sweat."

The last thing I wanted was to sample chili, but appearances, appearances. Spicy cumin and cocoa-scented steam curled around my nose. Mom had used stew meat instead of hamburger, and the meat was juicy and fork-tender. The sauce tasted of roasted tomato that gave way to the bite of habanero and made sweat pearl on my upper lip. Really, the chili was fantastic. Under normal circumstances, I'd have asked for a bowl, but my stomach was doing flips.

"It's great," I said. "You're going to kill them."

"Well, *that's* no good," Mom fretted.

"Nothing a decent beer won't cure," Dad said. "On the other hand, you discombobulate 'em enough they can't bid and make seven-no again, that'd be okay."

Mom looked huffy. "That was *not* my fault."

"I've got to go," I said, hoisting my backpack. Honestly, all this bridge babble made no sense to me anyway. "See you later."

"Careful driving home from the ER," Mom called after, and as the door closed on them, I heard her say to Dad, "And the next time I say two spades, that doesn't mean you should jump to four . . . "

———————

The air was laced with the musk of dead leaves and wood smoke. To the east, the sky was darkening to a deep cobalt blue. The first stars shone hard and bright alongside a hangnail of moon. The hospital was northeast, but I drove southwest, heading out of town and in the opposite direction from Cuppa Joy. I punched up random radio stations, but the music did nothing to settle my jumpiness. Eventually, I jabbed the radio silent. The dashboard clock said I had another forty-five minutes before I was supposed to meet Jimmy.

If I met Jimmy. I still hadn't decided.

There were other cars on the road, but they thinned out as I took a two-lane country road toward Cedar Ridge, ten miles away. That gobbled up fifteen minutes. Outside Cedar Ridge I stopped at a 7-Eleven, bought some gas and a Slurpee, then drove aimlessly through Cedar Ridge, sucking on my drink which was too sweet and so cold it made my sinuses ache. On down the main drag and then south to a strip mall with a Target, Home Depot, Starbucks, and Burger King. I got out at the Burger King, used the bathroom, then got fries and a Whopper that I took back to my truck. I'd been hungry but couldn't manage more than a few bites before my stomach knotted up again. The fries tasted like salty cardboard. Now that the sun was about gone, the truck was starting to get cold and I had to turn on the heater to warm up.

I shot a glance at my watch: 6:55. It would take me almost a half hour, maybe more, to make it back to the Cuppa Joy. If I went. Was I going? Really doing this? Well, maybe. Sort of. I would be late, so Jimmy would give up, go back inside, and the lot would be empty. I would cruise by once and then leave.

Well, I'm sorry, Jimmy. I could picture us talking, me plastering on an earnest expression. *But I was driving around and then I got something to eat and by the time I got there, you must've already gone back in and, well, considering what happened with that pastor the* last *time . . . You understand.*

Until that moment, that very last second, I really thought I was going to bail. Drive around, maybe show up at the ER after all. Or go home and say that the ER let me off early because there was nothing cooking and I was really wiped from the night before, blah, blah, blah. Snarf down a bowl of Mom's chili and say hi to all my parents' bridge club buddies and then go into the basement and flip aimlessly. Maybe goof around on the Internet. Or just go to sleep. I'd been so reliable for so long no one would think twice.

The shoulder on either side of Cuppa Joy was clogged with cars and motorcycles, so many that I couldn't get a clear view of the back lot and dumpsters. The marquee said the Penitents were playing at seven and nine, so this must be the crowd for the first show. Just my luck. I did one drive-by, couldn't see a thing, thought about bagging it and then decided, no, I'd come this far. Park the truck, walk back, see if Jimmy was still outside. He wouldn't be. That's what I told myself. He'd have given up for sure, and I was off the hook.

Full dark now, and cold. I shivered in my thin scrubs and black sweatshirt as I trudged toward the coffeehouse. I wished I'd thought to bring something warmer.

There was no one out front coming or going, though I could hear the band seeping through the walls. Maybe that's why I didn't catch the voices until I'd circled nearly all the way around back.

The first thing I heard was a short, angry rap. No words, really, just the impression of a voice. A guy? A girl? I couldn't tell. This was followed by the kind of staccato up and down you hear when someone's *really* pissed.

Oh boy. I stopped dead, heart knocking against my ribs. Someone had wandered out back and found Jimmy, I bet. No way I was getting caught. For a second, I contemplated the merits of a quickly executed about-face and sprint back to my truck, but there was something in the tone of those voices that made me hesitate. They sounded . . . were they arguing? I couldn't be sure.

Then I heard Jimmy, very clearly: "*No!*"

That wasn't good. He sounded freaked. I'd already flattened myself against the building's cold stone. The lone streetlight at the other end of the lot provided the only illumination. Holding my breath, I peered around the corner.

Jimmy stood halfway across the lot in a wedge of shadow. I recognized the ghostly blur of his apron and T-shirt. He wasn't alone. His back was against the passenger's door of an aging Taurus wagon—and there was someone with him.

"*No,*" I heard him say again, but whoever it was—and I couldn't tell if it was a girl or guy because the light was so bad—said something else. A thin razor of light cut the shadows around their faces, just enough for me to catch the barest details of a profile: the angle of a jaw, a hank of hair. Then the light was blotted out as the figure in black pressed close, and then closer.

Against Jimmy.

Jesus. My throat squeezed shut. Was Jimmy . . . Were they . . . *Christ.* My eyes jumped away. I didn't need to see this. I felt dizzy and sick.

And—yes—angry. Because what the hell, what the *hell?*

But then I thought, *Wait. It's cold. Who's gonna do anything like* that *when it's minus ten? They might be just talking, the other guy leaning in so they're not shouting.*

I wasn't sure, though. Because the way they looked, they *might* be . . . God, I didn't want to even *think* about it.

Then my ears pricked at a new sound, this very faint metallic squall. I peeked again just in time to see Jimmy dragging open the Taurus's passenger-side door. The other person was circling around to the driver's side. The dome light flicked on for just a second, enough time for me to catch the peak of a black hood, before cutting out. The engine cranked, coughed; the headlights and tails flared, and I saw that a chunk of red plastic was missing from the left taillight. The car began to roll out of the lot. Not hurrying. No squeal of tires.

They were leaving. Jimmy had gotten his ride after all, I guess. When I didn't show, that must be what had happened. Someone else came out, caught Jimmy out back. Jimmy was forced to explain. They'd gotten into an argument, but then the other guy agreed to drive Jimmy . . . to drive Jimmy . . . My brain hitched. To drive Jimmy *where?*

Jimmy hadn't sounded right. You don't say *no* like that unless . . . Jesus. Unless *what?* And now someone was taking him someplace. Jimmy hadn't struggled; he'd gotten into that car. But something wasn't right.

He said no. I quickly trotted back the way I'd come, retracing my steps in just enough time to see the car turn right and head west. *I heard him say no.*

Yeah, but so what? This wasn't my problem. This had nothing to do with me. Jimmy and Black Hoodie were going somewhere. They'd been doing . . . *starting* . . . something. Honestly, I didn't want to know.

But why had Jimmy said *no?* Had he been afraid? Or were they only arguing? That had to be it. Jimmy had climbed into that car. No one forced him; there was no gun to his head. I was late, he got tired of waiting. But where was he going? He'd sounded . . . weird. Scared? So he might be in trouble, gotten himself in deeper than he even knew.

Even if that were true, what was I supposed to do about it? I could tell someone, but I wasn't sure what I could say: *Well, Jimmy got in this car with this guy and maybe they'd been making out, I don't know . . . Oh, what was I doing? Well, uhm, I was meeting Jimmy . . . No, no, nothing like that, he wanted me to take some stuff to get copied and then mailed because his parents weren't supposed to know.*

Oh, yeah, that would really fly.

All this sparrowed through my mind in maybe five seconds, long enough for me to sprint to my truck, an idea already half-formed in my mind. Down the road I could make out the faint fiery glitter of that car's taillights. I knew these roads and the countryside pretty well, having either driven or run them for years. Southwest was Cedar Ridge, where I'd been. Directly west lay a state park, a whole lot of country, a couple farms, and then Hopkins, twenty-five miles away. There was a Kinko's in Hopkins, open twenty-four hours. Jimmy needed stuff copied, printed out, and sent. So maybe they were headed there. That would make sense. Sort of.

And this was out of my hands, wasn't it? I wasn't Jimmy's keeper. I wasn't his brother. I was just a kid who'd tried to help—and look where that had gotten me. Better I should just go home. Right?

Right?

Following a car is actually a lot easier than you imagine. Who thinks to worry about getting tailed in rural Wisconsin? In the countryside around Merit, you can see forever where the land's not covered by forest.

I was able to keep a good distance between me and the Taurus, which was easy to spot because of that broken taillight. Ten miles out, a deer bolted across the road left to right, but I was going slow and a tap of the brakes was enough to bring the truck to a crawl. I waited for the other deer, surely following, to take their turns, because everyone knows: there are always more deer. Sure enough, three seconds later, a doe galloped across. I spotted four more in a clutch off the left shoulder, just waiting for their chance, drawing straws to see who got to try to make me crash.

By the time all the deer bolted across, the Taurus had pulled ahead. I was nervous about more deer, though, so I didn't speed up too much. The last thing I needed was an accident I couldn't explain. Eventually, I caught a firefly flicker as the Taurus braked and then hung a right. I knew what was out there: Cachemequon Lake State Park, spreading north and west. It was only a couple trails around the lake, picnic grounds, one platform shelter for big groups, and restrooms. No overnight camping, so the park would be empty. I also knew that the road was gated off at the entrance so anyone coming after dark would have to park and go the rest of the way on foot.

Wherever that guy was taking Jimmy, it was most definitely not Kinko's. Still, I rolled past the access road and kept going. Went on another two miles, fretting, then pulled onto the shoulder to think.

Clearly, Jimmy and his mystery friend weren't in such a hurry to get to Hopkins. Jimmy and his friend were going to a closed park. So, what if the person with Jimmy was . . . and they were . . .

You know.

Look, just because I didn't have a girlfriend didn't mean I was completely clueless here. I knew what happened in parked cars, regardless of what it . . . if it was a girl or a guy, I mean. Because Black Hoodie could be a girl, right? Sure.

And maybe I'd misinterpreted how Jimmy had sounded. Maybe he wasn't saying *No, don't do that*, but *No . . . don't do that* here.

"Jesus." I pinched the bridge of my nose. I could feel the thump of a headache behind my eyes. This was none of my business. What was I going to do, creep up on the Taurus and offer condoms? If I cared so much, I should've said something in the parking lot. I should've been on time and helped Jimmy. Then Jimmy would've gone back to work and no one would be the wiser.

Shoulda. Woulda. Coulda. You know the drill.

I should have done and said so many things. Instead, I was driving a lonely country road in the dark, wondering if maybe Jimmy needed help dealing with his girlfriend. Or boyfriend. Or whatever.

I almost went home. I actually reached for the ignition key twice but didn't turn it because here's the thing that hitched me up, made me think: Pastor John and all those eyes on Jimmy at Cuppa Joy. I remembered how cowed Jimmy was the night before. His desperation had been palpable. He was so freaked out by the idea that his father would find out what he was up to that he didn't dare go to the post office, for crying out loud. His dad was monitoring his computer. So this same kid is going to get into a car, willingly, and let himself be driven twenty miles outside town to go make out? When he should be working? There was something really wrong with the whole freaking scenario.

"You're nuts," I said as I cranked the steering wheel and got my truck turned around. "And this is not going to end well, Benny Boy. You just wait and see."

The woods closed in as soon as I turned off the main road and started winding along the approach road to the park's front gate. The woods were blacker than pitch. Maybe half a mile in, my headlights swept over a panel van off the left shoulder, and I slowed, then hit my high beams. In the sudden flare of silver-blue light I saw that there was no one in the front seat. An orange tag drooped from the antennae. Just a broken-down van waiting for a tow.

The trees pulled apart as I reached the park entrance. My lights cut across the Taurus nosed to the right of the main gate. Nothing happened as I rolled up. No startled, bleached faces darted out of sight, and the windows were clear. As in not fogged up. I didn't know if this was good or bad, but I do remember the distinct feeling of not being relieved. If anything, I would rather have come on Jimmy making out with someone, *anyone*. Then I could've hightailed it out of there.

Instead, I killed the engine. Listened to the soft tick of the muffler. Thought, *Okay, now what?* If Jimmy and his friend were headed anywhere, it would probably be the shelter. There were lights there, tables. I knew the way; I'd come running out here a couple times before.

But was I really going in after Jimmy? What could possibly motivate me to do something so stupid?

Here's what finally got me off my ass: the cold. It wasn't freezing out, but it wasn't comfortable either. Now, maybe Jimmy's mystery friend had blankets, but I kept remembering how startled and upset Jimmy had sounded. So, all I would do was take a quick peek, long enough to make sure Jimmy wasn't in trouble, and then I'd get out of there.

———————

Padding down a trail of trampled dirt. My ears tingling in the silence. The night was too cold for insects and frogs, and only the lightest of breezes stirred the bare branches and fingered my hair. The shelter was about a quarter mile in. Somewhere, an owl hooted, and a few seconds after that a second answered and they kept on, tossing calls back and forth as I moved down the trail. After ten minutes of creeping along without a flashlight, I sensed the woods opening up. Maybe a hundred feet further on, I caught the silver-blue sparkle of a flashlight and knew I must be close. I crept to the edge of the trail, keeping well back of the mouth and out of sight.

Ahead, I saw the shelter: a peaked roof and wooden supports over picnic tables on a concrete slab and open on all sides. The flashlight I'd glimpsed lay on a table. Leaning against the table, in profile, were two people—and one was Jimmy. I still couldn't tell who the other person was; his or her back was to me and so there was only that black sweatshirt.

A sweatshirt.

A black *hoodie*.

No. Was it, could it be Pastor John? No, that was nuts. *I* was wearing a black sweatshirt, for chrissakes. Besides, it might not be a *he* at all. I just couldn't tell.

All I knew for sure was that this second person's hands were all over Jimmy. Maybe Jimmy was struggling, but I couldn't be sure about that either. His apron was gone, and the second person was fumbling at Jimmy's waist and then . . .

Oh, Jesus. Not struggling.

Kissing.

They were kissing, mouths working, jaws pumping, and—

No. The sight knocked the wind out of my lungs; I couldn't breathe; my mind felt like it was melting. *God, no.* I didn't want to see this. I might have taken a step back, but I don't know. I do remember thinking how dirty I felt, and the next I knew, my glasses were in one shaking hand. I couldn't be *seeing* this.

High above, the owls called to one another: *whoo, who-whoo, whoo.* Owls were bad-luck birds, death birds, and I had to get out here, fast; get as far away from this place as I could and never see or think about Jimmy ever again. What an idiot, I'd been so *stupid.*

The next thing that came to my ears was not the mournful cry of an owl or a groan or anything you might think, given what was going on over there. What I heard was a shout: a ululation so wild and strange, almost a scream—and that sound was wrong, it was so wrong that my heart jammed up against my teeth.

Jimmy! Gasping, I looked, my eyes snapping back just in time.

Two figures rushed from the dark woods ringing the shelter. I couldn't see them properly; I still held my glasses in one hand. So all I know for sure—the only thing I could be certain about—was they wore black, and as they moved under the shelter's lights, I caught a flash of yellow hair. One, I thought, had a rock. A *rock*. I don't know how big it was. Bigger than my fist, I think, but the rock was wavery and out-of-focus and I was far away and so stunned, my mind was still catching up to what I thought I saw when I realized something else.

The second person was clutching a stone in one hand and a hatchet in the other.

And they went straight for Jimmy.

Jimmy's head, all an amorphous blur, whipped around. He screamed, but then the others were there. The blond swung. There was a sodden *thunk*, like the sound of my mother's cleaver chopping raw roast.

Like that, Jimmy's shriek cut out. A thick gout of black blood spumed in an oily geyser, and Jimmy went down.

And then I was scuttling away like a crab, one hand clapped to stopper the scream pushing against my teeth, my eyes wide and staring, bulging from the skin of their sockets. My heel hooked a root, and I toppled back. My elbows jammed rock; a searing sensation of pins and needles raced down both arms. My glasses jumped from my hand, but I was too paralyzed to move, much less search for them. I just lay there, my breath whistling in and out of my nose.

And I heard it all, every second: the attackers' grunts. The thud of stone against bone, a sound that went wet and mucky. The dull chop of metal on ... something: wood. Concrete. Meat. And, finally, a long, lowing moan that went on and on and on.

Oh God. I couldn't be hearing this; I couldn't be here! Frantic, I stirred the earth with my hands until I found my glasses only a foot away. Jamming them on, I staggered upright, clawing air.

And then I ran.

Christ.

I ran.

OCTOBER 27

1125

TO ALL WHOM THIS MIGHT CONCERN:

So, yeah. I ran.

I didn't save him. I didn't save anyone. I didn't spring out of the woods to help my friend; I didn't scream or shout or try to scare those guys away.

Instead, I ran just as fast as I could, my feet pounding beaten earth. Panic and terror swelled in my chest. I sped for my truck, tearing down the trail full-tilt, and then my shoes hit asphalt and I was back in the empty parking lot, the glimmer of the spot above the ranger's kiosk lighting my way. I didn't know how much time had passed since those men burst from the woods. (Had they been men? I thought so, but I wasn't sure.) I think I covered that half-mile or so in less than three minutes. The miracle of it was that no one came after me and

I didn't knock myself out running into a tree. Chances were, the noise they made beating Jimmy covered any sound I made. Lucky me.

I bounded for my truck, wrenched open the door, fell into the driver's seat. I was shaking so badly that I had to hold the key in both hands to slot it into the ignition. The truck caught, the heater roared. Then I jammed the stick into reverse, twirled the wheel, and sent my truck screaming down the approach road. Thinking, *They had to hear that.*

My eyes kept darting to the rearview, but no headlights winked into view. Good. By the time I sped onto the main drag I was reasonably sure that whoever they were, they weren't after me. But Jimmy . . .

"Oh my God, oh my God." The words rode on thin sobs. I was shivering like I had the flu. My palms were wet with sweat and so were my cheeks. Or were those tears? I could smell the metallic stink of my fear. Every time I blinked, I saw the fuzzy black humps exploding from the woods and the peculiar flash of the hatchet and that spurt of stuff that looked like black ink but had to be Jimmy's blood. I was gasping, white-knuckling the steering wheel, my foot like a hammer on the accelerator. The truck bulleted past clots of deer on the right and left, their startled eyes leaping like green meteors from the darkness. The road was an infinite tunnel through which I hurtled like a rocket, trying to reach escape velocity—and now I believe I must've thought about exactly that: getting away, and how it would feel to keep on going forever.

Looking back on all that, it was a miracle I didn't crack up and no one pulled me over. But the road was deserted. I kept on until I saw the lights of Hopkins and then, four minutes later, the Kinko's. There were three cars in the Kinko's lot, all nosed in at the front where the light was. I could see a couple people at copiers inside. I slotted the truck in the farthest, darkest corner and killed the lights.

And then I hugged myself. I was bone-cold, my teeth chattering—and I heard myself sobbing, the sounds raw and ragged like something had broken in my chest: "Nonono . . ."

I don't how long I shivered and moaned and wept, but it was a while, long enough for the warmth in the cab to bleed away. My thoughts were all tangled up. Every time I clutched at a thought and tried dragging it in, I hit a snag and then my brain jumbled and snarled.

I couldn't tell anyone. Could I? My dad? What would I say?

No, Dad, you don't understand; these two guys jumped out of the woods and they started hitting Jimmy. They had rocks and an axe, and I ran . . . No, I didn't do anything, I was afraid so I . . . What do you mean, what was I doing there in the first place?

God. I couldn't tell my dad that. I'd turned tail and run. I hadn't tried to help a kid who thought I was his big brother. Worse, a kid who had a crush on me, who'd taken a picture and started rumors. A kid everyone saw me talking to in Cuppa Joy, right before they kicked me out because I was mad enough that, yes, I wanted to hurt that boy something fierce.

Yes, Detective, I was angry with Jimmy. Who wouldn't . . . What? Well, I don't care what people saw or thought they saw . . . Yes, okay, I grabbed his wrist and I was angry. No, I wasn't following *Jimmy. Well, okay, I was following him . . . Yes, I agreed to meet him in secret. Yes, I lied about where I was going and I didn't think about the black scrubs and sweatshirt, not really, I wasn't trying to sneak around and hide, it's not what you think. No, I wasn't involved with him. I worried that maybe he was in trouble . . . I don't know what I thought I would do. I thought maybe if he needed my help . . . Yes, you're right. When he needed my help the most, I ran.*

God, that sounded awful, and I was supplying all the words. That started me thinking about what I'd really done, too. Not just a whole lot of nothing; I'd practically pushed Jimmy into this spot, hadn't I? If I was that worried about him, why did I sneak around? Why hadn't I said something in the parking lot? Oh God. Maybe I wanted something to happen to Jimmy. Parker's mom, the psychiatrist, she was always talking about how our unconscious influences what we do, how we talk ourselves into believing one thing while we really mean something else.

So, what if I wanted Jimmy dead?

What if some deep, dark piece of me, the one that grabbed his wrist and thought about how easy it would be to snap his neck; the guy who would follow a kid and then spy and get *pissed* . . . what if that version of me ran because that's what it hoped would happen?

No, that was crazy. I had to calm down, or I was going to make a mistake. None of this was my fault. I hadn't started rumors or snapped pictures or taken advantage of a friend. If I was going to get out of this, I had to be cool, get myself under control.

Drawing in a shivery breath, I dragged my sleeve across my streaming eyes. One of the cars in the lot was gone. That made me sit up. Had they seen me? Heard me screaming and crying like a maniac? As I watched, a guy pushed out of the Kinko's. I could tell from his walk that he had a cell phone at his ear. His face lifted; he glanced my way, but something about his walk made me think he hadn't really seen me. But then, as he reached his car, I thought he glanced my way. Was he calling me in? Maybe someone had gone back into the store and told them there was some crazy kid in a truck bawling his eyes out. My dad always said how calls from ordinary folks on cell phones helped keep bad situations from getting out of hand.

I had to get away from here. I couldn't be stopped by the police. What would I say? And what if someone had seen me, that evening, at Cuppa Joy? I'd been so intent on watching the Taurus that someone could've come out of the coffeehouse or been in a car, and I'd never have known.

I had to think. Snot coated my chin, and I smeared my face clean with the tail of my black sweatshirt—and then I really looked at it and what I was wearing and thought, *Oh. Shit.*

Yes, Officer. I could hear myself now. *Yessir, I saw Jimmy with someone dressed all in black: black jeans, black sweatshirt . . . no, no, not like mine. Well, all right, maybe a little . . .*

The person I saw with Jimmy—kissing Jimmy, touching Jimmy, grinding against Jimmy—wore a black hoodie.

And Pastor John wore black.

No, no, that was crazy; why did my head keep looping back to that; what was I thinking? A lot of girls, *they* wore black. That girl in the band, the Penitents, *she* had a black hoodie. It was a girl out there with Jimmy; it could've been a girl; yeah, of course, it could . . . and that was *better?* How? Because Jimmy was still . . .

"Stop." I mashed the heels of my hands to my temples and *squeezed.* "Stop, stop stop."

Pastor John.

Wore black.

Pastor John wore black, all the time.

The guys who'd burst out of the woods wore black hoodies.

And so what? *I* was in my Angel of Death sweats—and . . . oh, Jesus . . . if someone at Cuppa Joy had seen me, or Jimmy and that other person talking in the back lot, they'd *assume . . .*

No, no, Officer, it wasn't me—

—kissing Jimmy, holding Jimmy, wanting Jimmy—

—*it was someone else.*

But that would be a lie.

Wait . . . *what* was a lie?

Being with Jimmy.

Kissing him.

Wanting . . .

"Shit." The word rode on a gasp. No, I hadn't wanted Jimmy. I'd never thought or even *felt* it until this second . . . "No, no, no." My fingers twined in my hair and I was gulping air. Christ, but it was suffocating in here. "I don't feel that, I don't feel anything, I didn't, I didn't *feel* it, I *didn't*, it was a *suppose*, it didn't *mean* anything . . ."

But no matter what I said, even to myself . . . it would never stand up. Wait, why not? *Think, think, think!* My mind whirled. Yes, it would all come out. No, wait, *what* would come out? There was nothing *to* come out.

But there was. I'd followed Jimmy; I'd

—*been obsessed—*

spied on him. What kind of maniac did that? How could I explain—and just what was I *trying* to explain?

I would never be able to live any of it down. Yale wanted

leaders. Georgetown looked for the innovators of tomorrow. If this came out, no college on Earth would want a person like me. I had turned tail. I had run.

Worse.

I had left Jimmy to fight for his life.

I had let Jimmy die alone.

———————

The truck's windows were turning steamy, and I cranked on the engine to get the defroster going. My eyes drifted to the dashboard clock. Only half past eight. It felt like a lifetime had passed.

I needed an alibi. I needed to be seen by people. I racked my addled brain, trying to think of what I could do that would explain why I wasn't in the ER.

The ER manager: *We were just talking about what kind of social life you could possibly have.*

Brooke. Brooke was having a party, a bonfire after the game. Would the game be over by now? I hadn't been to a football game in years, but maybe I could go now. The more people who saw me, the better. But . . . wait. I stopped with my hand on the ignition key. Wouldn't that look suspicious? All of a sudden, out of the blue, I appear at a game? No, that was no good.

So, okay, bag the game. Maybe I should just show up at the ER. Say I changed my mind. They'd all laugh, and then one of the nurses would offer me a doughnut and tell me to clean up room seven.

Or was that the wrong thing to do? I'd already called in

to cancel for the first time *ever*. Wouldn't it be weird for me to suddenly show up? What could I say?

Nurse: *Well, yes, Sheriff, we thought it was awfully strange when Ben just appeared and you know, he did seem a little upset . . . Mary, didn't you say you thought Ben looked as if he'd been crying?*

Okay, scratch the ER.

Except my parents thought I was there. Jesus, what if one of the other deputies talked to my dad? *Oh yeah, there was this real bad wreck and I figured on maybe saying hi to your boy, only he wasn't in the ER and the nurses said he'd taken the night off and I thought to myself, well, that's not like Tom's boy; Ben never takes time off.*

Stick to Plan B. Go to Brooke's house. At least that would square with the story I'd given the ER. If it came out, I could tell my parents that I'd lied because I thought they would freak out if I skipped a night of volunteering. Which was close to the truth, what with my mom obsessing and all.

Wait, wait . . . Flicking on the dome light, I patted my pockets and fished out pocket trash: coins; my pocketknife. Jesus, why was I carrying a knife? Crinkly balls of paper receipts.

Excellent. I'd driven around. Gone to a 7-Eleven, and I could prove it. I squinted at the blurry numerals: 6:28. Maybe too early . . . where was that Burger King . . . I spotted the grease-spotted bag in the passenger footwell. My half-eaten Whopper smelled like cold shoe leather. A long, rusty lick of catsup had dried on the wrapper, and I couldn't help but think of the oily squirt of Jimmy's blood as the rock connected.

Hold it together. Bile flooded the back of my throat and burned my tongue, and I tasted regurgitated fries. *Take it easy.*

I swallowed down a mouthful of puke, closed my eyes, waited for my stomach to settle. After a couple seconds, I rummaged around again, found the Burger King receipt, uncrumpled it. The time stamp was 6:48. Okay, okay, that was a lot better. This would establish where I'd been. Jimmy said that he took out the trash at seven, which meant he'd left the kitchen right around then. I had a receipt that showed me almost fifteen miles away, getting a burger and fries. Should I save the burger? No, that was stupid; I should chuck it. Normal people didn't leave food rotting in their cars. No, but wait . . . Wouldn't it look better to actually *have* the burger in the truck? Like I'd balled it up and forgotten about it? There were stories about how people went through trash cans to find receipts and crap that would place them somewhere else. And if they tested the burger, they'd find my DNA.

Stop, stop. I gnawed on a gritty knuckle. *Be cool. Stay calm. No one's going to test your DNA. Toss the burger but keep the receipts and the bag. Just in case.*

That's when I noticed my hands. The heels were scraped raw and grimy with dirt. I looked at my scrubs. They were filthy, streaks of dirt and leaf trash, and one of the knees had a rip and there was blood. *Shit.* Angling down my rearview, I barely recognized the wild-eyed, white-faced stranger staring back. Snot crusted my upper lip. My black sweatshirt was a mess of mud and congealing mucus. Dirt flaked from the elbows.

I couldn't go to Brooke's like this. I had to find a place to clean up. But to use a bathroom would mean having to stop somewhere and buy something. You had to get a key for the john. You couldn't just wander in.

I sat and thought about that a while but couldn't figure a way around it. I didn't know Hopkins as well as I did Cedar Ridge, but I figured there must be a gas station a little further on toward town. My only problem was that Brooke's house was in the opposite direction, a good thirty miles away. No way I could say I'd just swung by Hopkins for a little gas. Well, that was okay. All I had to do was keep calm. Pump a little gas—only that would be too suspicious, wouldn't it? Pumping only a gallon or so? An attendant would remember that. So maybe just get a quart of oil and put air in the tires, yeah . . . It would be risky because I'd have to show my face and there would be cameras. Maybe hide my face? Put up my hood? No, no, bad idea. Hoodies were suspicious. Leave the sweatshirt in the car. Better yet, ditch it, get rid of the scrubs after I got home, go out and buy another pair. That's how you got rid of evidence.

But wait. I'd been out to the park. If the police looked at my truck, could they tell?

Dirt in the treads. I got the Lariat headed into Hopkins. *Maybe find a car wash, scrub the tires.* I kept to the speed limit and my eyes peeled for cruisers, but I saw none. Three miles on, I spotted a Mobil station with a do-it-yourself car wash. I decided on a Supreme Plus, the kind of wash that included an undercarriage spray, then eased the truck into the wash station. Sitting inside the cab, listening to the whir of machinery and the roar of power-spray sluicing away grime and grit, watching as the mechanical arm spewed multicolored foam that smelled of sharp disinfectant and too-sweet flowers, I felt a stillness finally settling in the center of my soul, as if the water and soap coating the windshield could hide me forever. Or maybe it was just all that white noise made me feel safe, gave me an excuse to sit and do nothing for a time.

Getting the oil took me a couple minutes, mainly to screw up my courage to get out of the truck. But I had to get clean. I peeled out of my sweatshirt, mopped snot and crud from my face then turned the sweatshirt inside out and wadded it in one hand.

The convenience store attached to the Mobil station was brightly lit. A chime dinged as I entered. There were no customers and only a single attendant behind a counter to the left of the door. The store reeked of stale cigarette smoke, engine oil, burnt coffee, and brake fluid. The guy manning the register looked up from a magazine. "Help you?" he asked.

"Just getting some oil," I said.

"Last shelf on your right, at the back," the guy said and went back to his reading.

"Thanks." I walked down rows of freestanding shelves with snacks, boxes of doughnuts, razor blades, newspapers. I found the oil and grabbed a disposable paper cone. As I headed for the front, my eye fell on a traveler's sewing kit. I took that and then a small squeeze bottle of Hibiclens, a tiny square of Dial, and a box of gauze.

"Going on a trip?" the guy asked as I dumped my purchases on the counter. He moved his magazine to one side: *Guns & Ammo*.

"Ah, no, I just like to, you know, be prepared." So stupid. Too late, I remembered: surveillance cameras. All these stores had them. The urge to look around for the camera was powerful, but instead I grabbed a candy bar and added that to my pile. "Uh, you got a bathroom?"

"Sure. Around back." The guy handed me a key. I thanked him, paid for my purchases, took the key and my change, went back to my truck, grabbed my sweatshirt, and then went around back to the men's room.

The men's room was cold and reeked of the sour ammonia tang of urine and old farts. A lone fixture in the ceiling bled thin yellow light, and I could see the black carcasses of dead flies trapped in the bowl. The floor was grimy yellow and white tile. The toilet seat was up, and a ring of brown stained the underside, rim, and bowl. There was something wrong with the plumbing because water continually hissed from beneath the rim. A roll of toilet paper perched on the lip of the sink. There was no hot water spigot, and the cold water was so icy beads of condensation clung to the metal. Of course, there was no soap, but there was a hot air dryer attached to the wall and a stack of paper towels.

I washed my hands and arms with the Dial soap and then my face and neck, using paper towels to dry off. My scrubs top looked pretty clean because I'd been wearing my sweatshirt, so I unrolled the sweatshirt, turning it right side out. I scrubbed away the dirt and dried snot and then held it under the dryer, but it was still clammy when I tugged it back on. Then I put down the toilet seat and cover and pushed down my scrubs, balancing on one foot as I tugged them over my sneakers. No way I was going barefoot here. The gash in my left knee wasn't deep, but dried blood tracked from the wound down my calf. I used paper towels to wash away the blood and grit, then opened up the gauze and repeated the process with Hibiclens. After I spot-washed and dried my scrub bottoms, I cracked the traveling sewing kit, threaded a needle with black thread, and then repaired the rip over the knee.

The guy behind the counter cocked an eyebrow when I returned the key. "Thought you'd fallen in."

"No. Stomach flu," I said—and then thought, *Moron, you just bought a candy bar.*

"Nasty stuff," the guy said, hanging up the key. "You take care now."

"Thanks. Ah, you might want to check out the toilet. It keeps running."

"I'll tell the manager," the guy said, but he was already flipping to another page in his magazine as I left.

I spent another ten minutes feeding coins into a power-vac next to the car wash and vacuuming out the truck's footwells and seat. Then, as a precaution, I vacuumed my sweatshirt, which the vacuum promptly tried to eat. So incredibly stupid.

When I was done, I checked my watch: 9:42. A safe bet the game was over. Brooke and her friends ought to be at her place. Wait a second . . . where did she live? Then I remembered the night before in the parking lot and dug out my wallet. *Yes.* I exhaled in relief. Her address and phone number, scrawled on a scrap of paper. Still there.

———————

As I drove toward Brooke's house, it hit me: Jimmy had been dead for over an hour and a half.

Unless he hadn't been. Or still wasn't.

No, don't be such a maniac; he's dead. A chill finger crept down my spine. No one could survive something like that.

But what if he had? Hadn't he been moaning? So what if, by some miracle, he was still alive, right now?

Then I could save him. I could make this right—

A flash of silver out of the corner of my right eye, and then a deer streaked across the road. I wrenched the steering wheel to the left, the absolute wrong thing to do. The truck slewed, its tires squalling over asphalt. The world whirled and blurred beyond my windshield. Panicked, I pumped the brake, but the truck kept spinning in a blistering, squealing one-eighty before finally jerking to a halt and stalling out.

Jesus. Gasping, I clutched the wheel. *Kill yourself while you're at it.* My throat was raw, and I realized that I'd been screaming. Now, in the sudden silence, my ears rang. I could feel my heart thrashing against bone. That had been too close. If another car had been coming, I could've killed someone. Or myself. As it was, I was lucky not to have crashed or rolled over.

After another minute—when the shakes passed and I was sure I wasn't going to vomit into my lap—I cranked the engine, got myself turned in the right direction, and headed off again for Brooke's. I had to get hold of myself and focus. Concentrate. I couldn't do more than I already had. This wasn't a movie or comic book. I wasn't a superhero, and I'd heard that solid *thunk*, the crash of rock against bone eventually give way to the hollow, wet sound of tires over a smashed pumpkin.

Jimmy was dead. He had to be, and that was all there was to it.

Hah. HAH.

I know what you're thinking: *Joke's on you.*

"It's so nice to see you." Brooke's mom led me through the house. "It's been what? Three years? Five?"

"I don't remember, ma'am," I said, myopically eyeing a row of photographs on either side of the front hall. The newest ones were closest to the front door; I recognized what must be Brooke's graduation picture because we'd used the same photographer that very summer. Wandering past these photos was like walking back through time: Brooke at eighteen, Brooke at fifteen, Brooke in middle school. Brooke at the village pool, in a striped tank and one of those inflatable pink inner tubes snugged around her middle. A big goofy grin on her face, so I could see where she was missing a front tooth. "Been a while, I think. A long time."

"Too long." She saw me studying the pool picture. "I remember the day that was taken. When you were little, your mother would bring you to the village pool nearly every day of the summer. This was before she started working full-time again. We mothers would all loaf in the sun and gossip and watch you kids paddle around the baby pool. Only my little Brooke was afraid of the water. Lord knows why. No one could get her to go in, not me or her father or any of the other moms. Then, one day, you marched up and took her hand and walked her out to that pool."

I had? I didn't remember that at all. "And she let me do that?"

"Oh, not without some fuss. If it had been up to me, I'd have swooped down and rescued my baby, but your mother stopped me. She said it was good for children to take chances with one another. Well, she was right. You kept Brooke so busy she didn't have time to be scared. You even brought her a popsicle, but you made her eat it by the pool. You were so cute—you were only, what? Four? You were such a determined boy, so sure of yourself. You just wouldn't take no for an answer."

"I did? I *was*?" This was news to me. I mean, I knew that Brooke and I had hung around together when we were kids, but all I remembered was running in a pack. Until around fifth or sixth grade, I guess. Then the girls and boys started to split up into their respective camps. I wondered, too, what the hell had happened to that confident, take-charge kid, who knew what to do and how he thought. Because I was pretty sure that if I looked into the mirror right then, he wouldn't be staring back.

"Oh yes," she said. "There you are, with the ball, see? You kept throwing it into the pool for Brooke to chase."

I did see now: a little potbellied mini-me, in a pair of orange trunks, clutching one of those big, multicolored blow-up balls. A leggy woman in a floppy hat and blue polka-dot two-piece was grinning and clapping.

My mother, of course: egging me on, even then.

Brooke looked a little taken aback as I eased through the sliding glass door onto the back porch. A fire pit was going, and there were knots of people talking. Maybe thirty kids altogether, and most of them seniors, though I spotted a couple juniors. There was music; I recognized "Some Boys." Kids were shaking ice from cans of pop plucked from a Coleman cooler and scavenging chips and dip from big glass bowls. Marshmallows for s'mores spilled across the picnic table, and I watched as a kid—someone from Russian history—fed squares of Hershey's chocolate to his giggly girlfriend, who squealed, "Stop, *stop*," in that way which you knew meant *don't stop, don't stop*.

Stop, don't stop, don't stop, don't . . . there, in the dark meat of my brain: Jimmy, under the lights, and they were kissing and they were touching and *don't stop, don't stop* . . . and then there was the rock and blood and Jimmy *screaming* . . .

"Ben?" Brooke's mouth was crooked in a tentative half-smile. "Are you all right? What made you change your mind?"

"Oh." I fished a can of Diet Coke out of the cooler, shook off ice-melt, and popped the top. "I thought about what you said. I decided you were right. I need to get out more. You're only a senior once, right?"

"If you're lucky." Her gaze swept over my clothes. "So you came from work?"

"No. I mean, yeah," I fumbled. "I was going to the ER, but then figured that, you know, coming here was a better idea." Okay, so maybe not so much of a lie. At least half of that was the truth. Still, I'd have to watch how many lies I told and to whom, so I wouldn't get myself all tangled up. They always hammered that home on cop shows and in books: *keep it simple, stupid.*

She cut me a strange look. "Are you okay? You're kind of pale."

"Hungry." Another lie. But that gave me an excuse to break eye contact. Swear to God, it was like I suddenly worried she had x-ray vision, could see right through me. Turning, I practically sprinted to the picnic table—I know; she must've thought I was a maniac, and thank *God* she let me go because I don't know what I'd have done or said—and started loading a paper plate with chips and dip and veggies. Then I hustled to a free lounge chair and plopped by the fire pit. I swirled a Dorito in drippy red salsa—and, Jesus, that wet, smashed-pumpkin sound ghosted through my mind. My stomach tried crawling up my throat. I set the plate aside.

Some kids were dancing. I tried watching them for a while, but I was restless, uneasy, skin all prickly and fizzy. I knew now that it had been a mistake to come over, but I couldn't just bug out or duck back into the house. So I unfolded myself from my chair and wandered around. People were talking about other people and things I didn't much care about. I hovered, though, trying to look like I was listening, but my mind kept bouncing to the woods: Jimmy and the other person at the shelter. Jimmy and that other person touching. Kissing. Then Jimmy watching death swoop out of the dark woods. Jimmy screaming, and that spume of black blood.

And, just like that, I started to cry. Not sob, but my eyes stung, my nose itched. My legs got all wobbly. I quick ducked my head and struck out for the yard, moving out of the glow of the porch spots and into shadow. At the far corner of the yard I spotted a wood playground set, the kind with a fort and slide and walking bridge to another platform and swings and one of those two-seated gliders. I veered toward it.

All of a sudden, someone slid up on my left, melting out of the night. Spooked, I ducked even as my brain finally caught up: *You maniac, there's nothing there.* Of course, my Chucks went out from under me on the slick grass. I came down on my ass hard enough to send an electric jolt up my spine that squeezed the breath from my chest. What an idiot. Spooked by my own shadow. Just my eyes playing tricks. I kept waiting for people to come running, but I was too far away from the house and no one had been paying attention to me anyway.

After a few minutes, I dragged myself to my feet and staggered over to the swing set, settling gingerly onto the glider. My ass still hurt and my legs were tingly. The Coke I hadn't wanted but drunk anyway sloshed as I swung, back and forth, back and forth, gurgle, gurgle, gurgle.

But the motion was soothing, and I started to feel a little better. We'd had a swing set in the backyard of our old house, the one we'd lived in when Dad had just made chief deputy. The swing set had been green metal with chain swings, and I'd gouged deep ruts out of red dirt from countless hours of swinging. Once, I'd swung so high the legs of the entire set lifted right out of the grass. Mom had been pushing Mal, just a baby back then, and I remembered how loudly my mother screamed. She must've thought the whole set would topple.

Thing is, I wasn't scared, not all the way or straight through, if you know what I mean. I *was* freaked but also . . . exhilarated. Like, *Wow, I'm strong enough to do* that? Afterward, though, I think my mom made my dad set the legs in concrete, because I couldn't remember coming close to tipping that set again. Come to think of it, my dad anchored that sucker so well it'll probably be there when the world finally ends.

I swung awhile until my eyes stopped pooling and the shivers subsided. I was about to get off when something peeled out of the dark. This time, I didn't try jumping out of my skin.

"Hey." Brooke held out something wrapped in a napkin. "Brought you a s'more."

"Thanks." The napkin was still warm. The mingled aromas of melted chocolate and charred marshmallow spirited past. I'd thought I was hungry, I really did, but my stomach did another of those slow somersaults.

She dropped onto the glider seat opposite. "You don't want it?"

"No, no. Thanks. I . . . it's just . . ." Pulling in a breath, I set the napkin on the ground and tried again. "I think I'm coming down with something. You know, that I picked up in the ER."

She kick-started the glider. I really was done swinging, but I thought it would be rude to hop off now, so I stayed put. "Do you like it? The ER?" she asked.

"Yeah." Having her sitting right across from me was a little disconcerting. My eyes wanted to settle anywhere but on her face. "Sometimes it's boring. Not a lot happening. But when they bring in a big accident, then it's pretty exciting."

"You must see a lot of blood." Then she must've read my face because she said, "I'm sorry. Are you okay? Should we stop swinging?"

"No, it's okay." My forehead was suddenly beaded with sweat. I licked my upper lip and tasted salt. What had she asked? "I . . . uhm . . . I guess I don't think about the blood. I try to think like a doctor, you know? Figure out the problem and how to fix it."

Her nose wrinkled. "You make it sound like you can't think of people as people then."

"I guess. I don't think you could worry about people as human beings every single second, or you'd never get anything done. One of the docs said that's why they drape patients so a surgeon only sees the area he's operating on. That's why medical school anatomy labs have you start on the back, because that looks the least human."

"I heard once that some guy was doing a dissection and then they flipped the cadaver over and it turned out to be someone he knew from, like, a million years ago," Brooke said. "How freaky is that? All that time, he'd been cutting up the kid he used to play baseball with."

"I have to stop now," I said. I dug into the dirt hard enough to jerk us to a halt.

Brooke's head snapped forward and almost slammed into the vertical swing bar. "Hey," she said.

"Sorry." But I'd already hopped off. My stomach was doing those damn flips again. I closed my eyes. "I'm just . . ." I cleared my throat and spat. God, my mouth tasted like a toilet. "I should go. I'm feeling a little sick again."

"Do you want to go inside to lie down?" she asked. Her concern made my eyes go salty and hot. Brooke was so good, such a nice person, and Jimmy's dad was right for all the wrong reasons. I *was* filth, but not because of what he thought I'd done. I was scum for what I *hadn't* done, and Jimmy was out there, right now, in the cold . . .

"No." I hawked up another pukey gob. "But I probably should go home. Wouldn't want to make you sick."

Brooke walked me to the house. The fire had died, and it was cold enough now that people were starting to drift inside. Brooke's mom looked up from gathering smeary bowls of ranch dip and salsa. "Oh honey," she said, "you look ill."

"He thinks he's got the stomach flu," Brooke said.

"Well, stay away from me, dude," said one of the juniors.

"Maybe you should lie down first," Brooke's mom said. She tried to convince me to use her older son's room, but I begged off and said good night and thanks.

Brooke walked me to the front door. "I'm really sorry you don't feel well. But it was still nice to see you. Maybe we could have coffee or something. Like . . . Monday?"

"Yeah," I said, struggling for something approaching normal. "Sure. That would be great." And then I blurted: "I never apologized. For making you cry. You were only trying to help. Brooke, I . . . I'm just so sorry."

I don't know why I said that then. It just happened. Like all the words had piled up behind my teeth and couldn't wait to get out. That I had to say sorry to someone because I couldn't to Jimmy. If you know what I mean.

Brooke's face had gone very still. Except for her eyes, which were deep and dark, like bittersweet chocolate. We were close enough that she could've placed a hand on my chest. She could've touched me. She didn't, but I think now that I wanted her to. What I finally understood was what it meant when someone tried looking behind the mask and into those hidden places. I wanted her to see into me—and yet, I didn't.

"Thanks." Then, after a pause, she said, "I take back what I said. You know, that day."

I remembered that I hadn't heard what she'd said. But I didn't ask. Instead, I only said good night. But when I did . . . something flickered across her face. I think . . . she was disappointed. Yes, looking back, I really *do* think that.

I really do.

It was a little after midnight when I crept into the house. The lights were out downstairs except for the one above the stove, and no one was up. That was a surprise. I did a quick sweep of the kitchen, looking for the note I was positive must be there: *Jimmy's missing. Have you seen him? We called the ER. Where have you been?* But there was nothing except a platter of brownies in plastic wrap. I love my mom's brownies, but I turned out the light and went upstairs.

In the bathroom, I struggled out of my clothes. I would throw away everything, even the Chucks. Hopkins had its own police department, but Merit was too small, so the deputies handled evidence collection. But I bet that once someone found Jimmy, they'd get one of those fancy crime scene guys from Madison to come up. Those techs could analyze anything, even dirt. They might be able to tell I'd been in the park.

Yeah, bag the clothes in a black contractor's bag, so no one can see inside. Sunday was bagel morning in our house. I could set my alarm, be sure I got up before anyone else. Hell, before the bagel place even opened. *Then swing by the pizza place first. That's on the other end of town. No one will be there. Stuff the bag into a dumpster, then head the other way, grab bagels, be back home in a half hour, tops.*

Or maybe not. I could just wash the scrubs and sweatshirt. So what if I'd ripped the knee? The only blood was mine, and that wasn't a crime. I could even throw the Chucks into the machine. Yeah, pitching them was stupid. What if someone found the bag? Then they'd wonder why I needed to get rid of my clothes, and how would I explain that?

Slow down. Hot water rained over my head. I raised my face to the sting. *Don't panic. One foot in front of the other.*

I stood under the water until it started to run cold. Then I got out, dried off, and dug under my nails with a file. My nails were completely clean, but I really scraped the hell out of them before shearing them with a pair of very sharp nail scissors, right down to the pink quick.

When I scrubbed away steam from the mirror, I thought I looked better than I had at the gas station. Not as yellow. Or maybe that had just been because of the lights. I squeezed a worm of toothpaste onto my brush and was running the whirring brush over my teeth—when I heard something.

The phones, in my parents' room and downstairs. Ringing.

I froze, toothbrush still spinning, green froth dribbling down my chin. The phones rang again. I jabbed off the brush at the same moment that the phones cut off in mid-ring. Someone—my dad, the phone was on my dad's side of the bed, and any call in the middle of the night was always for him—had picked up. I strained to hear, but my heart was booming. Then I thought how suspicious it would be if I didn't keep brushing, like I was worried about the call. So I finished washing my teeth, spat out goopy green glop, and rinsed. My mouth still tasted like garbage.

Okay, just be cool. Knotting a towel around my waist, I tucked my bundle of clothes under one arm and opened the bathroom door. My glasses fogged. My skin prickled with gooseflesh as I stepped into the chill hall. My room was all the way down on the left. Only five steps away. I took them fast, making it just in time to flick on my light and shut the door before I caught the telltale *scree* of my parents' bedroom door.

But that was okay. No reason I ought to be hanging around the hall after midnight, all chatty. Or should I have been curious? How many people got calls in the dead of night? No, no, I had to calm down; my dad was chief deputy . . . but had I ever asked before? I couldn't remem—

A soft knock on my door. The hairs spiked all the way up and down my neck. "Uhm." I cleared my throat. "Yeah?"

"It's Dad." His voice was low and muffled. "Can I come in?"

"Uhm, sure." I backed up as the door open. My dad was buttoning his uniform shirt. *Shit.* I felt my heart try to seize up. "You going out?"

"Afraid so." He tucked in the tails then cinched his belt. "Maybe nothing. Missing person. Nothing official yet. Hasn't been long enough. Might be nothing more than a runaway, but . . ." He punctuated with a shrug. "Thought it might be good if I went on over, talked to the family."

That was right. In my panic, I hadn't considered that kids ran away all the time. Nobody mounted full-scale searches for at least, what? Twenty-four hours? Forty-eight? I'd have to look this up. But that meant no one had found Jimmy yet. The more time passed, the safer I was.

Yes, maybe. The voice was small, and this time I knew it was mine. *But why is your dad telling you about this at all? Has he ever stopped by to explain anything like this before?*

"You all right?" My dad was studying my face. "Look a little peaked."

"Just . . . I might be coming down with something." The paranoia started up again. Why was Dad asking? I tried to remember if we'd ever had a conversation like this. I couldn't think of a single instance. So, was he watching for my reaction? I tried to think of what would be a normal thing to say in a situation like this. Yeah, I'd ask who it was, right? Except I already knew Dad wouldn't tell. One of those law-enforcement confidentiality things. Just like he never brought up things until they were old news, things we'd have heard about already, and that was only rarely. I decided not to ask.

"Sorry to hear that," Dad said. "How was the ER?"

"I . . . uh . . . I didn't go," I said, then pushed on as I read the surprise in his face. "Brooke was having a party and I . . . well, I decided to bag the ER and go do that instead."

I waited for Dad to say something about college and responsibility. What I didn't expect was for him to clap his hand on my shoulder and smile.

"Good for you," he said. "You've been working hard, and you deserve a break. When I was your age, I did my share of partying. Young man like you, you got to cut loose now and again. This time of life is special. It'll never come again. You have the rest of your life to work. Only I'm not especially happy that you lied about where you were going. I know you did that because you didn't want to get into it with your mom, am I right?"

Among other things. I cut my eyes away, worried what he might glimpse there. "Yeah. It wouldn't have gone over really well."

"Then that's partly my fault. You make a reasonable request, you ought to be able to count on your parents to be reasonable, too. Look, I got to get going, but we'll talk more about this, okay? Only . . . no more lying. If, God forbid, something happened, your mother and I needed to know where to find you . . ."

"Right. I'm sorry."

"That's all right. Get some sleep now. I'm just glad you're home safe. Calls like I just got?" He squeezed my shoulder. "Make you realize how precious family is."

God. I was an awful person. The longest conversation I'd had with my father in I couldn't remember how long, one where he stuck up for me, and it was all a lie. I was definitely going to hell.

Come to think of it, maybe I was already there.

———————

I crawled into bed, bone-weary, convinced I would never sleep. Yet somehow I dozed off. My dreams were confused and fragmentary: awful, jagged snippets of Jimmy; the shelter; the wink of that hatchet in yellow light.

I had a terrible nightmare, too. In the dream, I was immobile, and that was because I was dead. It was one of those nightmares where you're in and out of yourself at the same time. There was me, floating above my body—and there was me, facedown: a cadaver on a cold steel dissection tray.

My parents were there, too, hunched over my body like green vultures in surgical caps and gowns. "Don't worry," my dad said. The keen blade of a heavy-duty scalpel glinted, wicked and sharp. "He'll feel every second."

All at once, I collapsed into myself. No more safe detachment for me. I was in my body, my nose mashed against icy metal. I felt the instant the blade plunged into my flesh. I gargled out a scream—my mouth worked—but my dad kept going, slicing through skin and meat along my spine. There was this wet ripping sound, like the kind I'd heard whenever my mom tore up old underwear for dust rags. But this time, she was tearing me apart, flaying skin from bones, and I was screaming, *screaming* . . .

"Ah!" Flailing, I jolted awake in a sweaty tangle of damp sheets. My heart was trying to blast out my chest. Gasping, I fell back, gulped, waited for my pulse to slow down.

When I was calmer, I checked the time: 7:15. Thin slants of gray slowed through my venetian blinds. The house was quiet. There was no warm smell of coffee, so Dad probably wasn't home yet. I didn't know if that was good or bad. I stumbled out of bed, dragged on some clothes. My mouth was rank as a sewer, so foul it was like something had crawled in and died. I washed my teeth again, only this time I used an old toothbrush I dug out of a drawer. The electric toothbrush would make too much noise, and I needed time alone.

Cranking up my computer, I did a search. Jimmy's name popped up only in references to his photography prize and thumbnails of that stupid picture and a frigging website the magazine had put up just in case someone in Outer Mongolia didn't know about the pictures yet. Google News had nothing about a dead Wisconsin kid. Neither did any of network affiliates' websites or CNN or the *Hopkins Press.*

I wiped my search history, turned off the computer. Then I started worrying again. Couldn't they load a program on your computer to figure out what web pages you'd looked at? I thought so. I had once used a recovery program for a paper I'd inadvertently zapped. Just downloaded it from the Web, and that thing pulled up documents I'd done in *sixth grade.* So I couldn't use my computer to do any more searches like this, not now. I had to be smart. Thank God I didn't have a cell phone. I might have been tempted to use mine last night, and then *that* would've placed me somewhere I couldn't afford to have been. Come to think of it, if your phone was on, couldn't they track you by GPS or something? Even if you didn't call anyone?

Maybe the news hadn't made the paper yet, but I just couldn't believe the word wasn't out already. Except how could I find out? I gnawed on the side of my thumb and thought about it. People—especially really old guys—loved to gossip. Dad always said the best way to pick up information was park your butt on a stool, drink a couple gallons of coffee, and keep your mouth shut.

And your ears open.

———————

The most likely place this early on a Sunday was a diner on Main. Farmers and field hands and workers getting off third shift at the plastics plant over in Ely came in early for breakfast. I could grab some coffee and there would be a newspaper, sure, but more importantly, there would be people. And people liked to gossip.

The diner smelled of stale smoke, bacon, and coffee. This early, there were only about ten guys either hunched over the counter or sitting at a clutch of tables near the windows. I slid onto a red vinyl stool about three places in from one end—close enough to hear anything the guys said, but not so close as to put me into the conversation. The waitress splashed coffee into a heavy porcelain mug and asked if I wanted anything. The idea of eating made my stomach turn, but I thought that not ordering something would look suspicious. So I asked for a fried egg sandwich with sausage, and she went away. I dumped about ten of those little things of creamer into my coffee, but it still tasted like dirty dishwater. No one was talking much either, except for the kind of conversations where no one finishes a single sentence because these guys had known each other so long, it was like they were telepathic. A guy two stools down was methodically going through the Sunday paper, putting aside each section as he finished. He spied me looking and waved a hand—*help yourself*—so I swiped a section and flipped pages. Not like I was looking for something, even though I was, and not fast but, like, random. But there was nothing.

Halfway through the sports section—a stupid thing to look through, but guys were supposed to like sports, and I was supposed to be acting like a normal boy—the waitress brought my food and refilled my coffee cup the eighth of an ounce I'd managed to choke down. I figured it would look bad if I didn't eat, so I took a bite of my sandwich. Mistake. The egg burst, squirting a gooey glop of runny yellow yolk-snot onto my tongue. I nearly heaved right then and there.

Someone said my name. I craned over my shoulder and recognized one of the farmers with whom I'd done milking for the Langes. I hadn't spotted him when I came in, but I waved, said hey. He came over and held out his hand. "Long time. You going over to the Langes, too?"

A sudden whooshing roar in my ears: *Going to the Langes . . . too?*

"Uh." I smeared a slick of egg yolk from my chin onto a napkin. "No, I just felt like going out for some breakfast. Why?"

"Harlan called this morning, early. About six. Said he was going to need an extra pair of hands. Didn't say why. I guess I figured you were on your way out there."

"No." Then added, like an idiot, "Sorry."

"Don't know why you should be," he said and then looked over my shoulder toward the front door. "Hey, here comes your dad."

My whole body went cold. My chest wasn't working right, like I was sucking air through a straw. I turned as my father and another deputy came through the front door. Of course, my dad spotted me right away. It was weird, knowing what I did, reading the expressions that sparrowed over his face: surprise, followed by an instant's quick calculation—*has Ben ever...*—and then a flit of something darker. Not bemusement or confusion or, even, curiosity.

Suspicion. As in, *This has never happened before.*

"Son." His tone was carefully neutral. "What are you doing out so early?"

"I . . . I just felt like getting out of the house. I thought maybe my stomach was better, but . . ." I gestured lamely at my sandwich in its puddle of oozy yolk. "I was just leaving. Uh . . . how did the night go?" Yes, that was okay to ask; he was my dad; he'd been out all night. Asking was normal—and, hell, I really needed to know what was going on. "Did, ah, did the kid come back?" Which I wanted to grab back just as soon as it was out of my mouth: *You maniac, he never said* kid; *he said missing person. He said runaway.*

"Mmm," was all my dad said. Which didn't sound noncommittal to me, and had his eyes narrowed in that cop-squint I knew meant he was replaying something in his head?

But then he was turning, nodding at the waitress. "Just coffee, Kathy." To the farmer: "You heading out?"

The farmer must've heard the same note in my dad's voice, because he cocked his head, said, "Yeah. Harlan called." Pause. "Something I should know before I go?"

At that, the diner went completely silent. It was the eeriest thing, like this dense blanket had come floating down to muffle all sound. Even the cook seemed to have paused.

My dad shot a quick glance around, then inclined his head. "Walk you to your truck," he said to the farmer. To me: "Hold up a sec, be right back."

Everyone in that diner watched as he and the farmer sauntered out, my dad gesturing with one hand as he spoke. Their conversation was short; the farmer gave a mournful shake of his head and looked at the ground; my father and he shook hands, and then the farmer was climbing into his truck.

I turned back in time to see at least a dozen eyes cut back to their plates, their neighbors, to empty space. I suddenly didn't want to know what they were thinking or had heard, and I sure as hell didn't want any of them listening to or thinking about me. I dug a five out of my wallet, threw it on the counter, got out of there before the waitress even opened her mouth. I probably looked suspicious as hell, but right then I didn't care.

Outside, my dad was watching the farmer drive away. "What's going on?" I asked.

"Nothing good." Dad's eyes ticked to mine. That cop-eye squint? Definitely not my imagination. "You heard from Jimmy lately?"

I had to play this just right. "Jimmy?" I tried to inject confusion into my reply and then started to worry that would

138

sound too calculated. *Be cool, stay calm; it's just a question.* "Uh, no. Not since, you know, the thing in the magazine." Too late, I remembered that was a lie too easily exposed; ask anyone in Cuppa Joy and they'd tell my dad I'd been there. But I couldn't take it back now. If—*when*—my dad found out, I'd say I was embarrassed about the whole thing. Yeah, that was good. "Why?"

"Well, it's not official yet, but . . . Jimmy left where he was working last night. Cuppa Joy? Didn't tell anyone where he was going."

A pause. My cue to respond: "Oh. Wow. So . . . he's the runaway?"

"Maybe." Dad was telling the story, but I saw how carefully he was watching, gathering information, measuring my response. "Staff there says he went to take out the garbage roundabout seven and then, maybe an hour or two later, they realized no one had seen him around. There were two dishwashers on that night on account of it being Saturday, and the other guy thought Jimmy was out front and the front people thought Jimmy was in back. Now no one can find him, and he's not answering his cell phone. Can't locate him by it either, so he must've turned it off."

Some mental alarm bell *dinged.* Wait a minute, what had my dad just said? Something really important . . . "Uh, wow," I repeated. "You think he's okay? Is there anything I can do to help?"

As soon as the corners of my dad's eyes relaxed, I knew I'd said the right thing. "Hard to know," my dad said, and sighed. "I sure as hell hope that boy hasn't done something stupid. Tell you what, though. If you hear from him, if he gets in touch, you tell me, all right? This is one of those times when the best thing you could do would be to rat him out. Don't get sucked into keeping secrets."

"S-sure. O... okay," I stammered, and I sounded so shocked that I was positive my dad thought my reaction was normal. Only he would've been wrong about why.

Because I had just figured out what, until that second, I had forgotten.

Jimmy had been waiting for me; he'd wanted to see *me* because he'd had a camera card full of pictures *for me*. More than that, Jimmy had said, *"I'll write it all down and then you can mail the package."*

So it was a really good bet that *me*, my name, would be there, on his body, somewhere. I was there, on a piece of paper or envelope. I was sure of it.

And Dad—my smart-cop dad with that tough squint—either misunderstood whatever was written on my face or hadn't being looking in the first place because, what the hell, I was his son and who would believe such a thing of his boy?

"I know." My dad reached over and cupped the back of my neck. His hand was rough and calloused, but cool. "I know. I'm sorry about all this, too. It's not right when bad things happen to good people, and that poor kid's had to deal with a lot. You've been a friend to him, but there's only so much a person can do. You should go home now, son. You don't look like you're feeling so hot there."

"My stomach," I mumbled. I was so terrified and exhausted, all I wanted was to burst into tears and hug my dad and tell him everything. He was my dad; he could make things right; he'd tell me what to do. But how would he feel about me afterward? Would he still love me? Would he be so proud of his son then?

I just didn't want to find out.

So I went home, like the good boy he thought I was.

———————

Sundays, I usually did a long run. If there was one day when I definitely didn't feel it, that Sunday was it. Only I didn't want to just sit, worry, and have flashbacks. Or start bawling again. Or tell somebody, let everything just come rushing out.

Besides, I had something new to worry about. Jimmy had that camera card. There was evidence on him, somewhere, that would tip off someone that Jimmy and I were supposed to meet. If my dad or one of the other deputies found all that first, I was dead.

"You have a nice run," Mom said. She was still in her robe, drinking coffee with Dad, who'd come home an hour after me and was now pushing scrambled eggs around on a plate. He looked like an old rag doll with most of the stuffing gone. "Oh, have you sent in your Common Application and supplements yet?" she asked.

"Helen, leave him be," Dad said shortly, then turned away from the astonished little *o* of my mother's mouth to look at me. "You sure you ought to run with that stomach?"

"I'm a little better, thanks. I won't push it, promise. See you." I banged out before they could ask any other questions.

———————

It seemed to take forever to drive to the park. It was still before noon, so most everyone else was in church. On the way out, I passed a couple cruisers, but no one seemed to be paying attention. One guy, though, raised his hand; probably recognized the Lariat. *Shit.* Well, nothing to be done. I kept to the speed limit and tried very hard not to think, but of course I did.

It occurred to me that Jimmy might not be there, not because he was alive or had stumbled off or was in some hospital—but because there were animals all over that park: coyotes, foxes, raccoons, martens. Birds always squabbled over roadkill. I knew that animals went after all the soft stuff first then dragged off whatever they could.

Jesus. A moan dribbled out of my mouth. *What if Jimmy's in pieces?*

Something was different about the road going into the park, but I couldn't put my finger on it. There were no other cars. I rolled up to the closed gate, killed the engine, sat a second. If there was anyone else around, I sure didn't see them. There was no one in my rearview, no movement in the trees. I checked my watch. Half past eleven. I needed to move. How long before Jimmy was declared officially missing and then people started looking in earnest?

Go. You can't afford to wait any longer. Go on, you coward, go.

The groan of metal as I shut the truck door was much too loud. Road grit squealed and popped under my running shoes. My heart pounded harder and harder as I retraced my steps into the woods. Now that it was daylight, I could see that the dirt in the center was softer. Worrying about leaving tracks, I eased off, skirting the edge of the trail, watching where I put my feet so as not to crush too much. If I did, and someone figured it out, they'd wonder why a runner wasn't keeping to the path. Maybe I should use a branch to scour away any footprints—but then . . . wouldn't that show up, too? Could you pull a finger-print from wood? Every twig snap sounded like a gunshot. The woods were eerily silent with only the *hoosh* of the wind, the occasional scuttle of small animals in the underbrush, and the hollow *thock-thock-thock* of a woodpecker hammering a tree. No owls this time, but above the trees a crow cawed, and then a group rose in a black cloud. Shit, crows were scavengers.

Not good. My feet felt like they were plowing through quicksand. *Not good, not good, not good.*

The woods thinned. The trees pulled away, and the trail opened onto that picnic area like the parting of a dense, dark curtain. The field in which the shelter stood was empty.

But the shelter wasn't.

———

Even from a distance of fifty feet, you'd have to be drunk or stoned out of your mind to believe that someone had decided the cold concrete was just the perfect spot for a nap. I wish I could say that if you didn't know better, you'd think that some-one had left behind a tumble of old laundry. I wish I could tell you anything but the truth.

I thought I was ready. Working the ER, I'd seen a lot. Guys who did headers off barns. Little kids run over by their dad's lawnmower. Construction workers in the wrong place at the wrong time when that girder decided to uncouple and gravity did its thing. There was one motorcyclist crushed by a semi; everyone converged, doing CPR and stuff, until a doc peeked under this towel draped over the place where the guy's face was then told everyone to stop. (The short version: no helmet.) Of course, I'd seen the mess that was Del.

So I thought I could take it. I thought that, when I saw Jimmy, I already knew what to expect.

Still, I stood there for a very long time, unable to move, scarcely able to breathe. There was blood, everywhere: a wide purple lake of it and more hosed onto the concrete, spray-painted onto the picnic table because, of course, Jimmy hadn't died right away, and the heart is a powerful pump.

From a distance, Jimmy looked . . . strange. The air *hummed*. Someone had draped a black shirt—a hoodie?—over his torso to cover his face and chest. Jimmy was on his back, legs splayed, his left foot missing a shoe. For some stupid reason, I zeroed in on that naked foot, his toes, the shoe that wasn't.

I forced myself to move, one foot in front of the other. That hum was so odd . . . and then Jimmy's chest . . . *lifted*.

Stunned, I let out a shout. I couldn't help it. Oh my God, he was *alive*? I watched, eyes bugging, as Jimmy drew another shuddering, squirming breath . . . that hoodie bunching and roiling as the air *brrrred* . . .

Flies. My own breath came out in a sudden *whoosh*. Not a hoodie at all, but a thick mat of noisy, hungry blowflies swarming over moist meat and jellied blood.

"Get away," I choked. Somehow I'd waded into that awful red-black lake and begun swinging my arms, trying to drive them off. "Get away, leave him alone, *go*!"

The flies churned and lifted in a droning inky fog, and then I saw Jimmy's face.

Or, rather, what was left.

———————

Ever run over a Halloween pumpkin? For kicks? Come on, you know what I'm saying.

A skull's like a pumpkin. It's got seams, too, because it's not one big piece but many floating plates, sheathed in skin and muscle, which eventually fuse together. Otherwise, we'd all be stupid pinheads because our brains wouldn't have enough room to grow. Not that I have that kind of excuse.

Jimmy's skull wasn't squashed. Despite those rocks and the pounding he must've taken, Jimmy's skull wasn't mashed to pulp either. Given the divots, I thought they'd put that hatchet to good use, though, because Jimmy *was* broken: his skull fractured into a jigsaw of jagged slabs in the ruptured bag of skin and hair that had been his face and scalp. Dusky bluish and purple goo spumed over the concrete because fresh brains are as soft as warm butter.

Yet, as bad as that was—and it was terrible—this was worse: there were grains of rice speckling Jimmy's eye sockets. More dribbled from the lumpy mess of both nostrils, dripped from his ears. Jimmy's teeth were broken, but rice clogged his open mouth and was sprinkled over the blood bib on his chest. Looking at that, I couldn't make sense of it.

And then I realized: *flies.*

This wasn't rice. These were *eggs*. The flies were laying eggs in all that good moist pulp that was Jimmy's face.

Vomit roared into the back of my throat. Gagging, I spun away, clapped a hand over my mouth. *Don't lose it, don't lose it.* I couldn't puke; I couldn't leave *anything* of myself behind. *Come on, you can do this.* I swallowed back a mess of stomach acid, bad coffee and undigested egg. *You have to do this.*

Then I looked at my hands. They were shaking. I hadn't

brought gloves. What an idiot. I stared down at my smeary sneakers. In my horror, I'd blundered through muck and gore. The concrete was stenciled with coppery prints, and I would leave more on the way to the truck. The deputies— my *dad*—would know someone had come back, and they'd wonder why?

One foot in front of the other. No help for what I'd already done, but I could be more careful from here on out. After thinking about it a few seconds, I untied my shoes, eased them from my feet, stripped off my running socks and then stuck a hand into each. Socks I could get rid of pretty easily. Bare feet could be washed.

Do what you came to do.

I balanced on my toes over Jimmy's body because footprints are like fingerprints. I didn't know about toe prints, but I wasn't like I had tons of choices. My toes squelched. The flies were settling down to feed again, their drone a low, unending thrum like the purr of an engine. Jimmy didn't smell yet, and he wasn't bloated. He hadn't been dead long enough. I saw, too, that the flies weren't the only things to feast on fresh meat either.

Jimmy's lips and tongue were gone. So were his eyes. His fingers had been chewed to the knuckles, and something had started in on his neck, ripping away flesh down to the sloppy pink, ribbed worm of his windpipe.

Jimmy's jeans were saturated and stiff with gore, yet the fly was open, the waistband pulled away. His underwear had been pushed down into a rust-colored accordion fold as if he'd been caught trying to take a leak. A wash of coagulated blood, studded here and there with clumps of Jimmy's hair, spewed over his thighs and down to his knees. Staring down, I just didn't understand . . . and then I remembered how sharp that hand axe looked and understood that after they'd taken it to his skull, they hacked off something else.

Easy, easy. Sheathed in socks, my own fingers were clumsy. Wriggling my way into first the right and then the left front jeans pockets, I found nothing except a bank slip that I put back. I tried working my stockinged hands into his hip pockets but failed because, light as he'd been in life, Jimmy was only so much dead weight now. I would have to turn him onto his side. Moving a body was bad, I knew that, because it told the police that there was something someone didn't want left on the body. No help for it, though. I stepped around to Jimmy's left side, making sure to keep clear of the muck. I didn't want to reach over and pull him toward me; I worried about getting smeared with gore. So I had to jam the heels of my hands into Jimmy's side, right at his ribs, and push.

His body, stiff with rigor, came away from the concrete with a sucking sound, like Jell-O turned from a mold. His right hip pocket bulged. Steadying the body with my left hand, I squirmed my fingers into the pocket, felt them skim a hard edge, and realized that I'd found Jimmy's cell phone. But there was nothing else.

I repeated the procedure, the drone of the flies fragmenting as I rolled Jimmy onto his right side. I remember that I hesitated, too, hand poised over his left hip pocket. If this was empty, I was out of luck. Or I still might be okay. Maybe Jimmy had changed his mind. But no, he'd been in back, waiting for me, right? Unless he'd *only* come out to dump the trash then gotten waylaid by that . . . guy? Girl? I didn't know.

Then I had another thought: what if whoever killed him was after the same thing I was?

I eased my fingers into his pocket. My breath caught, and then I was tugging out a folded envelope, still sealed, the paper soupy and dark brown with clotted blood. Easing Jimmy back onto the concrete, I backed out on tiptoe, my overstressed thighs and calves beginning to cramp and complain. Dark splotches marked where my toes stenciled the concrete, and I used the side of my fist, still sheathed in a sock, to smear the prints. Then I rocked back on my heels and unfolded the envelope.

Holy shit. There was my name in big block capitals, plainly visible through the muck. Anyone could tell at a glance who the envelope was for.

Okay, I had what I'd come for. Now I had to get away from here. How much time had passed? Fifteen minutes since finding the body? A half hour? Yeah, but best to make sure there was nothing left behind that might make people look at me. Then, get out.

But I found nothing else, not even a wallet—and that was weird. Jimmy said he got paid every Wednesday. Hadn't he decided to cash his check to cover my expenses? So where was the money? Had his killers taken it? Had this been all about a robbery?

As incredible as this may sound to you, that was the first time I'd actually slowed down long enough to wonder *why* Jimmy was murdered. For the money? Because they thought he was gay? Because he'd crossed them somehow? Who were these people? Why had he gone with that guy I'd seen in the back lot in the first place? And *was* it a guy? The more I thought about it, it could've been a girl. Way more likely than a guy, right? *Right?* Shit. I just didn't know.

But whoever it was and whatever their motive, Jimmy had gone because he trusted the guy or the girl . . . because they were friends? No, from what I'd seen, either they were more than friends, or the guy *wanted* to take things further . . . only Jimmy had refused? Jimmy had said *no.* I'd heard him. But then Jimmy got in the car. So maybe *no* wasn't really *no.* Maybe Jimmy changed his mind, gave in, and then . . .

"Jesus." My voice was airy and thin and sick. "*Stop* already." My thoughts were scuttling around and around in the rat's maze of my brain, and I had to find a way out, I had to leave. I was chilled and my ankles were cold, and there was nothing more I could do. Using the socks, I messed the prints left by my running shoes. Then, stripping off my stained socks, I turned them inside out the way I did with latex gloves in the ER.

I thought about saying good-bye or telling Jimmy I was sorry. I really did. But what good would that do? Looking down at him, though, I thought about how long it might take people to find him. The flies were bad, and I didn't like that animals had already been at him. Maybe I could phone in a tip or something, anonymously. But it was daylight now, and if they traced the call to the phone, someone might remember the Lariat—

"Phone." I wasn't aware I'd spoken aloud until I heard my own whisper. Of course, if I turned on his phone, they'd find him faster and before too many more things got at him, which I really did want. It also meant that I had to separate my gluey socks, ease my naked toes into bloody jelly, and roll Jimmy again, but I did it.

Jimmy's cell was a clamshell. I flipped the phone open—and then hesitated when I remembered something else: cameras. Cell phones had cameras, and Jimmy loved cameras. So, had he taken shots of me with *this*? Possibly—he'd managed with a digital camera, after all. Even so, that wasn't necessarily incriminating. Everyone knew about the magazine pictures.

But what if there were other people on the camera, maybe even the people who'd killed him? I might recognize them—and if so, I could still make this right.

I could imagine myself clicking through pictures, enlarging one, recognizing the killers. Taking the pictures to my dad. Coming clean about what had happened. It would be hard, but I would've ID'ed the killers. They'd bring in suspects, line them up as I stood behind a one-way mirror with my dad and said, *Yeah, that's him. The blond guy with the black hoodie.*

Then I'd be a hero. People would understand what had happened. Then I'd be good. Always. I'd been a good person before, but now I'd be better.

The problem was that I knew only the most rudimentary workings of cell phones. You flipped them open, you made phone calls. You could take pictures. There were other bells and whistles—surfing the Internet, text messaging—but I didn't know much about that. But I did know enough to understand that pictures were saved to either the phone's internal memory or a small memory card. But I couldn't turn on the phone to check whatever was stored in memory. The moment the cell went live, I was dead. Which left only the memory card.

The socks made it impossible to open the tiny rubber cover over the card slot. So I shucked out of one sock and used the edge of my thumbnail to pry open the slot, hoping that fingerprint programs weren't nearly as good as the ones on *CSI*. I spotted the navy blue of the card right away and pressed it with my fingernail. The tiny card popped out. I slipped it into the pocket of my sweatshirt and then closed the slot.

Then I turned on Jimmy's phone, laid it on the concrete, and left.

Afterward, I drove in my bare feet to another park that had lake trails where I knew there would be people walking their dogs and stuff. I didn't feel much like running, but I needed witnesses. By then, it was after noon, and the day had warmed up with the sun. My brain was foggy with fatigue and fear and my stomach was empty, so my form was crap. My whole body was shaky and shuddery. Every step shivered into the small of my back. I'd wiped down the shoes before starting out, but running without socks, which I'd chucked into a porta-potty, was bringing up blisters on my ankles. My gastrocs cramped up about five miles into it, and then I was hobbling off to a bench and cursing. I'd been so flustered I hadn't remembered to bring any Gatorade or water, but there was a concession stand and I gimped over and bought an energy drink. Got it down without bringing it back up. Then I went home.

My mom was still at the table, only she'd changed out of her robe and into jeans, and the kitchen smelled like soup. She looked up from the Sunday crossword. "How was the run?"

"Okay," I said. "I'm going to take a shower and then I got homework. Uh . . . did Dad . . . have they found . . ."

She shook her head. "I don't know. He was taking a nap when the dispatcher called him back in. I guess something's happened. He said he'd call when he knew." She hooked her pencil over her shoulder. "I thawed some of that pumpkin soup you like so much. Might settle your stomach."

My guts did a slow roll. "Pumpkin. Yeah," I said. "That would be just great."

Peeling out of my clothes that, this time, I knew I would have to get rid of. Another shower. Only this time I started crying. I thought I was done with that, but I apparently wasn't. Muzzling myself with both hands, I slid down the stall and huddled there, weeping, until the water ran icy and my skin burned. By then I was empty as an old corn husk. One stiff breeze and I'd blow away. That actually might be okay, too.

Once I'd locked my door, I dug out a pair of thin glove liners and put them on. Then I laid out the envelope I'd found on Jimmy's body and the micro-card from his cell phone on Kleenex. Stared at my name in block capitals. Fretted a couple minutes about how I was going to open the envelope and then thought about how stupid that was. So I ripped it open the envelope and shook.

A clear plastic case tumbled onto the Kleenex along with a piece of paper folded in a small square. Inside the case was a blue eight-gig CF card. Shit. I had no way of reading that. What an idiot. My mom had a little digital camera, but it took the other kind of memory cards.

I turned my attention to the paper. Dried blood had glued the folds together, and I wasn't able to tease the paper apart without rips. The paper was blotchy with copper splatters, but I was able to make out enough: instructions to print JPEGs 2, 14, 26, 30, and 42, as well as a completed application that Jimmy had loaded onto the card, with an address to which I was to send the entire packet.

Below that, Jimmy had penned this:

I'm so sorry for everything. You've been my only friend. I never wanted you to get hurt. There may be something wrong with me, but I can't believe it's wrong to feel about you the way I do.

Jimmy

———————

It took me a long time to figure where to hide the cards. I *did* think about mailing them to the sheriff's office and letting them deal. But there were so many ways that could go wrong and blow back on me, and I still didn't know what was on those cards either.

Besides, there would be no way to make this right if I did that. Because I still hadn't given up on that idea. I could make this right; I could still do *something* right.

I thought of slipping them between the pages of a book, but then all the movies I'd ever seen had cops shaking out books by their spines. Walking around with the cards tucked in a pocket was out of the question. No way I was shoving them into the toe of a boot or shoe, either. It would be just my luck for my mom to decide that pair of boots deserved a trip to Goodwill. She was always doing crap like that.

Finally, I dug under the stack of Kleenex still in the dispenser box, slipped the cards underneath, then patted the

Kleenex back into place. Maybe not the best hiding place, but it was the only thing I could think of to do.

And I flushed that goddamned note. My life had gone down the toilet. Somehow, it seemed appropriate to return the favor.

I had a lot of work, mainly for my university courses, and reading to do for English Honors. I opened my books, but I still couldn't concentrate. When I'd reread the same paragraph about the Jacobian of a gradient three times over without it making a lick of sense, I gave up.

Booting up my computer, I went to the Common App site. Reread all the lies I'd told about myself. I didn't recognize that person, the one who talked about how he'd discovered he wasn't in the ER for himself but for the patient. I looked at what I'd been doing my entire stupid life to this point: getting good grades and acing the SATs and subject tests and doing Key Club and Big Brothers and all that shit designed to make me seem attractive, someone a college would want. The person in these pages was a model citizen, a great student, a stand-up guy.

That person was a complete lie.

In that moment, I saw the application for what it was: a marketing gimmick, a sales tool—like the trailer for a movie— a compilation of my greatest hits.

Now, I am one hundred percent sure I was not the first kid to have that thought. But I was ninety-nine-point-nine-nine-nine percent sure that I was the only kid with that thought to run like hell when his friend got his brains bashed in with a rock and hacked to death.

But I didn't push <send>. I didn't close out the program either.

I don't know what the hell I was waiting for.

My dad didn't come home, and he didn't call. After faking my way through dinner, I managed to slog through my calculus and chemistry, and then I decided to try to read. I've always liked books. I mean, math was cool because there were these pristine equations and only one right answer, nothing vague. They had a certain purity. Books are way different. When I was younger, I used to program in these study breaks when I'd give myself permission to read a chapter out of whatever book I was on that week. Books are like these trapdoors into other worlds and problems, like Alice tumbling down the rabbit hole.

Now, if *Alice in Wonderland* were physics, you could calculate how fast Alice falls and when she'll hit bottom; if the hole's really bottomless, and assuming for infinite acceleration, could Alice ever reach a point where she was going so fast that she could break the speed of light? And as she gets closer to the speed of light, and because she's still in Earth's gravitational field, what happens to her? Does her head age faster than her feet? Unless she fell headfirst, in which case her feet would age faster.

Books aren't like that, though. Right then, we were finishing up *A Catcher in the Rye*, which I'd read about two years ago, so rereading it was no problem at first. The class was still back where Holden's just getting ready to call his old teacher, Mr. Antolini, but I'd reached the penultimate chapter, when Holden's gone to say good-bye to his little sister, only to discover that she's brought this big suitcase because she wants to go with him.

Well, so it turned out that reading was a bad move, too. I got this sick and fluttery feeling again because I couldn't help but read about old Phoebe and think of little Jimmy. Holden's sister was just a kid, and I'd always thought of Jimmy like that: really young, not very experienced, someone you had to protect. Even now, with everything that had gone on, I had a hard time thinking of him being just a year behind me in school. I could see Jimmy pulling a Phoebe. Showing up with a suitcase and wanting to run away with me.

Only . . . that wasn't right, was it? Jimmy had been trying to leave town. He hadn't talked about following *me* anywhere. *I'd* followed *him*. So whose fantasy was that, anyway? Why had I been thinking that Jimmy would want to go with *me*? God, did that mean I felt more for Jimmy than—

Jesus, stop it. I rubbed the naked space right above the bridge of my nose. I had to cut this out. Was it going to be like this for the rest of my life? I was driving myself crazy. Jimmy had made his own mistakes. They hadn't concerned me at all. Oh, some of them were *about* me, but I wasn't to blame. Jimmy had acted on his own all the way along. I was the one playing catch-up after the fact, trying to figure out what Jimmy had planned or intended.

Downstairs and in my parents' bedroom, the phones shrilled once, twice. I heard Mom answer. Pause. Pause.

And then she said, very distinctly, "Oh *no!*"

Okay. I closed my eyes, forced myself to breathe. *It's okay. You knew this was coming. Just relax.*

A couple moments later, I heard Mom hang up the phone and then her footsteps on the stairs. The floorboards creaked as she walked the hall toward my room.

And then she stopped.

But I could feel her, this presence, this *pressure* just beyond, out there, in that world. If I let myself, I could see her, too: a balled hand poised to knock, the other wrapped around her stomach because she thought she might be sick.

Then a quick double-rap. And: "Honey?"

As he watched his little sister, Holden Caulfield was positive there was no such thing as a nice, peaceful place on this earth. He was right about that, and in the end it broke him. Too bad for old Holden, he just couldn't do the math.

But I could.

Alice could fall forever. But the math said that after she reached a certain speed, the universe would pile up below her feet. Beyond the far horizon toward which she plummeted, time must eventually stop—and *that* would be peace.

It was simply a question of falling far and fast enough.

This was it, my Wonderland moment. Everything that happened from here on out depended on what I did next. I might not be able to rocket to the far horizon, but that didn't mean I couldn't reach breakaway speed. I could—but only if I was very lucky and very, very careful.

My application, the one I'd delayed sending for so long, hummed on my screen.

One foot in front of the other, right up to the brink.

I reached for the mouse.

I clicked <send>.

And, just like that, the ground swooned open, and I was falling fast and then faster and ever faster . . .

Escape velocity.

Then I went to open the door so my mother could give me the bad news.

OCTOBER 27

1314

TO ALL WHOM THIS MIGHT CONCERN:

The next day was Monday.

Mom hadn't said much the night before, only that they'd found Jimmy and my dad wouldn't be home for a long time. She didn't say anything about anyone wanting me to stay up, which was good because I was running on fumes.

But I still couldn't sleep. Every time I closed my eyes, I kept seeing Jimmy's body, matted with flies, lying in a lake of congealed blood. I kept checking the clock, only to find that two minutes had passed since the last time I'd looked. Sometime around four or five I must've dozed off, because my alarm jolted me out of a garbled bad dream I mercifully couldn't remember.

I stumbled downstairs in a fog. Mom and a subdued Mal were already at the table. The kitchen smelled of coffee and sweet French toast, which was normally Mal's favorite. Yet, for once, even she was only picking, cutting her food into smaller and ever smaller squares.

"Your dad got in about fifteen minutes ago," Mom said. "He's showering, but then he's got to go right back out."

"Where?" I asked.

"He didn't say. Poor thing, he's exhausted. He ought to stay home, but . . ." Her eyebrows tented with worry as she splashed coffee into my mug. "You don't look well at all. How's your stomach?"

"I'm okay." I blew on my coffee for something to do. Otherwise, I was afraid I'd fall asleep right there at the table.

"I'm not scheduled for anything today," Mom said. "You can stay home if you want."

"Can I?" Mal suddenly piped up. Thumbing her plate away, she looked at our mother, and I saw then that her lips trembled. "I don't feel so good."

"Certainly not," Mom said. "The only reason I offered was because your brother was sick yesterday." Then, softening, Mom palmed hair from Mal's forehead. "I know it's hard, honey. But this isn't your fault."

"We made fun of him." Mal's eyes pooled. "We laughed."

"Jimmy was what he was," our mother said. "You're only human."

I didn't know what either of those statements even meant. But watching Mom soothing Mal . . . my phantom fingers feathered Jimmy's hair. I could feel the ghost of his skin.

"We should get going," I said abruptly. I didn't think I could stand another minute in the house, not with them, or Dad just upstairs. If I stayed away from school, all I'd do was worry about when he was going to knock on my door and want to talk about the last time I saw Jimmy alive. Which the police were going to do anyway, just as soon as they talked to the people at Cuppa Joy.

Mom wanted to drive me and Mal to school, but I wouldn't let her. Mal didn't say word one the whole way but only stared, her expression white and pinched. I kept punching radio stations, but the noise was like nails on chalkboard scratching my brain, and I switched the damn thing off.

As we rounded a corner near the school, Mal suddenly stirred then pointed. "Hey, look at that."

News vans were lined up across the street from school. I recognized the logos for the local stations, including Wausau and Superior, and yet another from Green Bay, which was kind of a shock. The news people were standing behind a barricade of orange sawhorses, and I recognized a few of the deputies keeping the reporters off school grounds.

As I turned into the lot, another deputy held up a hand, then changed over to a wave as he recognized us. "Hey, kids," he said as I lowered my window. He was an older guy who'd been in the department nearly as long as my dad. "How you two holding up?"

"We're okay," I said. "Are you going to let the news people in the school?"

He shook his head. "But you better watch yourself. Those vultures might recognize you from that magazine. We're here to make sure the news people keep their distance, but there's nothing we can do once you're off school property."

"But I don't know anything," I said for what must be the bazillionth time. It seemed to me that was all I'd been saying for days now—first about that damned stupid picture, and now this.

"Yeah, but you were Jimmy's friend. Anyway, we can't keep them off once you leave school property, so just watch your step, okay? I think either your dad or the sheriff is talking to the school this morning. " A car beeped behind me, and the deputy backed away with a wave.

A trio of teachers was stationed at the front doors and kept shouting that everyone was to report to the auditorium after going to their lockers. In the senior hall, Parker and my other friends were AWOL, but I was surprised to find Brooke waiting for me. "Hey," she said as I walked up. "That thing about Jimmy's all over town. I'm really sorry."

"Yeah." Rattling open my locker, I dumped books, stashed my coat. "Does anyone know what happened?"

"No, but I'll bet that's what the assembly's about." She hesitated then asked, "Has your dad said anything?"

"I haven't seen him. I guess they have to wait for an autopsy or something." I banged my locker shut. "How'd you hear about it?"

"Are you kidding?" she said as we joined in with a stream of kids heading toward the auditorium. "It's all over the local news. I heard they might be calling in the FBI."

"Yeah?" A shiver shuddered up my body, like I'd stepped into an ice bath. My shirt between my shoulder blades was suddenly damp, and the walls seemed to close in. I'd never had an anxiety attack before, but I wondered if maybe this was what it was like. This whole thing was a nightmare I just couldn't seem to wake up from. I tried to think about the sheriff calling the FBI. Could they do that? That didn't sound right. Jimmy didn't seem like something the FBI dealt with. I thought the FBI only did serial killers or kidnappers.

"That's what they're saying." She peered up at me. "Are you okay?"

"No. Yeah." I blew out a shaky breath. "Just . . . it's all kind of unbelievable, you know? Makes me sick."

"I know. It's so weird, he was just in school a month ago. Now he gets murdered and . . . it makes me kind of look around, you know? Wonder who at school might do something like that?"

"Is that what people think? That it was someone in school?" I didn't know if this was good or bad. Mal and her friends had laughed at Jimmy. Kids made fun behind his back. So this might be a good thing, right?

Unless they looked at me. Which, of course, they would. No one would have to dig far for the whole Cuppa Joy mess. And there was the picture, the damn picture . . .

"I don't know," Brooke was saying. We were in the auditorium now. The air buzzed with excited voices. Teachers from the various grades were trying to direct kids into rows, but no one was paying attention and the room swarmed with bodies. Brooke tossed a look over both shoulders, then leaned in with a conspiratorial whisper: "Actually, I heard they arrested his dad."

Oh, thank you, God. The shock—the relief—was physical, a wash of emotion that left me suddenly limp. *Let them look anywhere but at me.*

"His dad?" I had to resist wiping sweat from my upper lip. "Really?"

She gave a grave nod. "That's the rumor, anyway. We all know he beat up Jimmy, so . . ." Her eyes clicked left, and then she'd thrown a wave to friends. Still, she lingered. "Would you like to sit with—"

"No." The last thing I needed was to be with Brooke. I didn't know why then. Now, I think I was afraid of . . . well, I was just afraid. Thankfully, I'd spotted Parker and the other guys and was already angling that way. "But I'll catch you later, okay?" I think she said something else, but it was lost in the crush—and, really, it was better that way.

"Are you all right?" Parker asked.

I dropped into an open seat between him and Robert. "Everyone keeps asking me that."

"Well, *duh*. He was your friend, dude." Robert shook his head. "You believe this?"

"There's some weird shit going down," Parker said.

Mark sat to Parker's left, and now he leaned forward. "I heard they think one of us did it. You know, a student."

Parker frowned. "Why would anyone do that?"

"Well," Mark said, and his eyes slid to me. "Because Jimmy was . . . you know. Like those guys and the Fletcher place."

"But it was the gay dude who burned down the house," Parker pointed out.

"Well, I heard they think maybe someone made an example out of Jimmy," Mark said. He was still looking at me. "Kind of like a warning."

I said nothing. Parker crinkled his nose. "Warning?"

"Yeah, like, you know." Mark rifled another look my way,

then lowered his voice enough that Parker and Robert crowded in to hear. "About being gay."

Parker let out a disgusted snort. "Dude, you don't know shit. Why you spreading rumors like that?"

Mark bridled. "Hey, I'm not the one starting them. I'm just saying."

"Well, you shouldn't be repeating them. Nobody knows anything about anything," Parker said.

At that moment, the principal walked across the stage. The hum of conversation died, but the air fizzed with expectant whispers. In the lull, I looked to my right and spotted two other people slipping through a side door. One was the sheriff.

The other—of course—was my dad.

I knew why they were there: to watch us. To see how we reacted.

To see if maybe one of us would give himself away.

Onstage, the principal cleared his throat. "As I'm sure you're all aware, one of our students, James Lange, died at some point this past weekend." He paused as if expecting to be interrupted. Yet the auditorium was quiet as a tomb. Not a cough. No whispers. "This is a terrible tragedy for his family and this community," the principal resumed. "I don't know what you've heard or what rumors are making the rounds, but I can tell you this: Jimmy Lange didn't commit suicide. He wasn't in an accident." The principal paused, then said, "Jimmy Lange—our student, your fellow classmate—was murdered."

Now there were murmurs and scattered gasps. Someone said, very distinctly, "Oh no!"

The principal held up his hands for quiet. To me, he looked like a pastor about to give a benediction. "Other than that, I have no information for you, nor would it be appropriate for me to speculate. I can only tell you that the sheriff's department is throwing the full weight of its resources behind this investigation. The Hopkins police department is also cooperating, and it's possible that state authorities may become involved at some point. To that end, it's highly likely that law enforcement officials will want to speak with those of you who shared classes with Jimmy, or were his friends."

There was a general rustling. I felt eyes shift in my direction, but I kept mine fixed on that stage.

And this is also the truth: I badly wanted to glance over at my dad. In fact, I remember wondering if I should. Wouldn't that be the normal reaction of an innocent kid? To look at his dad? But I didn't.

"Some of you knew Del, Jimmy's older brother. His loss was bad enough. The death of any young person is tragic. But Jimmy's is far worse." The principal's tone turned hard. "It's worse because I know that there were some of you who were unfair to this young man. Some of you are guilty of spreading rumors that drove him from this school. They fueled speculation about what should be a private matter and caused distress not only to Jimmy but also his parents. Those of you who participated in this should be ashamed."

"Oh, give me a break," someone murmured behind me. Someone else snorted, "Maybe they should just ask Jimmy's *boyfriend.*"

I felt the burn creep up the back of my neck. Parker turned around. "Hey, asshole, shut up."

"Yeah?" It was Snort. "You going to make me?"

Their voices weren't much above a murmur, but heads were

turning now, eyes flicking from Parker to the kid to me. To Parker's right, I saw Mark nudge Robert, and the two of them scooted forward a tad, either to catch the action or, more likely, be part of it. This I really didn't need. "Come on, leave it alone, Parker," I muttered. "It's okay."

"Yeah," Snort said, "leave it. Jimmy's boyfriend wants you to leave it."

"Listen," Parker began, but then I was turning around, fists cocked, my face hot with anger. I didn't know the kid, a freshman probably, but his smirk drained away as he got a good look at my face. He put his hands up.

"Hey, man, hey," he said, "I was just . . ." His eyes cut right, and then he abruptly sat back.

"Problem here?" It was the sheriff. I'd been so focused on the kid, I hadn't noticed that the principal had stopped speaking. Everyone was looking.

Okay, this was *so* not the way to handle things. I shot a glance at my dad, who hadn't moved from his post by that side door. The auditorium was gloomy, and he was too far away for me to make out his expression. I looked up at the sheriff. "No, sir," I said.

"Glad to hear it," the sheriff said. "But why don't the two of you come on out into the hall anyway?"

Parker spoke up. "Hey, Ben didn't do anything. It was this other kid."

"It's okay." I stood. "Really. I'll be all right."

If you think that watching Jimmy being killed was the worst moment of my life—well, other than my running away and letting it happen—you'd be right. But the hardest thing I ever did, after robbing Jimmy's fly-ridden corpse, was get myself out of that auditorium. My ears roared. So stupid to get dragged into this. The kid was a nobody, an idiot, but I'd reacted and that was my mistake. They'd question me now, and everything would come out because they'd grill me and I'd crack.

But maybe that was for the best. I could shift this weight from my shoulders. And I hadn't done anything, not really. I had to remember that. No one punished a kid who didn't do anything.

Even if the truth ruins his life.

———————

They put me in this little conference room with nothing but a table, some chairs—and a box of tissues. I'll tell you something: that damn Kleenex box nearly gave me heart failure. All I could think was, *Shit, they found the memory cards.* It took me a second to realize that box was the wrong color, wrong shape. Not mine.

A slim rectangle of window was inset in the door, and I could see people walking up and down the hall from the front office. Everyone who passed glanced and nodded, gave me that thin-lipped kind of smile that was more like a grimace.

Be cool. Stay calm. My teeth worried loose skin on the side of my thumb. *One foot in front of the other.*

A secretary popped in, asked if I wanted a cup of coffee or maybe some water. I didn't but worried how that would look. Like, whether punks or murderers felt so guilty they couldn't choke anything down. So I asked for coffee.

"I brought you a couple of creamers and a packet of sugar," she said, depositing these and a steaming Styrofoam cup on the table. She put a hand on my shoulder. "I'm sorry about your friend. I've lived here all my life, and I don't ever remember anything as bad as this happening. I can't imagine how hard this must be for you."

She was being so nice my throat got all knotted up. She wouldn't be so understanding once she knew about me. I swallowed around what felt like a stone. "I'm okay. Thanks for the coffee."

She squeezed my shoulder again and then left me alone. I played around with the coffee, took my time stirring in creamer and sugar. The coffee was terrible, like sugared mud. But it gave me something to do.

They kept me waiting about twenty minutes, long enough for the coffee to get bone-cold, the bell for second period to ring, and me to break into a clammy sweat. If they didn't hurry up, I was going to miss my calculus and chemistry classes at the university, and I couldn't do that. That would totally mess up my grades. Maybe I should tell somebody I had to get going. Then I thought that this was probably part of their strategy—to completely freak me out, soften me up so I'd be off-balance and say something stupid. The more I thought about that, the more I thought that was probably right. They'd found something; I'd left some piece of evidence behind—maybe a partial print from my running shoes or my bare toes or something—only the evidence wasn't enough to really connect me to Jimmy's murder. So they were sweating me, hoping I'd slip up and incriminate myself. Should I ask for a lawyer? No, that would be dumb; on cop shows, that's how they knew the guy was guilty.

Be calm, stay cool. The only reason I was sitting here was because I let some stupid freshman get under my skin. They'd probably been planning on talking to me all along. Of course they had; the principal said the police were going to question Jimmy's friends. My behavior only made sure it would happen sooner rather than later was all. I just had to be careful.

My thumb complained, and the tang of wet salt started on my tongue. *Shit.* I'd gnawed the skin to the quick. *Easy, easy.* I sucked away another bead of blood. Probably Dad would ask only a few questions . . . or would he? Would they allow my dad to do the questioning? Maybe not. Maybe that was a conflict of interest, like a doctor operating on her own—

The window darkened, and I looked to see the sheriff standing there. How long? Had I been jiggling my leg? I didn't think so, but I'd been chewing on my thumb . . . stupid, *stupid* . . . Jamming my hand under a thigh, I sat up straighter as the sheriff turned and spoke to someone off to his right. I couldn't see who it was. Then the sheriff craned his head back, peeped through the window, moved his head in a nod. Opened the door. He was smiling, but it looked fake to me. "Hey there," he said.

"Hi," I said, the word riding on an airy exhalation that cut off when I realized that the sheriff wasn't alone.

Two people filed in on his heels: my dad—and a trim woman in a dark brown, knee-length suit. She had a messenger bag slung over one shoulder. Her reddish-brown hair brushed her shoulders, and she wore square-framed glasses that made her look smarter than I thought she already was. Yet her smile felt real, and I found myself relaxing a little bit.

Dad just looked exhausted. There were big, purple bags under his eyes, and his skin was a thin, sickly yellow under the fluorescent lights. "Son," he said. "This is Special Agent Thorne from Madison."

Oh my God. I could feel the smile freeze on my mouth. A special agent. Brooke was right; they'd called the *FBI*...

"Angela," she said, holding out her hand like we were going to be friends and she was just one of the gang. "The sheriff and I wanted to ask you a few questions."

Her grip was firm. Her skin was soft and warm. As we shook, I threw an uncertain look at Dad—just the tiniest glance—but she caught it, real quick. "You can have your father stay if you want. Just for the record, though, until we've cleared up a few things, your father's not taking an active part in the investigation." Her voice was pleasant, but now I heard an undertone of accusation, a sort of hard cop-edge.

"Why not?" I asked. She still had my hand, and I didn't know whether I should pull back first. I decided to let her make the first move.

She waited a half sec, then let my hand go but kept those suspicious cop-eyes locked on mine. "Because you and Jimmy had a . . . history. There had been recent conflict between you and the Langes. It would be inappropriate for your father to be involved."

Translation: I was a suspect. Dad got involved with people we knew all the time, so Agent Angela was bullshitting me—unless she wasn't. Judges and lawyers weren't supposed to be involved if they had a personal stake in the outcome. I figured it would look bad if I asked if I was a suspect, so I said, instead, "Okay. But I have classes at the university. I have a test coming up."

"I'm sure they'll understand. If they give you a hard time, we can run interference for you." She flashed another smile, but this was one was a fake: no teeth at all, nothing that made it to her eyes. "Would you like your father to stay?"

Yes. But my dad didn't say anything, and that made me nervous. He was still my dad, but now there was a new kind of stillness about him, too. Like he was giving me that cop-eye again, only this time, the person he saw was not his son.

"No," I said. "That's okay."

"All right then," said the sheriff and clapped Dad on the shoulder. "We'll be outside." To me: "That is, unless you want someone else you know to sit with you while you and Agent Thorne talk."

"No, I'm okay," I said again. Then I thought, wait, wasn't the *sheriff* supposed to stay? To monitor things? Jimmy was killed in *his* jurisdiction. But would it look bad if I said something about that?

Shut up and stay cool. Keep your mouth shut.

"Is that coffee?" asked Agent Angela as she scraped back a chair to my left. "God, I'd kill for a cup. I've been driving since four."

The sheriff said, "I'll get you a cup."

"Thank you," said Agent Angela. "Just some creamer."

The sheriff nodded and then asked if I wanted a refill. I didn't, but I said yes because it would give me something to do with my hands. My dad filed out after the sheriff without a word or backward glance. Agent Angela waited until the door closed, then set her bag on the table, flipped up the front flap, and rummaged around before coming up with a small tape recorder about the size of a pack of gum. "You don't mind if I record this."

It wasn't a request, and I knew it would be bad to say no. She talked into the tape first, giving her name, the date, where we were, who I was, and what this was about. Then she squared the recorder on the table between us and said, "I'm sure you've got a lot of questions. You'll understand if I can't answer all of them."

I nodded. My throat was way too dry all of a sudden. "What happened to Jimmy?"

"He was beaten to death," said Agent Angela. She said it matter-of-factly, like, *nice weather we're having.*

"Beaten," I repeated and thought, *Oh shit, this is where she pulls out photographs or something and watches how I react.* All of a sudden, my voice cracked. "Like, how?"

"I'm sorry, but I can't tell you that. What I can say is that his body was found in a park outside town. Since we know that he didn't have a car that evening, he had to have been taken there." She crossed her legs and tugged at the hem of her skirt. She had a runner's legs. Her voice softened as she pushed the box of Kleenex my way. "I'm sorry. I know the two of you were close."

"Not so much." I looked down, thumbing away tears that seemed to keep coming no matter what I did, and mad that she'd seen me cry like a little kid. I'd be damned if I was going to use the Kleenex. "I mean, we used to be, but ever since his parents pulled him out of school . . ." When she didn't jump in, I swallowed. "Did he . . . was it . . . I mean, did he suffer?"

Maybe that was the wrong question. She cocked her head in a way that looked a little like a dog trying to understand whatever it was you'd just said. "Yes, I think he did. Horribly." She paused. "You cared about him."

I was saved from answering by the sheriff coming back with the coffee. Agent Angela turned off the recorder while we did the cream thing. I dumped in sugar, hoping that maybe the coffee would taste better than it had the first time. It didn't.

Agent Angela made a face as she sipped hers. "Ugh. Worse than cop coffee, and that's saying something."

"Are you, like, FBI?" I asked. The question just popped out.

She shook her head, then stretched to switch on the recorder again. "BCA, Division of Criminal Investigation. I do hate crimes. We think that maybe Jimmy's murder had something to do with his being gay."

"But . . . Jimmy wasn't gay," I said. "That is, he never came out or anything. That's just a rumor."

"Well, his photography was certainly suggestive," she said, sipping her coffee. "Wasn't that why his parents withdrew him from the school?"

"I don't know why his parents yanked him," I said, then amended: "Well, that's not true. They were mad because of those pictures. But that doesn't mean *he* was gay. All it means is *they* were pissed."

"But you just said the gay thing was a rumor. In my experience, most rumors have their bases in fact."

I shrugged. As tired as I was, I was also irritated, and these were stupid questions. She wanted to believe things went down a certain way, fine.

When I didn't reply, she said, "You didn't speak with him?"

Careful. "When?"

"This past weekend."

"No," I said, and considered that, technically, this was true. I hadn't spoken to him the night he died. "I saw him on Friday, though." That was okay to admit because it would come out anyway and had the virtue of being true. "I went to see him where he worked. The Cuppa Joy . . . it's a Christian coffeehouse outside town."

"Why?"

"Because," I said and stopped. She was playing games. If she knew about the rumors swirling around Jimmy, she knew about me. "I was pissed, okay? That stupid picture caused so much trouble, you can't imagine." I told her about the day Mr. Lange threw me off the property and then the way everyone at school had reacted. "So I wanted to see him. To clear the air. I mean, I was really angry. What he wanted people to think about him was his business. I didn't want to get dragged into his problems. He didn't even ask my permission to use that picture. I didn't know he'd taken it."

"But you remember when it was taken?"

"August. We were haying. I fell asleep. I thought I'd dreamed the sound . . . you know, the way cameras sound when you take a picture."

"So you never suspected the depth of his feeling for you?"

"No. I mean, *what* feeling? I cared about him, like, you know, a *friend*. I felt sorry for him, and he was just a little kid."

"He was a junior."

"He seemed younger to me. Kind of . . . lost after Del died. I thought I could help him. Instead . . ." I shook my head and fiddled with my cup. "I just made everything worse."

"How do you see that?"

"If I hadn't been there, he wouldn't have taken that picture. He might not have won anything, and then his father wouldn't have beat the crap out of him. What's with that, anyway? Don't parents like that get reported?"

"Believe me, we're looking into that. So what happened

when you went to Cuppa Joy?"

I went through it all: asking about Jimmy at the counter, Jimmy showing up at my table, the lady calling Pastor John. "Then Pastor John pretty much told me he didn't want *my kind*"—I mimed air quotes—"in his coffeehouse. So I left."

"Your kind." Agent Angela ran a finger around the rim of her empty cup. "You mean . . . gay."

"I'm not gay," I said. "I don't know if Jimmy was gay. Everyone's just *assumed* that he was, that he and I might have, you know . . . *done* something. It's nobody's business even if he was or we had. You want to look at somebody with a serious axe to grind, you ought to look at Pastor John."

"You don't like Pastor John," Agent Angela said. I noticed for the first time that her eyes were this deep, mossy green with flecks of hazel. I don't think I'd ever met anyone with eyes like that.

"He's a bigoted jerk," I said and meant that, too. So far I hadn't lied, and that was good. Okay, I had omitted stuff, but so what. "Why don't you ask him where *he* was the night Jimmy died?" As soon as I said that, I thought, *Oh shit, had she said Jimmy was killed at night? But, wait, wouldn't that be what would a normal person say?* This was how they tripped up killers on TV, when they said too damned much.

And then I almost, *almost* gasped because that was when I realized something important.

The night I saw Pastor John, he'd worn a black hoodie. He'd been wearing one the afternoon Jimmy's dad beat his son with a magazine. Except all Pastor John's hoodies had logos, didn't they? What about the person I'd seen Saturday night with Jimmy, *kissing* Jimmy . . . had there been a logo? I couldn't remember, exactly, but I thought that it hadn't. So what did that mean? It couldn't be Pastor John? What if he'd worried he might be recog—

"I intend to," she said, cutting into my thoughts. "So Friday was the last time you spoke to Jimmy?"

"Uh . . . yeah," I said. It was the truth, too. Thank God.

She nodded, then only stared. I kept waiting for a question, but none came. My nose developed a sudden, maddening itch, and I scrubbed it with the back of my hand. Then I glanced at my watch.

"You have somewhere to be?" she asked.

"Yes." My eyes snapped up. "I don't like missing class."

"Mmmm. I heard from your principal that you're valedictorian?"

"I guess so. So far. The year's still young," I said, trying to make a joke.

She showed a small smile. "Where do you want to go to school?"

"Yale." When her left eyebrow bowed in a perfect arch I added, "I don't expect to get in. But you never know unless you try."

She said the strangest thing then. "Well, that's pretty far away. From home, I mean."

I didn't know how to answer that, so I didn't. She let the silence stretch. The wall clock ticked. Finally, I said, "Did you have any other questions? If I leave now, I can still catch my chemistry class."

"Of course," she said and offered her hand again. This time I pulled back first. She said, "I might think of more to ask. Is it okay if I call or visit you at home?"

"Sure," I said. What else could I say?

"Thanks," she said, and then, as I scraped back my chair and stood, she held up a finger. "One more thing."

There was some old TV cop who used to do that, but I was blanking on the name. "Yeah?"

"If Jimmy was . . . *intimate* with someone in the school, or you thought he was, would you tell me?"

I had to think about that. Because it was a funny question. "No," I said, finally.

She did the eyebrow thing again. "Why not?"

"Because you asked two different things," I said. "If Jimmy was going out with someone, we would all know it and none of this would be a rumor. It would be a fact. If I only *thought* he was going out with someone, that would be a guess and it's really none of my business. I'd be spreading rumors. Believe me, I know what it feels like to be on the other end of that."

"That's an interesting distinction. But Jimmy's dead. The rumors can't hurt him, and many are built on half-truths. What if rumors helped us catch his killer? Would you tell me then?"

She was an idiot. The rumors could hurt Jimmy's family. They could hurt me. I realized how angry I'd become and wondered where all my fear had gone. "Half a truth is still half a lie." I said.

"Fair enough." Clicking off the tape recorder, she folded her hands on the table. "Thanks for speaking to me. I'll be in touch." No smile this time.

I knew then: she didn't believe me about *me.*

She believed the rumors.

———————

The other thing I got when I was halfway to the university: She hadn't asked me if I'd done it. Or where I'd been. Or if I had an alibi.

And then I thought, *Wait. She never read me my rights.*

What did that mean? What did that *mean*?

My university classes were a complete disaster, but I managed to get the notes on what I missed.

I banged back into the high school with five minutes to go before lunch was over, and I was, suddenly, ravenous. Like, I wanted a steak. When was the last time I'd really eaten anything other than that half a Whopper on Saturday night? So I grabbed a burger and fries from the cafeteria line and a carton of milk.

Brooke was sitting alone with a couple books spread on the table but made room as I slid across from her. "Hey," she said, not looking a bit surprised that I'd chosen to hang with her. (To be honest, I wasn't sure myself, and didn't care. Only later did I realize that being with Brooke made me look normal. So maybe my unconscious mind was trying to protect me, just in case Agent Angela had spies.) "I don't know why they don't just call off school," she said. "None of the teachers are doing their lessons, which kind of sucks because I stayed up late studying for a test. They have these grief counselors coming tomorrow. Some kind of SWAT team of crisis intervention or something. Like everyone's going to have a nervous breakdown."

"Stupid." I took a huge bite of my burger. It was rubbery and too salty and so good I almost fainted. I licked a dribble of catsup from my pinky. "It's not like Columbine or something."

"So I heard you got interviewed by a special agent from Madison. How did it go?"

"Okay," I mumbled around burger. I couldn't shovel the food in fast enough. "She was fine. I mean, I didn't have much to tell her other than what everyone already knows."

"I heard she talked to a couple other kids. Like Jimmy's lab partner in bio. And she spent a *lot* of time with the art teacher." Brooke scooted closer and lowered her voice. "*I* heard they're looking for more pictures."

My throat balled. All of a sudden, my burger tasted like road tar. "Yeah?"

Brooke nodded. "They want to look at the people in the pictures. They think that maybe Jimmy was killed because he took pictures he wasn't supposed to. Or that maybe," her voice dwindled to a whisper, "the pictures are *clues.*"

I had to take a long pull of my milk to get that knot of half-chewed cow and bread to go down. "What kind of clues?"

"I don't know. I also heard they took Jimmy's computer and stuff, you know, to analyze."

"Wow." Appetite gone, I put down my burger. What I'd eaten was trying to crawl back up my throat. "How come?"

"To look for the pictures, I guess."

"How do they even know he took them?"

"I heard that Mr. Badden was helping Jimmy get stuff together for some kind of special camp. Only after Jimmy left school, he didn't come back, I guess. So they think the pictures are somewhere on Jimmy's computer. Oh, and that lady you were talking to? Agent Thorne? She—" Brooke broke off as the bell rang. Gathering up her books, she stood. "I got to go."

"I'll come with you." After dumping what was left of my burger and fries, I said, "What about Agent Thorne?"

"I googled her during study hall, and guess what? She's *famous*."

Uh-oh. "How?"

"Tell you later," she said and then said goodbye and peeled off to the left.

Agent Angela was famous. Great. It was just so my luck that she would be. I'll bet she caught killers no one else could. Or maybe she'd killed someone really, really bad. I'd have to look her up, but not at home.

Because one thing was for sure: it wouldn't be safe to use my computer anymore.

My English lit teacher said that we should take time to talk about Jimmy's murder. I sure as hell wasn't going there. Instead, I zoned out, mentally reviewing my conversation with Agent Angela. I still thought I'd done okay, except for that one little slip about Jimmy getting killed at night. But now I also had something new to think about. Because I knew where those pictures were, and if I was right, Agent Angela wasn't going to find anything on Jimmy's computer or his camera because Jimmy had said as much. He'd wiped the internal memory. Maybe you could recover pictures the same way you could documents, though. Hell, the FBI or BCA or whatever could probably do anything.

But *I* had the pictures. I had the card from Jimmy's phone and—oh, hell—Agent Angela and the sheriff and my dad had to know *that* card was *missing* . . .

"It's like that section where Holden wakes up and Mr. Antolini is patting his head," someone said. I'd been so focused, I'd completely lost track of the discussion. "You know, Holden makes the assumption that Mr. Antolini is coming on to him."

"Wouldn't you?" a girl said. "Salinger set it up so the old guy was boozing and then Holden's sleeping in his shorts on the couch. It's pretty suggestive."

The English teacher said, "Yes, but is suggestion the same thing as fact? Remember, one of the main themes of the book is Holden's search for an identity and how that keeps eluding him. Wouldn't his wondering about his own sexuality count?"

The first kid was flipping through his book. "But what about right here, at the end, when Holden says that same thing's happened to him about twenty times in his life? Maybe somehow he *invites* guys to make passes. Or maybe he's in the closet only he doesn't know it."

"How can you not *know* something like that?" a third kid demanded. "I heard gay people always know they're gay, like, from birth, and they're just faking it so no one will suspect."

Right then I knew: I wasn't gay. I wasn't faking it. I was only me.

"People live in denial all the time," the teacher said. "Sometimes the truth is just too dangerous."

"It sounds to me like you're trying to steer us into believing Holden was gay," the girl said.

"No, no." The teacher held up a hand. "I was merely suggesting—"

"Look, you're always saying we have to stick to what's *in* the text, what supports an interpretation, and not let our own prejudices get in the way. Well—" the girl flipped, then jabbed a finger onto a page "—it says right here that Holden has second thoughts about whether he interpreted Mr. Antolini's actions correctly. Holden's *always* thinking about sex, and he's *always* worried that he'll suddenly turn into a queer. But why can't he just be confused? Why does that have to mean that he's gay?"

The English teacher gave a smile that was the kind of grimace you gave to a student who'd caught you out, and turned back to the first kid. "What made you think of Antolini in connection to Jimmy?"

"Well." The first kid fidgeted, and then damn if he didn't toss a glance *my* way. "I guess I was making a connection between what Holden thought and, you know, Jimmy."

"Can you be more specific?"

The first kid opened his mouth again, but I'd had enough. The same angry annoyance I'd felt with Agent Angela suddenly swarmed up my neck and made my arms itch. "He's talking about whether or not Jimmy was gay, okay?" I said. "You guys are talking about rumors that get started out of nothing. Because of a damned picture. It would be like starting a rumor that someone was sleeping around when it wasn't true. People make all sorts of assumptions, and those kinds of assumptions can ruin you."

Can ruin me. Hell, maybe they already had.

The first kid dropped his eyes. The girl shot this strangely triumphant look my way, but I didn't smile back. No one said anything. The teacher swept her gaze over the class, then let her eyes rest on mine. "You think that everyone here bears some responsibility for driving Jimmy out of the school." Not really a question.

"I didn't say that. His parents pulled him out. But I don't recall anybody coming forward and saying that he *wasn't* gay. No one defended him." *No one defended me.* "What I remember is how the rumors started about me and Jimmy on the basis of a picture and what some asshole who had never spoken to me said in some magazine." My voice was quaking by then. "People can only be responsible for so much, but one thing they can own up to is when they've spread rumors. Maybe if Jimmy's parents hadn't yanked him out of school, he'd still be alive because he could have come to one of *us . . .*"

I stumbled to a halt because I'd just remembered: Jimmy had done that. He had come to me. I told him to count on me, and I'd let him down. I let him die.

Silence. The teacher let it spin out. Finally, one kid said, timidly, "Well, *I* never believed the rumors."

That seemed to be the general signal for everyone to relax and ignore me and instead talk about reputations and people feeling safe and what people should be responsible for and blah, blah, blah. But that was good because the focus *had* shifted and then I could wonder who was really responsible—and who the hell I was trying so hard to convince that it wasn't me.

OCTOBER 27

2020

TO ALL WHOM THIS MIGHT CONCERN:

So that was Monday. I thought I'd be happy when school let out so I could go for a run and not have to think, but I hadn't counted on the news people.

When the bell rang and we all streamed to the parking lot, you could see them spill out of their vans and trucks so they could start shouting questions and training their cameras around the deputies who were trying to hold them back.

When I got home, there were a couple vans off the ditch, but no one camped out at the front door. Two off-duty deputies were posted at the end of our driveway to keep the reporters from coming up to the house. But I didn't go running. I could see it now, this tail of gasping reporters and cameramen, trailing cords and then probably calling in a helicopter to shoot video like they did for those high-speed chases on CNN.

At supper, Mom tried to make out like it wasn't so bad, even though a bunch of reporters had staked themselves out in the hospital lobby for a shot at interviewing *her*. "They'll get tired of all this eventually," Mom said. "Reporters always do."

No one had much to say to that. Mom asked about school, and Mal chattered on about the grief counselors coming and how stupid that was because it was like suggesting that if you weren't all upset about Jimmy, then there was something wrong with you. I didn't talk, just rearranged my meatloaf and mashed potatoes, which I usually like but couldn't stomach. Finally, Mom stopped trying to get anything going and the only sounds were the click of forks on plates. Dad just chewed his food, not looking at me much. Which I didn't think was such a good sign.

After supper, I was trying to do my chemistry when Dad knocked. He sat down on the bed with a heavy sigh, like he had the weight of a thousand years on his shoulders.

"How you holding up, son?"

"I'm okay." I wasn't, but I didn't need people to start offering sympathy for all the wrong reasons. "I can't concentrate so well." Which was true. Then I asked what was really on my mind: "Am I in trouble or something?"

Now I expected Dad to reassure me. Isn't that what fathers are supposed to do? But he only shrugged. "I don't know. I'm not in the loop. Why do you ask?"

I had to *explain* this to him? "Because of Agent An ... Agent Thorne."

"Like I said, I don't know." Dad paused. "Is there something you *should* be worried about?"

And, like that, I knew that my *dad* wasn't there at all. The only other person in my room, on my bed, was a *cop* being a cop, doing what cops do. "No," I said. "I didn't do anything."

"Then you don't have anything worry about, do you?" He hesitated, then added, "It's just . . . Son, you changed your plans the night Jimmy was killed. You lied about where you were going. You went to a lot of trouble to hide the fact that you were going to a party."

"You said that wasn't a big deal."

"Well, I'm not thinking like a dad right now. I'm thinking like a chief deputy."

Bullshit. That's what I wanted to say. *Bullshit, you've been thinking like a chief deputy the whole goddamned time.* "Okay."

Maybe he read everything I thought in my eyes or heard it in my voice, because his own eyes grew flinty. This time, when he spoke, the tentativeness was gone from his voice. What little warmth there'd been had leached away, too. "So I got to ask you: why? I know what you said about your mom and all, and I can almost buy that. But you've *never* lied about big things. What you did is . . . strange. Out of character."

"Is that how Agent Thorne's going to see it?"

"I can't answer for her. I'm asking for myself now. You want to explain it a little better?"

"I can't," I said. "I can't explain it any better than I already have."

"But you need to."

"Why?" I flung the word. "What for? Jesus, Dad, did it ever occur to you how hard it is to be so wonderful and fantastic and responsible all the time? Yeah, I never lie. I'm so good. I never do a damned *thing* except what you and especially Mom want."

"Now hold on, hold on." Dad was doing the air-pat routine with both hands. "That's not fair. You know I don't have the same stake in your going to some big-name school as your mother."

"But you don't fight for me either. You don't do anything. You just let Mom say what she wants, and I end up doing what Mom says. So who's really going to college? To medical school? *Mom?* She intercepts phone calls, for chrissakes." Why I was yelling at my father I don't know. But I suddenly had this idea that this was his fault, too, as much as mine. Kids are supposed to have role models, right? So I had this dad who took care of everyone else and solved their problems and worked hard to keep them safe—and this same guy couldn't help me fend off my mother.

There was this long silence. Through my closed door, I could hear Mal ask Mom something downstairs, just the slightest hint of a rising intonation in her tone. I wondered if they'd heard me. A tiny twinge of guilt twisted in my chest. I knew Mom only wanted the best for me. The problem was, I was no longer sure of where what *she* wanted stopped and what *I* wanted began. Or maybe I just needed to yell before my head exploded—and that was bad. Dad was like this soft wall, only absorbing what I said, while those eyes never left mine. The stress was going to make me do something incredibly stupid, like turn myself in. Yelling at this cop would only make him suspicious.

So I said, "I'm sorry. I didn't mean any of that. I'm just . . . upset. I don't understand how any of this happened."

"Nothing to apologize for. We're all upset," said Dad, and his tone was so understanding that I felt dirty and evil. My parents had this idea of their perfect kid; I was such a good person—no one would ever suspect me of leaving a friend to die. The best thing I could do was disappear before the truth came out. The truth would kill my mother. My father would never live it down. Oh, he might not say anything, and eventually things would settle down to some kind of new normal, presuming I didn't end up in prison. But the disappointment would never be far. My shame would hover the way a hawk's shadow slides over a dead field: a silent, black stain.

Dad pushed up on his thighs. "I heard that the ME's probably going to release the body back to the Langes sometime tomorrow. I don't know when the funeral will be, but I'm not sure you should go. There are going to be reporters, and then the Langes . . ." He shook his head. "You do what you feel is right, but those are my thoughts, son."

He left. I felt like a complete and total asshole because of what my rant had accomplished.

It stopped my father from asking too many questions.

———————————

Still.

Dad suspected something. Call it a feeling, because I couldn't put a finger on exactly how I knew.

That also made me think more about Agent Angela. Brooke said she was famous. So I decided *screw it* and googled her—and wished I hadn't. Because I thought I was probably in a lot more trouble than Dad knew.

Angela Angela had written a couple books and a lot of articles. She gave talks and stuff to other law enforcement people on something I'd never heard of: micro-expressions. I clicked through a website and a couple papers and got the gist of it. Seemed that reading micro-expressions—tiny gestures and facial tics and movements—was a kind of clue-in to what people were feeling or when they lied. There were other things, too: *gestural slips, mouth shrugs, hand shrugs*. Stuff your body did to give you away.

Which made me crazy.

I thought back to my conversation with Agent Angela. Had I acted surprised when she said Jimmy was beaten to death? I already knew he had been. I knew where his body was and how long he'd been there. Hell, I'd seen half of it go down. The website said that people who acted surprised for more than a second or so were faking it. But there were also times when if you broke eye contact, it was because you were remembering something. And then if you touched the back of your neck, you were lying.

Agent Angela was a frigging walking-talking lie detector. So . . . had she caught me? What had she seen? I skimmed another article she'd written on gender differences in lie detection—and discovered that guys frequently rubbed their noses when they were lying. Shit. I'd done that. So she must know something.

Is that what Dad was trying to tell me? Warn me about? The sheriff could talk about keeping Dad out of the investigation, but all law enforcement watch out for each other. Dad had given me an opportunity to tell the truth. He was trying to tell me that it wasn't too late.

But it was. The brief flare of hope in my chest died. I'd already talked to Agent Angela. I'd brushed off my father. I couldn't change what I'd said because I'd lied, and it was on tape. I didn't tell the truth any more than I had on that stupid college application and in those essays.

I'd come too far. There was no turning back. The only way to make this right was to catch the people who'd killed Jimmy myself.

If I could just figure out *how*.

––––––––––

The next day at school wasn't so bad. I mean, I was exhausted, not only from not sleeping but also because I had to be so careful. Normal people don't have to step out of their skins so they can keep an eye on what they say and do and judge how it will all look, but I did. It hit me that I'd become my own ghost image, like what I saw when I took off my glasses, you know? I was all blurry, like I'd taken this little sidestep out of myself and into a parallel universe.

The reporters were still at school. When I got out of the truck, someone shouted, "Hey, look over here!" Like an idiot, I did—and then I got to see myself on CNN and all the local affiliates later that night. But getting through the day wasn't as hard as I thought it would be. Maybe because I had myself pretty much convinced that, okay, I'd *lied*, but I still hadn't done anything *wrong*. I'd only been in the wrong *place* at the wrong *time*.

Whoever killed Jimmy had decided on doing it a while before I showed up, because it was so well planned. That panel van by the side with the flag, too: that was a stroke of real genius, because that was obviously how the guys had gotten there in the first place. Okay, so maybe it was a little bit my fault that Jimmy was waiting out in the parking lot, but it could've been any other night, and the outcome would've been the same, right? *Right?*

And what could I really have done to save Jimmy? The instant those guys burst out of the woods, Jimmy was dead. They hit him before I knew what was happening. If I'd shouted or rushed in, they'd have killed me. My only mistake was not calling it in right away. If I'd done that, they'd have found him a little sooner, was all.

All right, all right: finding him sooner also meant the flies wouldn't have had time to lay those eggs. Nothing could've made a meal of Jimmy's fingers and toes, his throat. His tongue. His eyes.

But that was *all* it meant. No matter what, Jimmy would still be just as dead.

Still.

Over that next week, I flinched every time the phone rang. I kept expecting someone to come to the door of whatever class I was in at the time and say that I was wanted down in the office. Or that Agent Angela would be waiting by my truck, the way detectives did in movies and TV.

Nothing like that happened. No one showed up with warrants to search the house or my locker. I heard that Agent Angela went down to Cuppa Joy to talk to Pastor John, but I already knew she would. The important thing: she didn't come back at me.

The news people said Jimmy had been beaten to death with rocks—which I knew was only half the truth because there was the hatchet. That was probably something the police were holding back for whenever they traced the hatchet to its owner.

The worst moment I had was when the news people also said Jimmy was alive for a couple hours before the cold and blood loss finally killed him. The CNN guy didn't say if Jimmy had been conscious at all, or if he suffered.

God. He'd been *alive*. And I'd left him there to die by himself, in pain and in the cold. I should've done something. I should've.

Coulda. Woulda.

Shoulda.

The best thing I could do was keep my head down and wait for everything to go away. To that end, I did my work. I said hello to my friends. I choked down food I didn't want. I listened to insightful discussions about Holden Caulfield's sexual confusion and never once lost my temper. I didn't speak up either, but you can't have everything.

The most important thing was that I didn't touch Jimmy's cell card or the one from his camera. I would have to be smart and wait a week, or a couple months. Or maybe I would never check them out. For all I knew, Agent Angela was having me tailed. If I went to Hopkins or maybe down to Wausau to buy a card reader and then find an Internet café, they'd know. I couldn't risk that. Not yet. Of course, I could flush the damn cards and no one would be the wiser.

But I hung onto those cards. I guess I thought that if I could somehow figure out what had happened to Jimmy, I could still go to Dad with that. Sure, I would be in trouble. I'd have explaining to do. By that time, though, I'd have figured out a good story. Then all would be forgiven and forgotten. I wouldn't be the kid who ran away and let a boy get axed to death. I'd be the hero who brought the killers to justice.

They released Jimmy's body on Wednesday. Agent Angela went back to Madison on Thursday, and thank Christ for that.

The Langes decided to bury Jimmy the next Tuesday. In Key Club, we talked about taking up a collection and either buying flowers or donating them to whatever charity the Langes wanted, which turned out to be Pastor John's ministry. That didn't sit well with me, but it wasn't my choice.

By Friday, things weren't normal, but they were getting better. Mom said things like this really blew over once the person was in the ground, which sounded kind of harsh to me but was probably true.

The other thing was that since the news people didn't have anything, well, *new* to report, they were reduced to recycling stuff everyone had already seen. Then some blonde college girl got kidnapped down in Florida, and all the news stations were more interested in that than some maybe-gay kid in a tiny town in Wisconsin no one had ever heard of. The sawhorses across the school disappeared, and Mom stopped worrying about reporters jumping out of the bushes. Dad just put his head down and went about his job. He and I didn't talk at all. I caught him dead-eyeing me now and again but let it slide. There was only so much I could control.

At school, Jimmy ceased being the only topic of conversation. People stopped avoiding me, and Parker and the other guys were suddenly around a lot more. "Anybody bothers you, man, you just tell us," Parker said. "We'll take care of it." Then he invited me to hang at his house that Saturday night. His parents would be gone, and he was throwing some kind of combo-party with some people from Holy Name, which was a private Lutheran school in Hopkins. The problem was that Saturday night was ER night, too. I told Mom about it and so, of course, she was about a millisecond from nixing it. But then Dad jumped in and said I should go have some fun once in a while; school had to be a pressure-cooker, and I'd earned it. Stuff like that. Mom shut up, but when she put the dishes in the dishwasher afterward, there was a lot of banging. She even broke a glass and swore.

Also, that week, for the first time ever, I bombed a history exam. My teacher was very understanding, though, and said I could take it again on Monday. She said she knew that wasn't my best performance and it was clear the whole Jimmy thing was weighing on me. At least that was true.

The jumpy, jumbled, prickly feeling in my chest began to subside. By Friday, I could go an hour or so during the day when I could concentrate on what we were learning in class or contribute to a discussion and not think about Jimmy at all.

The other thing that happened was I started to sleep more than just an hour or two at a time again. Not all night yet, but four hours beat no hours at all. When I did wake up— usually from some bad dream I could never fully remember but which always seemed to center on bloody meat and flies and monstrous, black-hooded men with hatchets chasing me through the woods—I could read myself back to sleep in a half hour or so. Probably a doctor would've said that my mood got better because I was sleeping more.

Whatever.

The party on Saturday started out okay. Since Parker's parents were both doctors, they lived way north of Brooke in what Mom called a starter-castle. It really was kind of a mansion. The party wasn't really my speed: kegs and agonizingly loud music so people had to lean in and shout into your ear. Actually, it was a good thing the house was so far out. No neighbors to complain, and way less likely that my dad or one of his friends would pay a visit.

I also discovered an upside to celebrity. The guys at the front door—football players from Holy Name—recognized me, gave me a cup, and didn't make me pay. I filled my cup from the keg, which was kind of dumb because I don't even like beer, and started looking for people I knew. The house was so crowded I was starting to sweat, so I stepped out onto the patio, where it was much cooler. My glasses fogged up, and somehow that suited my mood. Everything turned misty and faraway. Or maybe that was only me.

Parker and the other guys I knew were perched around a hot tub with their girlfriends. They were already pretty drunk, and Parker kept spilling beer into the hot tub and laughing and spraying more beer out of his nose. When he and his girlfriend started stripping down, I went back into the house.

I knew then it had been a mistake to come. It's hard to describe how I felt, but it was like this: I was in this little bubble of space, cut off by a force field. People and noise swirled around, but nothing touched me. I was isolated, self-contained, in a universe all by myself. Like hiding behind my fogged-up glasses. It was horrible.

"Hey," someone said into my ear, and I looked down. This girl I'd never seen before smiled. She had the whitest, most even teeth I'd ever seen. Her hair was honey-blonde, her neck was long, and her eyes—a bright, surreal turquoise—slightly feline. "I'm Cass. I recognized you from the news," she said matter-of-factly. "You with anybody?" When I shook my head, she tilted her head to one side. "I thought you looked a little lonely." Those unreal eyes dropped to my cup. "You're not drinking?"

"I don't drink much." I looked for a place to put my cup and found none. Shrugged. "Not in the mood, I guess."

"Been kind of a cruddy week."

"You could say that."

"Well, we can't let it go to waste," and then, with an impish grin, she reached over, took my cup, and tipped half of it into hers. "That's better," she said. "Come on. Let's go find a place to talk."

I was so out of it, I just followed as she threaded her way through the crowd. After circling through the dining room, kitchen, and family room, we finally ended up perched on the stairs, me against the banister and her with her back against the wall. Cass gave me a frank look. "You don't look so good."

"Like I said." I took a sip of my beer, realized that I really didn't want it, and carefully set the cup down on a step. "It's been a bad week."

"Tell me about it." She did the eye-roll. "Those news vans have been *everywhere*. How have you avoided talking to them?"

"Just lucky, I guess."

"You don't want to be on TV?"

"Not really. I mean, I don't have anything to say."

"But you knew Jimmy pretty well. How'd you guys get to be friends, anyway? He was a sophomore, right?"

"No, he was a junior. Sophomore when I met him, though."

"How'd that happen?"

So I told her about Del getting killed and my helping out, and before long I was telling her about the summer. Reminiscing like that felt . . . good. Like those memories were okay to keep. My throat got kind of dry, and I found my beer and took a couple sips. I'm really not a drinker, and I got a little floaty. Not drunk. Just . . . relaxed. She was a good listener, too. When I told her about the frying pan in the trough, she threw back her head and laughed, and that's when I noticed that she had this really nice neck.

"I can see it," she said. Her blue eyes sparkled. They really were amazing. She tipped her beer into my suddenly empty cup. (And how had *that* happened? I didn't remember finishing that beer at all.) "It would be a great scene for a movie. Why do you think his dad was so hard on him? Unless . . ." She gasped, her red lips molding a perfect *O*. "You don't think that maybe he was *abusing* Jimmy, do you? I hear that he was so *mean*."

"Well," I said and took a long pull from my cup. "I always wondered that myself. I mean, I didn't see bruises or anything. But he was really harsh, and when the magazine stuff came out . . ." I told her about the scene in front of the barn. "I thought he was going to kill Jimmy."

"I *saw* those pictures." Her too-blue gaze slid right, then left, and then she was learning in closer. "I wondered about him and Jimmy. I mean, it's so . . . suggestive. Oh." She put her hand to her mouth. "Sorry. I know you don't want to talk about that. How hard that must've been for you."

"No, it's okay," I said, and I really wasn't angry. "Everyone else makes assumptions, why shouldn't you? That's what you want to know, right? Okay then, for the record: I'm not gay. I don't know anyone who's gay. Nothing happened between Jimmy and me."

"Hey, it's okay." She touched my arm. "I'm not making assumptions. I don't know you. It would be wrong. But that doesn't mean something didn't happen between Jimmy and his dad."

That made me ill. I was glad I hadn't drunk much more beer, or else it would have come right back up. "You don't know the family. I can't see it."

"It might have happened," she persisted.

"I don't see it," I repeated.

"But it might've. I've done some reading and it's not exactly something anyone will advertise."

"Well . . . I don't know. Maybe. But I still can't—"

"Sure. Of course. It makes perfect sen—" Her blue cat's eyes shifted to a spot behind me, and the set of her face suddenly hardened.

Puzzled, I craned my head over my shoulder. The look of complete and utter amazement on Brooke's face was unmistakable. "Hey," I said. "How long you been standing there?"

"Long enough," she said. Her eyes didn't leave Cass.

"Uh, Brooke, this is Cass...uh..." I realized I didn't know Cass's last name. "Cass."

"Yeah, I know her," said Brooke. To Cass: "Cassidy Struthers, right?"

"You guys know each other?" I looked from Brooke to Cass, whose expression was stony now, and then back to Brooke.

"You could say that." Brooke's eyes sparked. "She's a reporter."

"What?" My stomach bottomed out. "*What*?"

"Yeah. Fox, I think. You haven't been watching the news, but I have." To Cass: "Isn't this trespassing? Does Parker know you're here?"

Picking up her empty cup, Cass stood. "Well, I guess I'll be going now." To me: "It was very nice talking with you, Ben. If you ever want to talk again—"

"Nice? I didn't want to talk to you at all. You tricked me. How could you do that?" I demanded.

"A: I'm sorry. B: No, I didn't, not really. C: It's my job." Cass fished a business card from her hip pocket. When I didn't take it, she laid the card on the step. "If you want to talk some more, just give me a call. I'll see myself out."

"Parker could have you arrested," Brooke said.

"Oh, I think that would be *no*." Cass gave another dazzling smile with those amazing teeth, which—come to think of it—made perfect sense now. How many TV reporters had rotten teeth? "Then Parker would have to explain all this underage drinking, wouldn't he? Besides, I wasn't trespassing. I crashed the party, that's all. Nice to meet you."

"Wait a minute." I recovered enough to struggle to my feet. In the process, I knocked over my cup, sending a spew of piss-colored liquid streaming down the stairs to puddle on hardwood. "You can't use anything I said. You didn't identify yourself. I would never have said—"

"Yes, I can, and yes, I did. I gave you my name. You didn't ask for my last name, nor did you ask where I worked. See you around, maybe," and then Cassidy ducked out the front door and was gone.

Brooke found paper towels, and I cleaned up the beer mess. As we worked, I said, "What are you doing here? I didn't think this was your kind of party."

"Speak for yourself." She made a face. "I came with Liz and Trevor. It's Saturday night, I didn't have anything else to do, and I didn't want to be alone. What's your excuse?"

"The same." I threw my sopping wad of paper towel into a trash can beneath the kitchen sink. The house was beginning to stink like a brewery. Parker wouldn't need someone like Cassidy Struthers to rat him out. His parents could get drunk on fumes. "Listen . . . you want to get out of here? I have my truck. Want to, maybe, get some coffee?"

"Sure." She smiled, and I thought that, of the two, I preferred hers over Cassidy's. "Give me five minutes to tell Liz and Trevor."

"Look," Brooke said, spooning up whipped cream, "you got to stop beating yourself up about this. You didn't know."

I shrugged. We sat in a booth at a Denny's just outside Merit. When I was little, my parents used to take us here for Sunday breakfast because my dad liked the pancakes. The place was pretty full for a Saturday night, but they were mainly older people—like, with walkers and pilling cardigans. This was probably *their* idea of a big night out. We'd taken a back booth, and I faced the door, which made me feel better for some stupid reason. Brooke and I both ordered sundaes and coffee. Normally I like chocolate sundaes, but tonight the sludge of chocolate sauce, the way it oozed over whipped cream, reminded me of that lake of congealing blood. I hadn't taken but one or two bites before I had to put down my spoon.

"I can't believe how stupid I was," I said.

"She took advantage of you. She had to know it would be on your mind."

"That's an understatement. God, she's going to twist my words around, I just know it."

"What'd you tell her?" Brooke listened as I sketched in the details, then said, "Well, the stuff about Jimmy being abused . . . you've wondered about that."

"There's a big difference between wondering something privately and saying it out loud." I squeezed my head between the heels of my hands. "I can't stop thinking about—" I almost said *the whole thing, Jimmy and those flies and the way pieces of his skull were all humped like slabs of broken ice and all that blood.* But I caught myself in time. "I can't stop thinking about the whole thing."

"That's understandable. Maybe you should talk to one of the grief counselors." She skimmed whipped cream from her upper lip with her tongue. She was completely unself-conscious about it, which I liked. In fact, I liked watching her enjoy herself. It made me feel a little better, like if I could make someone else feel good, maybe I wasn't so evil. "I heard they can tell you how to relax and stop thinking."

"I guess you have to want that," I said. "I'm not sure I think it's that easy to forget. I'm not sure I should."

"No one's saying you have to forget Jimmy. But life goes on."

"Not for Jimmy. I keep wondering what was going through his head up until the minute he . . . they . . ." I looked away, swallowed. "What would it be like to know you were going to die?"

She stopped, her spoon halfway to her mouth. A glop of strawberry ice cream dripped back into her glass. She replaced the spoon in her dish and wiped her lips with her napkin. "You want to talk about it?"

"That's all anyone wants," I said, fiddling with a sugar packet. "Me, to talk."

Cupping her mug, she blew on her coffee. "It sounds like you want to."

"No, I don't. You could drive yourself crazy doing that. Sometimes, when I was younger, I'd listen to the news and they'd talk about people driving their cars off the road and landing in a lake and the car sinking. I would always wonder what that was like: being trapped in that sinking car, the water rising around your chest, creeping up your neck. You know you're going to die. You know there's nothing you can do. Even after the water closes over your face and you're holding your breath, you think, *I'm going to die*, and yet I'll bet until the last second you don't believe it. You know, some people like that, they don't drown? They die of suffocation. They hold their breaths and their throat muscles go into this spasm, all because the body's hanging onto the hope that a miracle's going to happen and they'll be saved. I'll bet that's what it was like for Jimmy. Even as those guys were beating him to death, he probably thought, *No, this can't be happening, I'm not really going to die.*"

Brooke was quiet. I sighed, scrubbed my face with my hands. "I'm sorry," I said. "I'm really tired."

"You look like you've been carjacked." Her eyes grabbed mine. "What's going on with you? You've been all . . ." Her fingers waggled in the air. "Frazzled. It can't be just Jimmy. I mean, *you* didn't kill him."

Words crowded up behind my teeth. I felt this huge push to tell Brooke what had happened. Just get it off my chest and then everything would sort itself out. It hit me that this was probably why Catholics felt so much better whenever they went to confession. A couple Hail Marys and stuff and they were home free. Maybe I should see a psychiatrist. They were like priests, right? They couldn't tell the police anything. That way, what I knew could be someone else's problem. Like, maybe I could go to Parker's mom. She was a psychiatrist.

What I said was: "I didn't do anything to stop it." Which was, come to think of it, the truth.

Her eyebrows knit. "What could you have done? Jimmy's parents pulled him out of school. He wasn't your responsibility."

"But he was a friend. I . . . cared about him." Then added, fast, "Not in the way people were thinking. Just, you know, someone I spent time with. It makes me crazy that people make assumptions on the basis of nothing."

Brooke carefully sipped her coffee. "So . . . what are you

more upset about: that he's dead, or that people might have the wrong idea about you?"

"Both," I said. "When the whole magazine thing came out, I was so pissed. I wanted to strangle Jimmy. Then he got killed."

"But *you* didn't stone him." At my look of surprise, she continued, "That's what our pastor called it. Back in Bible times, they stoned you if you were a murderer or adulterer. Or if you were gay. Heck, they still do it in Iran: bury you up to your chest and then throw rocks until you're dead. They even have rules about how big the rocks have to be: not so big that it kills you right away, but not so tiny there's no damage. They want you to suffer, and for a long time."

"That is sick," I said, but I was thinking about that second guy and his rock when one would've done. Hell, they'd had a hand axe. What did they need rocks for in the first place? Is that what they thought they were doing, stoning Jimmy the way the Bible said? "So that's what your pastor thinks? That some religious nut-jobs did this?"

"Kind of. He said Jimmy was an example of how gossip could get out control and destroy someone—the same way it's destroying you."

I gargled a laugh, but I'd never felt more like crying in my life. "I'm fine."

"No, you're not. I don't know exactly what's wrong, but something's happened to you. A couple weeks ago, before Jimmy died, when I asked you to help me with the worms, you were . . . *mean*."

I thought back to her tear-stained face. God, how could I have been so awful? Then I almost laughed out loud. Hell,

I'd been nothing *but* awful since that stupid picture. Worse, I was turning into something I no longer recognized. Who and where the hell was *I* in all this? "Is that what you were screaming?"

She pinked. "Sort of. I said you used to be a nice person."

Maybe that was true. "So why are you out with me now? If I'm so mean?"

"Because you're in trouble," she said, simply. "And that's what friends do."

———————————

I drove her back to her house. We didn't talk, but that was okay. It was a comfortable kind of silence, and I wasn't mad. Instead, I felt . . . calm. The night was cloudy and there were no stars, but my mind was clear for the first time in what felt like forever.

The road went over a series of rolling hills and then undulated from side to side like a snake. Darkness pressed in all around, like a tunnel gradually closing down until it seemed we were the last people on Earth. I felt as if I was driving into a black hole, and the further I went, the more the world and life I'd known didn't exist.

I kept thinking about that. I could keep going north until I hit Lake Superior. I could sleep in my truck and then, come morning, I could drive to the ferry in Ashland or Bayfield or something. Load the truck onto the ferry—or, better yet, leave the truck behind and just walk aboard the ferry and let it carry me across the lake into Canada. It would be like when Jesus instructed his apostles to take nothing with them but the clothes on their backs and to shake off the dust of the cities of unbelievers from their sandals.

"You ever think about just leaving?" I asked. "Driving and not turning around and never coming back?"

"Sure." Her voice was so soft, like velvet. "When I was younger and we'd go camping, I'd feel this great weight slipping from my shoulders the further away from home we got. Like this heavy blanket, and then we'd cross into Minnesota or Canada or wherever, and then the blanket fell away and I was free." She fell silent a moment, then pulled in a long breath. "I guess that's what college will be: a chance to get free and clear where no one knows you and you can start all over again." There was a soft squeal of leather as she turned to face me. "Is that why you're going so far away?"

"I haven't gotten in yet."

"You will. Your grades are too good. You've worked for this your whole life."

"I don't know about that. Lately, I've been thinking that maybe my *mom's* been working for this her whole life." It just came out. "She sees my being a doctor the way a mountain climber thinks of Everest. Hump that summit and you've made it."

"Yeah, but they have to get back down without getting killed."

"Don't think this isn't killing me," I said. I had no idea where that came from.

"I'm sorry," she said. "Is there something else you want to do more?"

The first and only time so far that I'd opened this door was with Jimmy. Now, here was Brooke. She would understand, too.

I could tell Brooke, and together we'd come up with something I could do to make things right.

But, wait, didn't I already have a plan? Yes, of course, I did. The cards. Identifying the killers. So what was happening now? What was I doing?

"Yeah, sometimes. Don't get me wrong. I want to help people." Even as I mouthed the words, they felt foreign, something you said to an admissions counselor. "But people are . . . messy. I'm not talking about blood and stuff. I'm talking emotions. People aren't like math or physics. There, the equation is the equation. There's no emotion involved."

"Well, if that were true, there wouldn't be physicists fighting about string theory, right? Or what's beyond our universe? Even math breaks down eventually."

"But only because we haven't manipulated the equations the right way or discovered a new theory. There are rules in math."

"And no rules to the heart," she said, softly. "If you didn't have a heart, you wouldn't feel excitement or satisfaction. It wouldn't feel good to solve the equation, right? Why would you even bother? Maybe you have to have both. I guess it's a little bit like having faith."

I thought of Jimmy and Pastor John. "No. I think religion is evil."

"Religion isn't the same thing as God or faith. Religion's just the structure."

"Don't tell me you believe in God." I didn't like the way that came out. "Sorry, I didn't mean it the way it came out."

"Yes, you did." But she didn't sound offended. "That's okay."

I was silent a moment. "So . . . do you?"

"I don't know. I don't believe what our pastor talks about. Like, I know he feels that killing Jimmy was wrong, but the way he presented the whole stoning thing . . . it sort of felt like an apology, too. Like we should all understand if some people get carried away by what the Bible says. I don't think that's any excuse."

"See, that's what I mean," I said. "That's the religion part."

"Right. So I think that's wrong. But I also think that our brains are kind of preprogrammed to want a god. Like the way you feel awe or how cool something is? Sometimes when I meditate, I get to this place where my mind goes completely open and I get this overwhelmed feeling. Like I'm so full of good I'm going to bust."

"Shut up. You meditate?"

"Yeah." She sounded a little defensive now. "I do yoga, too. That's not so strange."

"No," I said. The idea of Brooke stretching and posing on a mat was something to think about. "I just . . . didn't know."

She mock-punched my arm. "Don't be a creep. How'd we get on me? We were talking about what you feel."

"I'm not so interesting." I felt suddenly tired. "I don't know what I want anymore. Remember when we were doing the worms and you started talking about those stupid pigs?"

"I was just talking."

"No, no, you said something really important. You said that the animal's whole life was all mapped out before it got started, and it would never know any different." I shot a glance, but all I saw was her profile glimmering in the dashboard lights. "Well, what's so different between that pig . . . and me? I feel programmed. I feel like I don't know what my own thoughts are. I don't know where I begin and my parents leave off . . . and that kind of freaks me out."

Her voice was almost inaudible over the hum of the road. "Why?"

"Because I don't want to think like this. I want to go back to being the way I was. Yeah, I complained, but . . . I honestly didn't think very much." It was on the tip of my tongue to tell her about writing and my short stories, but I bit the words back because it suddenly hit me *why* my stories weren't good and couldn't get any better: my mind was in shackles. I wouldn't let myself think differently. My stories were locked in a drawer the way I'd been in lockstep with the path my mom decided was right.

"What changed?"

"Come on. You have to ask?"

She was quiet for a beat. "Maybe you should just tell your mom you want to keep your options open."

I laughed. "My dad's the chief deputy, but my mom is a steamroller. She crushes everything in her path."

"Then you're already beaten before you get started. Maybe you're looking for a way to fail," she said.

I said nothing because there was nothing I could think of to say. We drove in silence for a few minutes. Brooke's road came up on the right, and she pointed out the turn. The truck dipped and bucked over the dirt road. In the distance, Brooke's house stood on a rise. Two windows on the second story fired with light, like candles in the sockets of a skull.

Brooke said, suddenly, "You know, I'll bet your mom doesn't know how she comes across. I'll bet your parents care about how you feel. I don't think they'd want you to do anything that would make you unhappy. Parents aren't evil. They just don't know, and they can't unless you tell them."

"You know what my mom would say? That I'm too young to know what would make me happy. That I don't have enough experience in life. That the things I think I want don't really matter."

"Is there something you want more than to go to college?"

Yes. I want Jimmy to be alive. I want to go back and be the person I thought I was. Instead, I pulled into Brooke's driveway. The truck crunched gravel that popped and pinged against metal. "I don't know. I'm just afraid that if I go to college, I'll get plugged into this path, and once you get started, it's hard to get off. I've been programmed my whole life. I've been a pig," and then I gave kind of a crazy laugh. "We all have. Go to school, get good grades, go to college, get a degree, be a doctor, be a lawyer, whatever." I thought of Holden and Phoebe on that carousel. "What if you want to get off the merry-go-round, but you're not the one at the controls?"

"Unless college is how you *do* get off," Brooke said as I swung around the circle in front of her house. "Maybe *this* is the merry-go-round, and college is when you get to control the ride. In a way, if you get a scholarship or do something that puts you out of your parents' reach, then *you* decide."

That was almost word for word what Jimmy had said, and look how well *that* turned out. I stopped the truck. "But there will always be someone else higher up. Even in college, you're not totally free. There are rules. You have to get good enough grades to stay in and keep the money coming. There are always strings attached and obligations and people counting on you.

No one's ever completely free."

"Okay, probably not, unless you go off somewhere so you're totally alone," she said. I couldn't see her face well in the dark, but I knew she was staring at me. "I think, though, that you'd be lonelier then than you are now."

Right then, I probably could've kissed her. She wouldn't have stopped me. The thought was startling and warm at the same time. I'd never thought of Brooke that way. But I think we could have kissed because we were connecting in a way I hadn't with anyone before. Maybe if I let myself relax with Brooke, those horrible thoughts of Jimmy would fade because I would have something new and pure to replace them with. It would be like a new life springing up to replace something that had been lost. Brooke would save me.

As soon as those thoughts winged through my mind, I knew they were loony. Nuts. I didn't want to spoil the moment, and I didn't want to ruin things and, honestly, the idea that Brooke was my salvation sounded kind of desperate, the way-out-there nutty idea of a complete maniac.

Even so, I didn't want Brooke to get out of the truck. I knew this moment would never come again. Remember what I said about Alice falling down the rabbit hole and how, at the far horizon she'll never reach, time has stopped? That's what this was like: a bubble outside of time. This was peace. Maybe I'd fallen far and fast enough and had to give myself permission to stop.

Nothing lasts forever, though. I didn't do anything to keep us in the bubble. I knew I couldn't and shouldn't. I wasn't the person Brooke thought I was. From the moment I turned and ran from Jimmy, I stopped being anyone I recognized.

So I let the moment slide past like water in a stream and then it was gone, and we were saying good night and thanks for talking and stuff like that.

I don't know what Brooke thought. I don't know if she was disappointed. I thought she might be. When she slid out of the truck, she turned back, one hand on the door. "If you want to talk, just call."

"Okay," I said, throwing the truck into reverse. "I will." Knowing I wouldn't. I waited until she'd disappeared into her house before I backed out and drove home.

Mom was waiting up when I got in, and asked how the party was. She seemed disappointed when I told her it was fine.

Of course, everything I said got splashed on the TV news the very next day. Not looking too much different from the party— meaning, she looked fabulous—Cassidy Struthers gave her report, interspersed with shots of the Langes' farm, the school and, finally, the park. There was this child psychiatrist expert, too, who made some connection between abuse and what she called *risk-taking behavior* but stopped short of suggesting that suspected sexual abuse had anything to do with sexual choice, even when Cassidy pressed her, which she did a couple of times and looked disappointed when the psychiatrist wouldn't budge.

My parents watched in grim silence. As soon as the segment was over, though, Mom looked at me, and then Dad. "They'll sue us," she said.

"That won't happen," Dad said. "That's the last thing on the Langes' minds right now. Not as if abuse wasn't thought of before. Agent Thorne already went down that alley, and it was a dead end." His eyes swiveled to me. "What were you thinking, son? Talking to a complete stranger like that?"

"She didn't identify herself. She looked like, you know, one of *us*." Dad's mentioning Agent Angela made me nervous, too. This was one thing we hadn't talked about. Would she now reappear and demand to know what else I was holding back? "It's not like she was wearing a sign: 'Hi, I'm a lying, scheming asshole who looks young enough to crash a dumb keg . . .'" I bit back the rest, but I'd already said too much.

Mom's mouth dropped open. "What did you say?"

"Keg?" Dad's eyebrows shot up. "There were no parents at this party?"

Mom: "Honey, you *know* how we feel about unsupervised . . ."

"Look," I interrupted. "If this stupid lady hadn't been there, you'd never have known. If it makes you feel better, I didn't drink anything, okay?" All right, I lied. Big deal. Not like it was the first time. "And I'd really appreciate it if you didn't get on the phone with all the other moms. I didn't talk to that reporter to get people in trouble. I only needed to be with other people, that's all."

"You can talk to a strange girl, and not to us?" Mom sounded hurt.

"*Mom*." Man, I should've stopped right there. "Not everything revolves around you!"

"I *never*—"

"*Yes*." I cut her right off. "You think that way. You do. Not everything is about me wanting to sabotage my getting into college either. There are lots of things I don't talk to you guys about—and what about the things you *do* know? Mr. Lange *hit* Jimmy in front of other people! He beat him up. His mom was there. So was his stupid pastor. Jimmy came to school all banged up, and the principal didn't do anything. People are always talking about helping teenagers and protecting kids. Well, where *was* everybody? How come a pastor would let a kid get that kind of beating?"

"Oh, I'm sure it wasn't that bad," Mom said.

"I saw him. You weren't there. How do you know?"

"Stop," Dad said, "both of you." To Mal, who was trying to blend in with the wall: "You have something to do, I'm sure."

"No, I'm done with all my work," Mal said.

"Fine. Then you won't mind cleaning your room."

"My room's clean."

"Then go clean *my* room."

"Dad . . ." But she shut up fast when Dad shot her a dark look. "Fine."

"Thank you." He waited while Mal flounced upstairs and then called after: "I need to hear a door."

"*Fine!*" Her door banged hard enough to rattle the window frames.

Dad waited another second, staring at the ceiling like a cat homing in on a mouse scratching in the attic. When the ceiling creaked, he nodded and then returned his attention to me. "Son, I don't know if you realize how bad things might get again. Jimmy's funeral is next week. Of course, we expect the news people to be all over that like fleas. Now that this has happened, they're sure to come back and camp out again at the bottom of the driveway. And you can bet that Agent Thorne will be giving you a—"

The phone rang. We all three stared at it. It was Dad who finally answered, listened, and then looked at me.

"Agent Thorne," he said, "we were just talking about you."

"I don't think you're telling me everything." Agent Angela's moss-green gaze pinned me like a worm to a dissecting pad. "I think there are things you're leaving out."

It was Monday night. School that day, with the sudden return of reporters, had verged on the absurd. Now Agent Angela and I sat on either side of her trusty tape recorder, which she'd placed on our kitchen table. Mom and Dad were upstairs; Mal was at a friend's house.

"You didn't ask about Jimmy and his dad," I said. I had to put a hand on my knee to stop my foot from jiggling. "You didn't ask me a lot of questions."

"All right, fair enough. But this was something you didn't think was worth volunteering? Even after you knew that Jimmy was beaten to death?"

"No, I didn't. I'll bet you already knew about this anyway." I didn't point out that I didn't see *why* telling was up to me.

"What I already knew isn't material. What you failed to volunteer *is.*"

"It wasn't just me." I gnawed on the side of my thumb, worried if that was some kind of gestural slip, and then figured to hell with it. "Go ask an adult. Go ask Pastor John why *he* didn't say anything. Or the *school.*"

"Believe me, I intend to. But." She aimed a finger at me. "Is there anything else *you* didn't think worth mentioning?"

"There's nothing."

"All right, then what about you? Where were *you* the night Jimmy was killed?"

There it was. But I was prepared. It was a good thing I'd spent time reading about her and micro-expressions and lies, because I'd probably have held eye contact, trying to make her believe what I said. One of her papers said that liars also stared at you to see if you bought said the lie. So I made sure to look away as I recounted driving around and going to Brooke's party, like I was dredging up the information. "And then I came home," I said.

"I see." Her mouth was a crack over her chin. "Of course, no one was with you when you went to Hopkins."

I shook my head. "But I'll bet I have the receipts. For the gas and the food. They'll have time stamps."

"Really?" Agent Angela's steady green gaze was disconcerting. "Tell me, you always save your receipts?"

"Yeah, actually. I don't have that much money. I have a budget." That was an outright lie. I looked at the ceiling and then back. "Look, I keep track of what I spend because I have to. You want to see the receipts, or not?"

"No." Sighing, she stopped the recorder, dropped it in her purse. "But you're lying about something. I don't know what. I wish I did. But I'm not a mind reader. Right now, I have nothing that ties you with Jimmy's death."

I sat up like I'd gotten zapped with a cattle prod. "I didn't kill him."

Her eyes were like a cat's, deciding whether to play a bit more with that mouse or chew off its head. "I didn't say you did. In fact, I know you didn't. But I think you know something

217

about who *did*, and for whatever reason you've decided not to share that information. So let me clue you in on a little fact. If you are intentionally withholding information, you could be in serious trouble. You could go to prison as an accessory after the fact." Her face relaxed and so did her tone, but those eyes were green ice. "Look, if you're in some sort of trouble, let me help. If not for yourself, then think of your folks, your sister. Think of how much harder it will be for them if it comes out that you're involved in some way. If that is true, you can say goodbye to any future you think you have."

What she wasn't saying—what she didn't seem to understand and what probably no one would—was that confessing now would still effectively end my future. No college would take me. My life would be over. No matter which way you cut it, I was screwed—unless I hand-delivered Jimmy's killers myself.

"I'm not involved," I said. "I've told you everything I know."

When she left, I knew she wasn't satisfied.

Tough.

———————————

So the ruckus at school went on until Tuesday, when the reporters figured out I had nothing to say and no intention of talking to anyone.

Except one thing I realized after that crummy weekend? Talking to Brooke loosened something in my chest. For the first time in a while—well, since Jimmy, I guess—I felt connected.

No. I just reread that, and that's wrong. Jimmy and I never *connected*. Not that way. I liked him, and he cared way too much about me in ways I didn't want to think about. But we weren't connected.

Never.

OCTOBER 27

2213

TO ALL WHOM THIS MIGHT CONCERN:

Jimmy was buried on Thursday of the following week. The school excused anyone who wanted to go. Pretty much the whole junior class went, as did most of Jimmy's teachers and about half the sophomore and senior classes and kids whose families belonged to Jimmy's church.

I'll be honest. The fact that all those sophomores and seniors went surprised me. I knew Jimmy didn't have many friends, unless there was a whole other part of his life I didn't know about. The more I thought about it, the more I figured the others went for the curiosity value. Or to get themselves on TV, because, of course, CNN and all the major networks were there. Jimmy was still news. I know the art teacher, Mr. Badden, didn't go. I'll bet he was told the same thing I was: stay away.

I followed that advice. I didn't need Mr. Lange yelling at me to feel any worse. Also, I didn't want to upset anyone. Considering how pissed the counter lady had been when I showed at Cuppa Joy and Jimmy had been *alive*, she'd probably crash her car into my truck or something. Honestly, I was afraid of being blamed and getting lynched. By then I'd read about how psychiatrists went to their patients' funerals, even if the patients committed suicide. (Don't ask me why; I was curious, I guess.)

Anyway, I couldn't decide if that was insane or really brave. A psychiatrist's job is to stop crap like that, isn't it? But then he goes and shows at the funeral. It's like he's making himself a target, walking right in with a big old bull's-eye on his chest and daring the family to take their shot.

But maybe the psychiatrist knows what we don't: that when people set their minds to kill themselves, they don't believe they can back out. Maybe a suicidal person thinks there's no choice, or this is his last, best shot at making things right. If he doesn't go through with pulling the trigger, that's just one more thing he's failed to do right.

I can't relate to that.

On the other hand . . . you're not in Afghanistan, and I am.

———————

Anyway.

School that day was very strange. Quiet. Although the school's K-12, the high school's upstairs and separate from the middle and elementary schools. Unless you have band or chorus, or need to use the library, you have no reason to go downstairs for anything other than lunch, and upperclassmen have the latest lunch. So the halls were pretty deserted. I didn't see Brooke all day, and that . . . didn't feel so hot. Everyone seemed to speak in whispers, but no one avoided me. Thursday was one of the days I didn't have to go to the university, so I had more free time than usual. We had substitutes for some classes, and they let us do whatever we wanted, which was both good and bad, because I had too much time to think.

For want of anything better to do, I started *Catcher in the Rye* again and then thought I should probably find another book. Rereading the same words over and over again was kind of creepy, too much like some weird Bible study. Or like being caught on the carousel with Phoebe, where you'd never grab the brass ring. Or revisiting memories of flies and brains and blood.

At lunch, I ate with Parker and the other guys and their girlfriends. I let everyone talk around me, drawing comfort from the swirl of conversation. I thought again about that bubble of space. I was already so focused on leaving school it never occurred to me, until then, that a normal person would feel uncomfortable and unhappy existing alongside other people instead of *with* them. But I was okay with it. I'd been doing that little sidestep out of myself all my life: becoming a ghost, going through the motions of my day, my soul nothing but a still, hidden center.

Or maybe this was what it was to be already dead.

———————

Turned out that it was a good thing I'd stayed at school. The funeral made the national news, of course. On CNN, the

222

funeral was all the news, all the time. But the microphones and cameras weren't the worst of it.

Jimmy had become a cause célèbre, everybody's poster child. Mal said things started to spiral out of control when this gay rights group, bused in from Madison, started a shouting match outside the cemetery gates with a bunch of people from Jimmy's church. To the gay-rights people, Jimmy was a martyr, a kid who hadn't dared come out about his sexuality in the current oppressive climate of rural Wisconsin. (Told you there were no gay people here.) To the evangelicals, Jimmy was a symbol of the dangers of earthly temptations and a godless existence and blah, blah, blah.

Anyway. That all died down, too.

A couple weeks after Jimmy's funeral, Dad said the Langes were going to put their farm up for sale. Seems that Mrs. Lange couldn't bear to stay where the memories of her dead kids were so strong. That got everyone at school talking again, but only for a day.

Life went on. Agent Angela never called or came back to town, probably because there just wasn't anything more to find. Over time I stopped worrying about her lurking around every corner because it was all too exhausting. That she went away so completely felt a little . . . too convenient, though. Like a trick or something that happened in books to lull the bad guys into giving themselves away. But you can't live your life worrying about shit like that. Believe me, I've tried. You get tired out real quick.

I stopped staring at myself in the mirror, too, wondering if I curled my lips or did a half-shrug and what all that meant. I slept more hours than not. I got through whole days without thinking of Jimmy more than once or twice. It got to the point that Jimmy snuck up only at weird times and if I saw something that reminded me of things we'd done together. Like the one Tuesday I passed a farmer working a forklift on one of those big bales, and then my throat closed up, my heart fisted, and I began crying so hard I had to pull over. Thank God, Mal wasn't with me that afternoon; she'd have asked too many questions.

The memory cards stayed at the bottom of that stack of Kleenex. I never thought of *them* either.

Well . . . unless I had to blow my nose. That wasn't often.

The terrible thing was, just when I thought things were getting better, I started to feel this horrible urge to tell someone what had happened. I guess half-confessing to Brooke and retelling it all to Cassidy Struthers started something going in my head. I used the library computer to google hotlines and things like that, but nothing seemed appropriate. Parker's mom, the psychiatrist, was out too. If I were in her place, I'd tell someone and to hell with ethics. I mean, we're talking *murder*. And what was I going to do? Sue her? I couldn't imagine being a shrink or psychologist or therapist and some kid you know comes in and tells you, *Oh, I witnessed a murder, and oh, by the way, I ran and saved my ass and then I went back and now I've got the evidence the police would kill for.* I mean, hello? This is a kid who goes to school with your son. Would you want your kid hanging around with some maniac like that?

Besides, I had a plan, didn't I? Pulling pictures off the cards and then going to my dad? Only the more I thought about it, the stupider that sounded. Like a little kid's daydream, the kind where you think about being a superhero. Still, I didn't get rid of the cards.

But I did do another search: *online confessions.* I know. Completely dumb. You wouldn't believe what came up. All these sites—GroupHug and FessUp and LightenYourLoad. I actually went to a few and read through a couple of the posts. One big rule I figured out right away was that you couldn't comment on anyone else's confession. I guess the point was for you to get it off your chest and then move on and not feel as if anyone was judging you. Someone might write *I slept with my best friend's boyfriend and I don't feel bad about it,* and then a bunch of people would send a hug or kiss or whatever.

Most of the confessions I read were pretty tame. Things like *I want a cigarette so bad I'll sleep with anyone and I'm only twelve.* Or *My girlfriend is a whore and not as good-looking as her Facebook picture.* I ran across one guy who wrote about beating up his girlfriend's ex-boyfriend and not telling anyone. More than a couple people confessed that they wanted to die or thought they were going crazy. (Hello? A cyber-hug was going to help with that? I mean, what could you say?) Not a single post about anyone witnessing a murder, anywhere.

Then I stumbled on an article about how the Catholic Church wasn't allowing online confessions because confession was supposed to be a sacrament. The problem was, nobody was actually *going* to confession anymore. More people felt comfortable confessing anonymously; they felt *better* because they could read the sorry-ass confessions of other people and think, heck, compared to those losers, their problems were nothing. One priest talked about how wrong that was because confession was about forming a guilt-free relationship with another human being and being absolved, not thinking you were so much better. In fact, I found this other article where some guy said how entertaining it was to go and read what other people thought. That didn't seem right to me. This wasn't supposed to be for someone else's entertainment. This was serious stuff.

I even ran across this article about old-time sin-eaters: beggars, mostly, but also people you could pay to come and sit with a dying person or by a corpse and then eat bread either touched by that person while he was still alive or placed on his body once he was dead. Sounded to me a lot like transubstantiation, only in reverse: instead of the bread turning into the body of Jesus, the food turned into sins that got taken into someone else and cleansed the soul of the dead person. The downside was the sin-eater was considered unclean and had to live outside the village—which was crazy, because that poor guy had voluntarily given up himself to swallow all the villagers' sins. Okay, sure, it was also one way of making a living, but it was in the village's best interests for their sins to be gobbled up—and now they wanted nothing to do with the guy? He should be an outcast, cut off, and hold all that filth inside and live like a bum? Wasn't that a sin, too?

In the Old Testament, that kind of shit didn't happen. Like, when someone did something wrong—when Miriam gossiped and got leprosy and all that—her sin was right there, on her skin, plain as day. She got exiled from the Jews' camp so no one else would be contaminated by her sin . . . but they didn't leave her in the desert. They didn't make it so she could never come home again. Instead, they waited for the sign of her sin to go away. They waited for her to heal, and they welcomed her back home. I'm not lying; go on, look it up if you don't believe me.

So, how was it right for an entire village to exile this one sin-eater, make him poorer than poor, the lowest of the low . . . when he was doing *them* the favor? When he was a goddamned saint for offering himself up like that?

I mean, come to think of it, that kind of crap had been going on for . . . well, forever. Since Jesus, right? Dying on the cross and all that? Look at it the right way, and you see that Jesus was this ultimate sin-eater—and people *worshipped* him. (And you have to wonder about the whole communion thing, too. I mean, think about it. Jesus ate all our sins, and we're supposed to eat him. But if his body holds our sins, then . . . See? You can drive yourself crazy thinking about stuff like this.)

But, by that logic, a sin-eater was as brave and selfless as Jesus. Hell, he was about as close to Jesus as a person could possibly be.

So to treat a sin-eater like that for your filth and guilt and sin . . . that's not a little screwed up?

―――――――――――

Now, here's also what I thought when I read and thought about all that.

Holding the secret in the way I was? Keeping it way down deep in the dark?

I was cut off too. I was in exile, stuck in the desert outside the camp: a sin-eater, with no way of getting rid of the filth and guilt and crime I'd swallowed unless I went to my dad or Agent Angela—

And that just wasn't happening. Because it would be like Jesus all over again. They'd crucify me.

I thought, too, about being with Brooke in that little bubble of time and space. Telling her would've been the same as giving her a bit of bread, a drink from my cup. It would poison her. Of all the people I knew, she deserved to become my sin-eater least of all.

And, hell, look at me now: stuck in Afghanistan.

But I did think about posting to an online site. I really did. For about five seconds. I thought, *I can write it all out. Maybe if I write it down, I'll be able to make sense of the whole thing and understand why I did what I did. Why I can't tell the truth now. Why telling the truth—spewing all that sin—would destroy everything.*

Then I thought about all the movies and TV shows I'd seen where they could trace people over the Internet. Sure, it wouldn't come back to me personally; I was using the school computer. But that was too close. In fact, I would have to drive all day to use an Internet café that was far enough away so this couldn't be traced back to me—and even then, things could go wrong. Someone might remember my face, and I was pretty sure that when you used a computer in a café you had to leave a driver's license or sign in or something. I just couldn't risk that.

Besides, I had a plan. Wait a while, and then look at Jimmy's cards and see if maybe I recognized someone. Yeah. I had to hang onto that. Stick to the plan. It's when you didn't stick with the plan that things went south.

———————

Then it was November.

Thanksgiving was a couple days away when my mom picked up the phone one afternoon, said *hello*, listened, and then turned to me, her eyes wide. "It's someone from Yale!" she stage-whispered as she handed over the phone.

My stomach did a flip as I pressed the handset to my ear. "Hello?"

"Hi, my name's Patricia Kramer, and I'm a Yale alumna for your area." A woman, very pleasant. Sounded about my mother's age, but like she was an executive. I could picture her in a suit. "I understand you've applied to Yale early action. I know it's a little late in the game, since early action decisions are made in mid-December, but I'd very much like to interview you, if that would be all right."

"Yeah," I said, dazed. "Sure, that would be great. When? Where are you?"

"Wausau, but I would come to you."

"No, that's okay. I go to Wausau all the time." I didn't, but she didn't have to know that. "They have way better bookstores." I know: total non sequitur. Why had I said that? I was so shook, I was babbling.

She didn't seem to notice, or maybe prospective students always babbled. "Of course, if you'd prefer, we can do that," she said. We worked out a time for the Saturday right after Thanksgiving, and she gave me her home address. "About noon? I'll make some sandwiches. You'll probably be sick of turkey. How do you feel about pastrami?"

"Uh, fine. That would be great, Ms. Kramer."

"Patricia. Actually, everyone calls me Pat. See you this coming Saturday, then," she said. "Oh, and don't worry about being nervous. Everyone is."

"Oh, honey!" My mom pulled me into a big bear hug. "Sweetheart, this is a *very* good sign. I'm so *proud* of you."

"I'm not in yet," I said. But she was right; this *was* good.

I just wished I could be happier about it.

Thanksgiving came. We ate turkey and stuff. My mom's sister and husband and their five little kids, all boys and blond as corn tassels, came down from Minneapolis. It was kind of nice, having the house full of little kids running around. Dad had the day off for once, and he and my uncle and Mal (who actually likes football and has this pink jersey with a big 4, even though Brett's gone to pasture) and I watched the games, which meant I didn't have to talk to anyone.

Afterward, we took those little kids out for a game of touch football, which was fun because we heaped up a bunch of leaves on either end of the yard to mark the goal lines. Then the adults and Mal and I spent most of the game grabbing little kids and slinging them into the piles. They screeched; Mom fussed about leaves in the house, but she was pretty happy gabbing and drinking wine in the kitchen with her sister, and no one really much cared. So it was good.

It was also the last time any of us was happy.

I'm really glad I didn't know that then.

———————

Then it was Saturday and time to go down to Wausau.

And, like that, I felt like I was coming out of a holding pattern, or maybe awakening from a dream. I'd told myself I was waiting for the right time to look at Jimmy's cards. Now, here was my opportunity.

That night, I got onto the computer and looked for cafés and coffeehouses in Wausau. At each website, I noted which ones had Internet access. I found four.

Which was three more than I needed.

———————

The day I drove down to Wausau was clear and crisp. The further I got from Merit, the greater the impulse got to just keep driving. I hadn't thought about leaving for a while, but the feeling recalled what Brooke had said that night we drove back from the Denny's. I knew—*felt*—what she meant about getting lighter and freer.

Patricia Kramer lived about ten miles west of Wausau, off I-51 and about five miles from Rib Mountain and Granite Peak. Wausau is a real city—thirty thousand people, more than two restaurants that aren't fast-food places, a Starbucks, condos on the river that bisects the town. Like a lot of northern Wisconsin places, Wausau used to be a big paper-mill town. So there are these old historic homes east of the river, all colors of the rainbow like you see in San Francisco, and even a couple of Frank Lloyd Wrights that I've never been in but which you can tour for a price. The landscape is all rolling hills and valleys, and then, as you head south, Rib Mountain pushes up on your right. In winter you can pick out the ski slopes amongst all the cedar and pines.

Pat Kramer lived off North Mountain Road, a little past the golf course north of the mountain and down a dirt road hemmed on both sides by tall spruce. The road opened up only at the very end into a large field. Two white swans floated on a pond off to the right, and a clutch of mallards scuttled along the edge. The road drained into a circular drive that ran right to the front door. The house was a mix of rustic and Swiss chalet: natural stone, logs that reminded me of those Lincoln Log kits I built stuff with as a kid. A lot of glass, too, soaring to cathedral points. A red, detached garage with double-wide, white scrolling doors and as big as a small barn hugged the woods left of the house. A shiny beige Jaguar hunched in the driveway.

Pat was about as I'd pictured her, only prettier, with chestnut hair and dark eyes. She wore black slacks and a charcoal gray sweater adorned with a single strand of pearls. She led me through the soaring front hallway and past a large painting on a south-facing wall. The painting was huge, easily seven feet high and wide, and you couldn't help but stop and stare.

The artist had chosen to paint a blasted, blighted tamarack bog: dead limbs strewn everywhere, trees canted at bizarre angles. A river of animals—fox, wolves, squirrels, fishers—streamed across the painting from right to left. The sky was choked with all sorts of birds. I recognized pileateds, downies, red-breasted woodpeckers, blue jays, thrushes, cartwheeling hawks, as well as scores of others, large as a half-dollar and painted small as a pinprick. Strange horned creatures as tall as a man and with spines running down their backs slithered along the dark pine frame. There was something about all those animals' terror and single-minded intensity that rooted me to the spot.

"You like that?" Pat asked. "It's a Uttech. He's a Wisconsin painter, lives down in Saukville. I love his work."

"What are they all running from?"

"Well, that's the mystery, isn't it?" But then she pointed to a blotch of what I'd initially thought was lichen on a rock. "Tom almost always puts in some sort of Ojibwe spirit, either a wendigo or what he calls trickster spirits. You could say that the animals are running from the evil the spirits represent. Or maybe the world in the painting is out of joint and the thing that's spooking the animals also allows for the primitive spirits that inhabit the woods to become visible."

"But no people. Maybe *they're* the evil the animals are running from," I said.

"Why do you say that?"

I pointed at the ruined forest. "Who else would be stupid enough to do that?"

I honestly don't remember much of what Pat and I talked about. I do recall that her kitchen was all light wood and cream tile and very bright, with bars of sunlight streaming through skylights. I also remember that she made Reubens: stacks of fatty pastrami and corned beef, tangy slaw, and melted Swiss cheese that were a heart attack waiting to happen. Any other time or any other me who wasn't about to sneak off to search through pictures taken by a dead kid, I'd have had two. As it was, I choked down a half-sandwich to be polite.

She asked questions I expected: why Yale, what could I bring to the school, stuff like that. I gave her my sales pitch, which went well as far as I could tell. She even laughed when I said that the first time I saw pictures of Yale, I thought of Hogwarts, and I didn't even like Harry Potter. She told me about Spielberg using the Sterling Library for the last Indiana Jones movie. We also spent a lot of time talking about cooking, of all things—which I used to like to do; hadn't I shared that with Jimmy?—and then I found out that she was a lawyer, having gone to Yale undergrad. She'd even run across Jodi Foster one afternoon as Foster was crossing the green and Pat was hurrying to the law library. After getting her degree, Pat had stayed in Connecticut, but she'd moved back ten years ago.

"Believe me, I had no intention of ever moving back to Wisconsin when I graduated high school. I wanted as far away as possible, see the world, the usual." She toyed with her coffee cup. "But real life intervened. My father got sick, and I was the only family left. My mom died when I was in law school. Cancer. Anyway, I took care of Dad. Then he died. I was all set to go back to Connecticut. But we'd made a life here by then, built this house, had children. And the more I thought of going back to what the East Coast had to offer, the more I realized I didn't need that anymore. People and their needs change."

"I guess I need to get away," I said, without stopping to think about it. "I've always dreamed of getting away. Like, there's got to be more than Merit and the Badgers and grilling brats on Sundays and watching the Packers. I wouldn't mind living where no one knows my name."

She paused. "I guess all the media attention's been hard for you. First the magazine, then your friend."

Now, I know this sounds silly, but I wasn't expecting that. Of course, she had to know. Hadn't I bragged about Jimmy's prize on my application, just like my mom wanted? "It hasn't been easy," I hedged. "It's not so bad now, though. It's not like I did anything wrong. I just wish . . ."

She cocked her head. Her pearls glowed in a bar of sun. "What?"

"I just wish he was still alive. So I could tell him I'm sorry for being mad. I was, you know. What he did started all sorts of trouble and rumors. But he shouldn't have to die for something like that."

"Oh." Her perfect, pencil-thin eyebrows tented. "I'm not sure I understand. Wasn't all that a collaborative effort?"

Oh, shit. "No, no," I said, trying to regroup. "That part was okay. I guess he and I never . . . we didn't think of the . . ." Shit, what was the right word? "We hadn't thought of the subtext, the hidden meanings." Okay, that sounded more like the artsy guy I was supposed to be. "I mean, I think that whoever killed him did it because they thought he was gay."

"Oh," she said again. "You do? You think Jimmy's being a homosexual was the motive?"

Either she'd been out of Wisconsin way too long, or we lived in parallel universes. Or maybe it was because she'd been out of state and places where kids didn't giggle and gossip and ruin reputations. Where people didn't get beaten to death. "Well, yeah," I said. "I really, really do. I mean . . . nobody really knows if he was."

"You were his friend," she said. "You were his collaborator."

"Uh . . . for his art, sure, and I was his friend, but it wasn't something we talked about."

"I see," she said and nodded as if she really did. "I imagine his death has been very traumatic for you on so many levels."

"Yeah." And then, I don't know what came over me, but I just said what was on my mind. "Ever since Jimmy died, my life's become like that painting you have in your hall. It was one thing, and then people got in there and thought the wrong thing because they saw the wrong thing, and they ruined it. Like that painting could be a metaphor for a person's life, or their soul."

"I see," she said, only this time, her tone held a subtle shift, one in which you could hear that she was now an adult who had no idea what the crazy kid was going on about. But you had to give her credit: she kept trying to understand. "How do you mean?"

"Well, if a forest is pure—if that's where all the wild things are—that could be like a soul. Only some evil destroys it, whether those are rumors that ruin reputations or an actual catastrophe, you know, like a tornado or something. But mostly I think the evil's internal. That is, the bad feelings that get stirred up are like the demons and tricksters in those paintings." I stopped talking then—*finally* and about five minutes too late—and thought, *Oh, snap. Now she'll think you're a* complete *maniac.*

But Pat's eyes were serious, so maybe I'd made some sense after all. "Like you said: only people destroy so completely. So how do you repair that? How can anyone repair their soul?"

"I don't know," I said. "Maybe all you can do is find another forest and hope for the best."

———————

At the door, we shook hands and she said, "It was very nice to meet you. I enjoyed our talk. You're a very thoughtful, very sensitive young man. I think you'll do well wherever you end up. Anyway." She took back her hand. "Best of luck."

Ouch. That felt like a kiss-off. She hadn't said that I'd do great at Yale or that she was giving me this sterling recommendation. All that drivel about forests and destruction and ruined lives. She was probably making a recommendation to the nearest psychiatric hospital. I figured I'd pretty much blown it.

But then, as I drove away, I wondered if maybe that hadn't been my plan all along.

———————

I'd already stopped at a RadioShack in Merrill, ten miles north of Wausau, and picked up a USB card reader. Then I made my way back to Wausau and to the café, which was right on a corner next to a gourmet coffee and wine place overlooking the river.

I parked but didn't get out of the truck right away. Instead, I sat and wondered what the heck I was doing. Here

I'd just talked to some lady about how people can wreck their souls. Well, wasn't that what I was doing? All that stuff with Jimmy had died down, inside and out. I was never going to be the normal guy I'd been before—whoever *that* had been—but there was no need to dredge all this up again. People had moved on.

Everyone but me, it seemed.

The café was crowded and noisy. The smell was amazing: coffee and fresh cinnamon buns. I couldn't help but think of Cuppa Joy, but instead of come-to-Jesus pamphlets, there was a stack of *Onion*s and real-estate glossies. Most everyone in the place had a laptop, but I spotted a trio of desktops in separate carrels at the very back. I ordered a latte and settled into the carrel furthest from the front door.

The latte was excellent. No foamy crosses this time, or doves. I wasted a few seconds checking e-mail and then decided that I was only putting off the inevitable. My heart was pounding as I tweezed out first the card reader and then the envelope into which I'd slid the two data cards. I shook out the cards into the palm of my hand. Just two tiny squares of navy blue plastic. Just two little atomic bombs. Maybe.

Before I could think my way out of doing it, I slotted the card with Jimmy's pictures into the reader and hooked the reader to the computer. Then I double-clicked on the drive and waited while the computer churned. A folder appeared: *Sample Portraits*. I double-clicked on that and settled back for the slide show.

There were twenty portraits, all in black and white. About half were men. Most were nude, and many were black. I don't know anything about art, but I could see Mapplethorpe's influence in the attention Jimmy paid to the men's bodies, delineating the line of muscle straining against skin. By contrast, though, Jimmy's work was much softer and gentler; the men's bodies weren't as aggressive in their poses or their sexuality. This wasn't about being in your face. There was this one picture entitled *Sleep* that was absolutely breathtaking: a black kid, maybe no older than me, lying on his back in bed. His body was relaxed, his head turned to one side, a drape of sheet crossing from his left hip to curl just under his right arm. His arms were thrown over his head, the hands dangling limply off the edge of the bed. The image was a little misty, no sharp edges at all, as if the photograph had been taken through mosquito netting or gauze: a picture at once both peaceful and wistful and erotic—and eerily similar to the picture Jimmy had taken of me.

I clicked through the rest and drew a blank. I didn't know any of these people. I didn't recognize them. I was thinking that the pictures were a dead end—until I came to one of a girl. At least, I think it was a girl. Like the photo of the black kid, the body and face were muzzy and ill-defined, and there were a lot of shadows like . . . like a movie where someone's slowly peeling out of these fingers of darkness that seem not to want to let go.

God, how do I explain this? I know . . . there's this old show my dad loved when I was a kid. Not *The Fugitive*, but the guy was always on the run . . . wait, I got it: *The Prisoner*. It was all about a spy who was trapped on this island and no one had a name, only a number. (Sort of like the Marines, ha-yuck, ha-yuck.) Anyway, that's not the important part.

This is: the way the bad guys caught anyone trying to escape was by sending this great big bouncy white balloon after them. That thing would catch and then swallow a guy right up, gulp him down the way a fish takes that hook, worm and all. The part that always creeped me out was when the outline of the guy's face would press against and deform the skin of that bubble. If you didn't know that it *was* a guy, that outline wouldn't help you. All you'd get was the impression of a face, and all that stretchy balloon deforming into a gummy white mask.

That's what Jimmy had done with these shadows. Instead of white, though, these were inky so that all you got was darkness and the barest suggestion of a face.

But was it a girl? A guy? I couldn't tell. Look at a guy, any guy, and you *know* it's a guy because of the Adam's apple. Guys' Adam's apples are visible, big as a knucklebone. A girl's neck is smooth, the Adam's apple invisible, like in the swan of Brooke's neck.

This person in Jimmy's picture, it could've been a guy, except the Adam's apple was in shadow, nothing but the gleaming jut of a chin and then a splash of black over the throat. So it might have been a girl, too. I just couldn't tell.

And here's what was really creepy: the moment it occurred to me that he or she—or it—might be both.

———————

Anyway.

Jimmy's picture, the one that really snagged my attention, was a full frontal. So you'd think I'd be able to tell if this was a girl. But like I said, I couldn't. Let's say, for argument's sake, that it was. I don't know why it's important for me to believe that right now, but it is, so go with it.

The girl's legs were crossed one in front of the other, a little like a ballerina, but so you really couldn't tell what was, you know, in her lap. Or not in it. If you know what I mean. No body hair at all, either. Her skin was as flawless as marble.

More shadows cut her torso like daggers, in diagonals, so her body was fractured; you only saw triangles of shimmery light. Her long dark hair twined from beneath the thing she wore—and it was the only thing, and I'm getting to that— and then down around her breasts like seaweed. But the thing was, there were so many inky fingers of shadow sculpting and pulling and kneading her body, her breasts could've been as flat as . . . well . . . as mine. I mean, you know: a guy's . . . chest. The dome of her left breast or chest or whatever was just a ghostly shimmer. Her waist was long and willowy, as thin and frail as Jimmy's, and a tiny silver hoop glinted in her belly button. So, yeah, it probably *was* a girl. Guys don't do that. I mean, I don't know any . . . *I* never would have thought of that.

Anyway, all that wasn't what made my heart stutter. What made me literally gasp was what she wore, the only stitch of clothing she had on.

A hoodie.

The picture was in black and white, and the hoodie was as dark as those shadows. In fact, the picture was entitled *Black Hoodie.*

A black hoodie. A slim girl—or a thin, lanky guy—in a black hoodie.

———————

Of course, it was just so my luck that there was nothing in any of these files to identify who the models were or when these were taken.

I closed the pictures, ejected the drive, and exchanged the camera card for the one I'd taken from Jimmy's cell. Jimmy had snapped seventeen pictures with his phone, and almost all, with the exception of two he'd taken of the farm, were shot in Cuppa Joy. All were band pictures and pretty clear, and then I remembered what he'd said about several groups paying him to take publicity shots. I had no idea why he'd take these candids with a phone camera, but maybe this was part of his process, I didn't know. Most had been taken across the room; I could see the table where he and I had sat. None of the pictures were particularly artistic or interesting. Just random shots of various bands. I clicked through them anyway, just on the off chance I'd spot something.

One picture flashed onto the screen, and I recognized the Penitents' setup: that acoustic guitar and the logo on the drum set. The band was playing, and they all wore theatrical black with silver chains. The lead singer was an older guy with burly arms and a fleshy, grizzled face. His nose looked stuck-on, like a smashed hunk of Silly Putty, and I thought he'd probably broken that a couple times. There was something weird about his hair, or maybe it was the way the lights fell, and then I realized that he'd dyed an entire hank of hair an eerie white. Like Morticia in the Addams Family. The other three guys—the drummer, bassist, and keyboard player—were all younger, and yet they had the same squat, fireplug build. Related? Maybe a dad and his kids? Older brother and his younger sibs? Could be either.

There was nothing to find here, though. I felt absurdly

disappointed, but then considered that maybe this was for the best. All right, there was *Black Hoodie*, but all that really told me was that Jimmy had this serious hang-up on a particular item of clothing and couldn't decide between girls and boys, and so go figure. I'd get rid of the cards, toss them into the river and the card reader, too. No one would ever know I'd been here, and I could get back to my so-called life.

As I was about to eject the card, my eyes drifted to the right-hand corner of that picture of the Penitents. Someone stood just off the main stage, in shadow and profile, but I recognized the roadie I'd seen the night I went to Cuppa Joy. The way she stood, I flashed back to *Black Hoodie*. Was it the same kid?

On impulse, I took off my glasses. The world instantly shifted and slewed sideways; Black Hoodie, that girl-roadie, doubled to an oily smudge. If you've ever seen double in your life, you'll know what I'm talking about. I stared, recalling that willow-reed of black pressing against Jimmy and Jimmy's killers rushing out of the woods like shadows escaping the boundaries of a nightmare. Even if my vision had bordered on the bionic, everything had happened too quickly and I'd been too far away to get a good look at Jimmy's killers. Heck, I hadn't even managed a good look at that panel van with the orange tag, either, and couldn't have said if it had rear windows or not. There had been a couple of panel vans in the back lot the first time I'd gone to Cuppa Joy, I remembered that, but good luck trying to figure out if the van I'd seen off the shoulder that night was one of them.

I went back to the picture of the Penitents. I stared so long at that girl—if it was a girl; it could've been a boy, the picture was that dark and grainy—that my eyes watered. I just wasn't sure. The lighting was terrible on that side of the stage. But if it was the same girl, if she was the one I'd seen by the Taurus the night Jimmy died . . . I tried to remember if I'd noticed a Taurus wagon during my first visit but couldn't. The lot had been pretty dark, after all, and I'd been looking for a parking spot not playing Encyclopedia Brown, for heaven's sake.

I didn't know the first thing about working with pictures or how to make them less blurry—if that was possible. I knew about Photoshop, but only in theory. The only person I knew who had the program was Mr. Badden, and he was obviously not an option. Maybe I could hire someone, but I didn't have the first clue how to go about that. More importantly, how could I explain how I'd come to have the pictures? The cards? Someone would eventually put two and two together.

Looking back, I know that should've been the instant I called Agent Angela, turned the pictures over, and took whatever she might dish out, which I was certain would be plenty. Of course, I didn't. Instead, I surfed until I found the Penitents' website. I found out their real names and that they were from Hopkins. There were a couple of pictures of the band, but none of the girl. In some of the pictures, the band members wore black hoodies. But that didn't prove anything. *I* had a black hoodie, for chrissake.

So now what? I went to the drop-down menu that gave the Penitents' schedule. They were due to play at Cuppa Joy that Sunday, the very next day. Tomorrow.

Then I ejected the card, finished my latte, and started home. I crossed the river again, but I didn't drop anything into the water. Maybe I should've, but I didn't.

On the way home, I detoured to Hopkins and cruised the neighborhoods. I think I had this half-formed idea that I might spot the girl—might, in fact, stumble on where she and her family lived—and then I would . . . I would . . . What? Confront her? Rescue her? I didn't know. Rolling through town, I spotted knots of kids on sidewalks—and they all wore hoodies. Guys. Girls. Some kids that I couldn't tell what they were because, without clues like long hair and pink, little kids in black hoodies could be anything. Most looked happy. I thought. Hard to tell, actually. What can you tell from a face?

When I finally pushed into the kitchen, Mom only pestered me a little about the interview, but then Dad got her to back off. I escaped to my room and slid the cards back under their stack of tissues and tried not to think about them.

OCTOBER 27

2328

TO ALL WHOM THIS MIGHT CONCERN:

That next day crawled by. Sunday night, I lied to my parents about where I was going. Surprisingly, I didn't feel nearly as bad or paranoid this time. Maybe lying was getting easier, like all I'd needed was a little practice. Or maybe I was getting used to living a lie. There was nothing I did that was not calculated; every move I made, everything that came out of my mouth, I thought about first in a kind of mental hiccup. Like those five-second delays broadcasters put into place after Janet Jackson's wardrobe malfunction, there was always this infinitesimal lag between what someone said to me and what I answered in return. I couldn't recall the last time, other than at Pat Kramer's house, when I'd spontaneously done or said anything where I wasn't standing to one side and evaluating. I was permanently outside myself, having slewed sideways into a ghost image, the two *me*s never converging.

For some reason I still don't understand, I took a great deal of care getting dressed. I had new black scrubs by then and dragged on a black hoodie I'd bought that afternoon at this skater place in the mall. Everyone in the store wore black or gray or olive drab, and with all those hoodies, it was like walking into a hoodie convention. I spent longer than I thought I would picking out a new sweatshirt, halfway tempted to get something sketchy with a logo. In the end I went for plain black.

Now, in front of my mirror, I pulled on the sweatshirt, zipped it to my throat, flipped up the hood. I'd lost weight in the past several months, and my face was cut into angles and planes, my cheekbones as sharp as blades. My eyes peered from deep caves. I could've modeled for that painting, the famous one where the guy's standing on a bridge, hands clasped in horror to his cheeks as he screams into an angry blood-red sky.

Or—hell—I could've been that girl, *Black Hoodie*. Squint a little bit, go a little muzzy. No sweat.

I'd decided to time my arrival to a point when the band was maybe halfway through their second set. That way, everyone would be looking at them and not watching the door. The front lot was packed again, cars and trucks lined up like beads on either side of the road. On a whim I tooled around back, and while there was no Taurus wagon, there were three panel vans, and all three with side windows. So that didn't do me much good. Any one of those vans could've been the one I saw.

After that, I parked a good quarter mile away. My truck was distinctive and would be remembered. I didn't want that.

The coffeehouse was jammed, standing room only, which was okay by me because the more people there were, the less likely it'd be that anyone would notice me, the lone heathen, in the mix. My black-on-black ensemble fit right in; almost everyone wore a hoodie or black tee, probably because of Pastor John. So I wasn't that conspicuous, which was good. I got myself a plain coffee (thankfully, the same woman wasn't behind the counter) and slid into a free spot along the far wall, slouching into a wedge of shadow.

The Penitents weren't bad. They were in the middle of a solo acoustic piece. The lead singer, the old guy with the Morticia Addams streak, was performing, his gravelly voice edged with just a hint of country twang. I wasn't really following the lyrics—something about getting saved, I was sure, or what a friend I had in Jesus only I had to open my heart. Instead, I tried picturing him as one of the men I'd seen burst out of the forest—and I couldn't, not really. I had been far away, and everything happened so fast.

I turned my attention to the crowd, scanning faces, alert for one person in particular. As far as I could tell, the roadie—Black Hoodie, as I'd come to think of her—was nowhere around. She might be in the wings, of course, or maybe waiting in one of the vans out back. Sipping coffee, I let my eyes drift over the crowd, touching on faces here and there, never lingering too long. No one looked familiar.

The piece ended, and the lead singer was acknowledging the applause when he moved into a bolt of light from an overhead spot. That hank of white hair flared a brilliant sunburst yellow, and my mind jolted back to the hooded killer with the rock. But that person had been a blond . . . hadn't he? I straightened out of my slouch. My pulse quickened and my mouth went dry. What if I was mistaken? What if the killer's hair, or only a part, had really been *white*, and what I'd seen was *that* reflected in the sickly yellow glow of the lights in the park shelter?

Forty minutes, four songs, and an encore later, I still wasn't sure. By then it was almost eleven; the band was done; the house lights had come up along with a surge of conversation and a general milling of people for the counter or front door. Now was the time. If Black Hoodie *was* with the band tonight, this would be when she'd appear to help with breakdown and carting the band's equipment out to their vehicles. If she was here, though—and if she really *was* Black Hoodie—how would I approach her? I couldn't do it in the coffeehouse. There were too many people. Maybe it was better to go out to the back lot, see if I could catch her there.

Before I could move, a hand clapped onto my left shoulder. Startled, I jumped, slopping tepid coffee on my scrubs. I twisted around, my heart already sinking down to my toes, because I knew who had found me out.

"Hello." Pastor John's voice was pleasant enough, but a quick flare of displeasure fired his eyes. He wore his trademark black jeans, black hoodie and large silver cross. His hand slid from my shoulder to grasp my forearm as if he were afraid I would pull away—which I would've, if I'd been thinking. Either because of the crush or the noise, Pastor John's face was only inches from mine. When he spoke again, he leaned in so close, his breath tickled my ear. "I thought I told you to stay away."

"I, ah, I just wanted to see the band." My eyes bounced from Pastor John's face to the stage, where the musicians were packing up their gear and then back. "I'm not bothering anybody. I was just leav—" My voice choked off in my throat as a slim figure in black slid onto the stage: the girl roadie, in a black hoodie. I couldn't see her face well, but I thought: *Yes, she could be the one in the picture. Definitely.*

"Don't lie to me. What's your business here?"

Out of the corner of my eye, I saw the girl—was it a girl? So thin, and there were so many shadows . . . yes, of course it was; it was a girl—winding electrical cords, and then I think she knew she was being watched because she stiffened. Her gaze swept the room and, somehow, fixed on mine. Some indefinable emotion rippled across her face, and her lips parted. She recognized me. I saw it plain as day: she knew that *I* knew. Turning away, the girl grabbed the handle of a small amp and practically ran from the stage, almost tripping over the metal legs of a crash cymbal.

Can't let her get away.

"I told you," I said to Pastor John, "I came to see the band. It's a free country; I'm not causing trouble, and I'll just leave, I'll leave right now, okay?" I tried pulling away, but he wouldn't let go. "Look, I'd just like to go home."

Pastor John had followed my gaze, and now his grip tightened. "No, it's not okay. What's your business here?"

"What do you mean? I'm listening to the band. I don't know what you're talking about."

"Liar. I don't know what you think you're going to find here, but your answers don't lie with a *person*, man *or* woman." His voice grew louder and conversations at tables near us died.

"Your answers lie with God, and you would do well to ask His forgiveness. Don't think I don't know a trickster when I see him."

"What are you talking about?" I asked, my voice rising on a new note of desperation. There were only a few pieces of equipment left on the stage, and the girl hadn't reappeared. She was hiding, lying low; she'd get away. "I just want to go home."

"You *are* home: in Satan's embrace. His Sin lives in your heart and rides your breath."

"Amen to that," said a woman at a table to our left. Her breasts heaved indignantly, and the white fish logo on her tee seemed to porpoise out of a black sea.

"Satan has taken up residence in your soul, your body, and you'll never be clean, never be free until you admit your guilt. I *know*," Pastor John hissed into my ear. "I know more than you think. You had something to do with Jimmy's death, didn't you?"

"What?" Now I didn't bother trying to look calm. "*No!*"

"Liar! Your sin is written all over your face. You may have fooled the police, your family, your friends, but you can't fool— "

"Get the hell away from me!" With something close to a sob, I jerked free with such violence that I staggered back on my heels, lost my balance, and careened into a nearby table. Mugs and plates toppled with a glassy crash; coffee slopped onto the floor; and one guy yipped as my hip connected with his elbow and sent his drink sheeting over his face. I felt hands dragging over my sweatshirt. Someone hooked my hood, and then I was nearly yanked off my feet as my breath choked off. My vision swam molten red, and then a clean bright spike of fear skewered my chest. These people were going to kill me, lynch me, stone me, string me up! Bucking, I kicked out, flailed blindly, heard someone yelp, and then the pressure around my throat was gone and I was spinning away, barreling toward the front door on a riotous wave of manic shouts and angry curses. Pastor John screamed something, and a knot of guys near the door closed ranks to block my way, but I was sprinting, muscling my way through, moving fast. I took the door at a dead-out run, straight-arming the pushbar with such force that the door exploded open with a shivery, splintery crash that might have been the sound of that frosted glass oval shattering. I don't know if it was and still don't to this day, because I did not look back.

But I was free. I was out, and I was never going inside that awful place again, never.

There was only one path left for me. A surge of cold wind blasted my face and stole my breath, but I kept on: arms pumping, feet pounding the earth as I ran as hard as I could into the night, into the dark.

I had only one thought: find the girl. Find Black Hoodie before it was too late and she got away and took the truth with her. This would be my only chance to know for sure; I would have no other.

Darting along the front of the building, heels skidding over gravel, I wheeled around a corner, frantically searching the shadows. It was full night, no moon at all, only that sickly dull glow from the lone streetlamp splashing over the dumpsters.

For a moment I stood there, chest heaving, breath sobbing in and out, and I thought, *She's gone; she saw me and she knows that I know and she left.*

And then there was movement deep in the shadows and inky silhouettes of parked cars. Black Hoodie appeared out of nowhere, pulling together out of the darkness the way a spider gathers its web.

"Why are you following me?" Her voice—and yes, it was a girl's voice; I know it—was tremulous, her face a silvery blur like a steam cloud about to fragment in a stiff wind. She sounded scared and very, very young. "What do you want? Who are you? I don't know you."

"I—" I couldn't speak. My eyes were adjusting to the dim wash of orange light, and now that I saw her—now that the moment was finally upon me—I wasn't sure, at all, if she was the girl in the picture or the one I'd seen that night with Jimmy, or if that person—in the picture or beneath that shelter—

—touching Jimmy, wanting Jimmy—

had been a girl at all. How could I be so sure? Maybe if I got her under a bright light? Yes, maybe then. It had been dark that night in the park, and hadn't I thought it might have been

—Pastor John—

a very thin man? Boy? Or was that what I was primed to see because of all the rumors about Jimmy? About me?

Only *were* there rumors about me? Weren't those only about Jimmy?

Wait, wait. Of course, there'd been rumors. That kid in the auditorium that day I met Agent Angela, he'd called me Jimmy's boyfriend. Of course. What was I thinking?

But now that I saw this girl, I thought: *I don't know anything.*

I don't know what I really saw other than rocks and a hatchet and Jimmy and

—kissing Jimmy, grinding against Jimmy—

blood, all that blood.

It had gone so fast, the whole thing. So maybe this was all in my mind. Not the murder, of course not, but the rest. Was I only *trying* to make pieces fit that had no business in the same picture?

"Well?" she said, less timidity in her voice now. She must've sensed my confusion. She came no closer, but she didn't shrink away either. "What do you want?"

"I . . . I just . . . I just want to talk," I stammered. "Please. I won't hurt you. It's just . . . I want to talk about Jimmy."

"Jimmy." Her tone was flat, not a question, and then there was a note of genuine puzzlement. At least, it sounded genuine to me. But five minutes before I hadn't been entirely sure this was a girl. "You mean the boy who used to work here? The one who got killed? What about him?"

"I saw you with him. That night." My tongue was thick. I felt as if I were feverish and moving in a dream, the gluey words pulling themselves out of my brain like taffy. "I came around back, and I . . . I saw you with him."

"You've made a mistake," she said, and now her voice firmed, held a note of both relief and decisiveness. "I mean, we talked once or twice, and he took a couple pictures of the band, but I didn't see Jimmy that night, except in the coffeehouse. He helped us bring in some of my daddy's gear, but that was all."

"No." I took a step closer, feeling the story I'd concocted for myself unraveling. "You're lying."

"No, I'm not."

"I know about you," I said. Why wasn't she scared? Could I be wrong? No, *no*, this was right; this was the real story; this was the truth. "I know about the picture. I've seen it."

"What? What picture?"

"Don't," I said. My voice quavered. "Don't say that. You know what I'm talking about. You *know*." I took another step toward her, my hands outstretched. "You must've gotten into trouble. Is that it? Your parents found out and you got into trouble for posing nude—"

"What?" Her voice thinned to a squeak. "Naked? *Me?*"

"And so they used you to lure Jimmy out to the woods . . ."

"No. *No.* You're *crazy.* Stay away from me!"

"But I can help you." Her face blurred and broke apart, and I realized that my cheeks were wet. "Let me help you. I can save you. I can save us both and we can do the right thing. You made a mistake, you got into trouble, you made a bad call, but that's because you didn't think there was any other way out."

"I don't know what you're talking about." She moved back with a small, stumbling step and then another, her hands pushing the air between us, trying to ward me off. "Get away from me. You come any closer, I'll—"

"Problem here?" The voice was deep, maybe ten yards off to my right, and I whirled around. The lead singer's white streak shone like the tail of a comet. "He bothering you, Evie?"

"Oh, Daddy!" And then she was stumbling toward him. She threw herself into his arms, and as he folded her up, I saw—*really* understood, for the first time—how young she was. Mallory's age. Heck, *younger.* Just a kid, and I . . .

I . . .

I didn't think Black Hoodie was a kid. *I* could've been Black Hoodie, and I was almost a man.

God, why hadn't I brought a copy of the picture to compare? Because, deep down in a secret dark vault of my mind, I knew that this girl and Black Hoodie weren't the same person at all? Because I wanted to retain some last vestige of an illusion that I might be clean again? That I wasn't to blame?

Evie said, "He's going on about that boy who used to work here, that Jimmy. You know, the one who took pictures? And now he's talking about . . ."

"I *saw* you," I said again, desperate to convince them both. No, that's not right. I was working myself up in an effort to convince myself, and maybe if I just kept talking, said what I believed was the truth often enough, what I wanted to believe *would* become real. "I saw you. You got Jimmy into a Ford Taurus wagon. You drove him to the park. I have *proof.*"

It was too dark for me to see the man's face clearly, but the night suddenly felt crowded and I turned. Two other men—the other boys in the band, as it were—stood there, waiting, watching, listening. I was surrounded. They were all of a piece, a family: a father and his sons and his only daughter, their little sister. And *Jimmy*, what had he done to them—if anything at all?

That tiny voice at the back of my mind hectored: *Nothing, nothing at all, this is all in your mind, you're trying to make connections where none exist because you're a maniac; you're insane; you could be Black Hoodie . . .*

"Evie," the father said. He gave her a little push. "You go wait in the van, you hear?"

"But, Daddy, he . . ."

"No buts. Go on. We'll be right behind you." She went, reluctantly, looking over her shoulder at me all the way. It was impossible to read her face, to tell whether or not there was a plea in there. Or only fear. Or, maybe, relief.

The father waited until the van's sliding door clapped shut, and then he turned. I shuffled back an involuntary step and felt the others close in behind. I could've run, I suppose; no one put a hand on me. But I was paralyzed, a terrified rabbit pinned in headlights.

"Let me make this as simple for you as I can," Evie's father said. His voice was low and saturated with menace. He was close enough that I smelled his sour breath: stale cigarettes and old coffee. "You stay away from my daughter. You stay away from us. You're sick. You're imagining things. I don't know what you think you saw—"

"I *saw*," I croaked. "I followed you. You were waiting for Jimmy in the park that night. She was the one who lured him there . . ."

"That's crazy talk," he said calmly. "You didn't see us, son, and if you're so certain, why haven't you gone to the police? To your father?" He must have registered my surprise because he gave a small nod. "I know who you are. Everyone here does. I'm not going to make a big deal about this. But my heart is heavy for you, son. Lord knows what kind of sickness you've gotten yourself mixed up in."

"N-no," I said. "No, that's wrong. I haven't *done* anything. You did it, *you* . . ."

"You sure about that? Sure those eyes of yours aren't playing tricks? I've lived through a lot, and let me tell you: sometimes you get something stuck between your teeth, worked real tight in there like gristle, and you pick and you pick, but it just won't work itself loose. That's what's happened with your mind. If you have proof, talk to your father. Talk to the sheriff. Otherwise, leave us be."

"I saw you," I said, weakly. "I saw the rocks and hatchet. I saw your *hair.*"

"That so? You saw all that, and didn't help, didn't scream? You were that close and you let that boy die?"

"I . . . I . . ." *I ran. I*

—wanted Jimmy? Needed Jimmy? W-wanted—

Nonono, what am I thinking, what am I doing, what am I? I only saved myself!

But I couldn't say that. I couldn't say anything.

"That's right," he said, as if he'd read my mind. He jabbed a hard, blunt finger in my chest. "You think about that. You think about the fact that you're alive and that boy is dead. If you saw something, if you were *there* . . . you could've saved him. That boy might be alive today."

No, I thought dully, *I'd be dead, we'd both be dead.*

But, then again . . . maybe not.

"But you didn't say anything then," he said. "You haven't said anything since."

"I'm saying it now." Then, more firmly: "I'm saying it *now.*"

"You're saying *nothing.* Just like you *did* nothing." He paused, and in the silence I heard only the thud of my heart. When he spoke again, his voice was curiously gentle. "We're going to forget about this. We're good Christians, and our Lord tells us to forgive. No one wants trouble here. So I forgive you this error in your ways, this delusion in your mind, this sin polluting your soul. You're obsessed, son, and that's a dangerous thing. It'll destroy you in the end, and I'm sorry for that, but I can't let you pull us down with you. So . . . do what you got to do the right way. If you're so sure we're guilty, then you tell your father. Tell the law. Tell our Lord. Otherwise, don't you ever come near us again, boy, you hear me? If I see you around again, I'll have to take action. I'll have to take *steps*."

"Yeah?" I wanted to sound brave and knew I only sounded small, like a ten-year-old facing up to the biggest bully on the playground and trying not to piss his pants. "Is that what you call what you did to Jimmy, taking *steps*? You saw or heard about that picture, about *Black Hoodie*, and decided that couldn't come out?"

"I don't know what you're talking about. We're going now," he said, taking a step back. "We're going, and we're not to see you again. And son? Get yourself some help."

I said nothing, neither agreed nor disagreed. Instead I stood, rooted as an ancient oak, and listened to the scuffle of footsteps as his sons broke ranks. I watched as they piled into their vehicle; I stood there as the van's engine coughed, turned over, then roared to life. I saw Black Hoodie's face once more, pressed to the glass and utterly blank, the dark shadowy mask so perfect, so flawless. Numb, mind reeling, I stared as the van passed by the dumpsters beneath that lonely sodium vapor—

And then, in that sudden twinkle, Black Hoodie's lips moved and formed words:

Help me.

———————

No.

I closed my eyes.

I had not seen that. I only *wanted* to because if I were wrong, then I had nothing but my memories and my guilt, and how could I live with that? Yes, it had to be just a trick of the light, what I wanted to see. Right? *Right?*

I didn't know, couldn't decide. I watched the van turn out of the lot and start west, the same route that Taurus had followed the night Jimmy was killed.

It's a dare. They're taunting me. They're not roaring out of here, not speeding away. They want me to follow, and that girl . . .

The paralysis that had me suddenly fell away. I'd let them shake me, frighten me into believing that I couldn't trust what I knew or had seen. I had to do something. That girl, Black Hoodie, was counting on me. I turned for my truck, thinking furiously. I would have to be fast about it before they got too far ahead.

Something rushed from the shadows. Crying out, I brought up my cocked fists to fend off a blow, and Pastor John took a step back.

"Whoa, hang on," he said. "Take it easy."

"What?" I forced my bunched fists to relax. "What do you want now?"

"Isn't that what I should be asking you? What were you doing? Why were you bothering those people?"

"What?" Sudden comprehension dawned. "How long have you been standing there?"

"Long enough. This is my land, and I'm within my rights to follow you anywhere I want and stand anyplace I please. As for those good people . . ."

"*Good* people—"

"These accusations you're slinging around . . . You could

ruin lives this way. You don't want to be responsible for starting a campaign of rumor and innuendo."

As incredible as this sounds, I managed a laugh, brittle and bitter. "Like what was done to me? Jimmy? You all think you know the truth, but you don't."

"Then tell me," Pastor John said. "Tell me the truth. Do you honestly believe what you said?"

It was on the tip of my tongue to say that I did, but the words hitched in my throat and I thought, *I'm out here, alone, in the dark. Pastor John wears a black hoodie.*

"What kind of car do you drive?" My voice had an alien edge. "Where's your car?"

"What are you talking about?"

"Your car," I said. *This is the plan. They've worked it out this way because the longer he can keep me here, the further away that van gets.*

That insidious small voice nipped my brain: *But what did you see, what did you see, what did you* really *see? The girl didn't know what you were talking about.*

"What?" Pastor John's

—*Black Hoodie's*—

face was in shadow, but I had to hand it to him, his confusion sounded so genuine, I'd never have guessed if I hadn't *known* what he was doing. "What does my car have to do with anything?"

"I have to go now," I said, pushing past. He made another abortive grab, but this time I eluded him. "Don't touch me. Don't try to stop me."

"Son, I'm only trying to stop you from destroying yourself. You're in no shape to drive. Have you been drinking?"

"Wouldn't you like to think so," I choked. I was nearly out of the lot, and now I broke into a jog. "Stay away, just—"

He called after me, but I didn't stop and although I expected him to run after me, he didn't do that either. I only looked back once, when I made it to my truck, but he had disappeared.

I never saw Pastor John again.

I was already a good fifteen minutes behind. I knew from their website that the Penitents were from Hopkins, and they'd headed west, so I gunned the truck and peeled away from the shoulder, gravel pinging against the undercarriage. Once on the straightaway, I dropped my foot on the accelerator and pushed up my speed. My headlights drilled the night; the darkness scrolled past in a moonless blur.

My thoughts churned. If Pastor John had heard everything, he didn't seem surprised. Didn't that mean he was in on the whole thing? Of course, it had to be. His aim had been to slow me up, keep me from following, and if he *had* heard, then he *knew* what I had for proof—

And yet, what was my proof? Was Black Hoodie a girl, a boy, Pastor John

—me—

Evie? And if she was, what did that really prove? Where was the motive for murder? The only thing I could come up with was that Evie had posed for Jimmy. The father found out.

He tried to get Jimmy to give them the picture, only Jimmy wouldn't and . . .

And that was enough to kill for?

Far ahead, a red flare of taillights. I was catching up, but I had to go faster, faster! I stomped on the gas. The small green mile markers by the side of the road flicked by. Yes, I would catch them, I was catching up, I'd be riding their tail in minutes.

A sudden bend, and then I was jinking the wheel to the right in a squeal of tires. Coming out of the turn, the black tongue of road straightening and then I hammered the truck, heard the high growl of the engine . . .

And there! Taillights bobbed and dipped and disappeared and then blinked into view once more as the van crested a hill. They would have to slow down; the van was even less maneuverable than my truck.

And would the girl know? Would she have looked back, understood what I was doing? Maybe that's why I was catching up because she saw me and so she'd done something to distract them, maybe she was fighting them . . . because, yes, because I told her that *I* would save us both, I would rescue her from herself. Oh God. I had to catch them. Then we could go together to my dad. She would tell him the whole story and I'd produce the pictures and they'd arrest her father and brothers and then everyone would forgive me, I could forgive myself. If I could just *catch* them . . .

I whiteknuckled the wheel until my hands cramped. A deer-crossing sign flashed on my right; a row of mailboxes smeared to a blur. Far ahead, there was a silver smudge on the horizon: Hopkins. Would I have to chase them through town to their house? My headlights dipped, then rose and cut a rectangle of green sign out of the black: **Cachemequon Lake State Park 3 miles.**

The park.

My heart thumped in my throat, and I felt a queer spasm of premonition. I had been down this road before, the night Jimmy died. Were they leading me back to the scene of his murder? Of course, that was the only thing that made sense. They weren't running *away.* They were running *back* to where all this had begun: to the point where the locomotive of my future jumped the tracks in what seemed another lifetime.

Ahead, the brake lights flickered and flared once, twice. Tapping the brakes. Slowing down. Yes! They'd have to do that to make the turn into the park. I couldn't let them get all the way into the woods because then they would

—kill me—

use the darkness to their advantage

—and make it look like a suicide. Because they've all seen you at Cuppa Joy, they know how wild you were, and they'll say, Sheriff, there was something real wrong with that boy—

So, if I could just stop them on the road before they got all the way into the woods, if I could head them off!

"Go, go," I chanted. The needle inched to eighty, then eighty-five, then ninety. "*Gogogogogo.*" Another curve, a flash of something silver to my right that my brain didn't catch up to until I was well past—

—Deer? Had those been—

and then the truck was skidding. Cursing, I wrenched the wheel right then left, felt the truck slew and the world outside turn, heard the squall of tires as the truck bucked and tried to slide sideways. A fence post and then another flashed in and out of my headlights, and then the truck left the pavement, bouncing and bucking first onto the soft shoulder before wallowing through high grass. I jinked the wheel a hard left, jabbing on the brake until I was at near stop then gunned the truck again. Gravel spewed under the tires, striking metal with a hollow, spattering *pock-pock-pock* as the truck gathered itself and dug in, grappling back onto pavement.

Frantic now, I scanned the road ahead. Had I lost them? Where were they? Was that . . . Ah, there, *there* they were: that telltale flare of brake lights. They were teasing me, daring me to follow.

"Well, you got your wish, you bastards." Sweat filmed my skin. I was gritting my teeth hard enough that my jaw hurt. But I was closing now. "I'm coming for you, I'm coming—"

A flicker of something to my left, a swift flash, and then the buck was galloping across the road directly into my path. I just had time to scream before I did the absolutely wrong thing.

I swerved.

In the next instant, the truck rocked and groaned and a thought as physical as a stiletto speared my brain: *I'm dead.*

There was a sudden, bone-crushing *bang* as the truck plowed into the buck. Even above the squall of brakes, I heard the deer's high, bawling scream, and then it seemed as if our screams twined and mingled and there was nothing but sound and motion and a fury of light. Shrieking, the buck catapulted against my windshield. The animal hit with a tremendous hollow *boom*, and the windshield burst in a hail of gummy glass.

And then the truck was rolling, the world turning in drunken circles, bouncing like a tiddlywink: once, twice, three times before the road was gone altogether. The wheel was torn from my hand; there was a choke of exhaust and grit and pulverized metal and blood. A tremendous jolt snapped my neck with the force of a whipcrack. My forehead slammed the steering wheel in a stunning, nauseating blow that sent my glasses flying and sheeted my vision a blistering white and then black. A second late, there was a heavy ka-*BANG* and a splintering scream of wood. My truck slammed broadside into a fence—and then, mercifully, died.

By some miracle, the truck had landed right side up, but the impact had done something to the driver's side door, which had popped and now hung at a weird, drunken angle like the shutter of an abandoned house. The headlights were still on, hazy dust swirling in the nacreous shafts. It was suddenly so quiet, so still, I thought I'd gone deaf. Stunned, I slumped, my hands still in their death grip on the wheel. There was something sticky in my eyes, and when I put up a shaky hand to smear away the wet, I smelled copper. Blood was sheeting down my face, dripping from my chin. There was more blood in my mouth, and a stripe of pain was painted from the ball of my left shoulder to my right hip. When I tried taking a deep breath, my chest felt full of broken lightbulbs. I moaned, but I heard that and so I wasn't deaf, thank God; at least I still had my hearing. But the sweet, choking fog of gas was strong, and I thought that the tank might have ruptured.

That's when I heard the moan: a long, lowing gargle.

It took me four tries to jab my shoulder harness's release. My fingers were stiff as pegs, and I couldn't make my hands cooperate, but I finally managed it, heard the sharp *snick* as the mechanism ratcheted. Then I was slithering from the driver's seat in a shower of nubbly glass, dropping to the chill earth on hands and knees. The impact jarred my chest and vibrated into my bones, and I groaned.

As if in answer, that odd lowing came again. The sound came from my right at some point beyond the truck. Something stirred the grass with a dry rustle. Without my glasses, the world was a chaotic blur of shadow and filmy light, yet I caught the wink of two silver-green coins sparkling in the silver-blue wash of my headlights—and then I understood.

Of course. That was why the van's taillights had flared. They'd been braking, but not to turn. They had slowed to avoid the deer.

The buck was still alive, and as I staggered nearer, the blur of its legs resolved and I could see that they were twitching as if galvanized by tiny electric shocks. A riot of blood and mangled intestine and ruptured bowel boiled from its burst abdomen, and I gagged against the stink. When my shadow fell across its face, the deer bawled again, its huge eyes rolling with pain and terror.

"Oh God." I crouched by the dying animal. It groaned. Blindly, I reached for its head, felt the ridge of thick bone beneath its skin. Cradling its head in my lap, I felt the sharp, thready kick of its pulse beneath my sticky fingers. "Oh God, I'm sorry, I'm so sorry, Jimmy, I'm sorry, I never meant for any of this to happen, I'm so sorry, I should've helped you, I should've . . ."

Something rumbled in the far distance, and I looked up as headlights scythed the darkness. Blinking, I put up one gore-slicked hand against the bluing glare that turned the buck's blood a thick, festering purple. The van halted twenty yards away, engine still running, and then I heard the frantic *ding-ding-ding* as the driver's-side door popped open. A crunch of shoes against asphalt and then a man's voice: "Holy God . . . Cheryl, call the sheriff, get an ambulance out here, hurry!" The swishing sound of grass against pants legs as someone ran for me, and then an oval blur of a face. "Kid, are you okay? Christ, you're bleeding like a stuck pig. You hang on now, we're getting help."

"Call my dad," I said, my voice cracked and wet. The buck moaned. "Call for my dad. He'll take care of it, he won't let it suffer."

"There now, it'll be okay," the man said. He reached an awkward hand to pat my shoulder. "Your head's bleeding bad, kid, I got to put pressure on it . . . here, let go of the deer . . ."

"No," I slurred. Incredibly, I kicked like an exhausted, cranky little kid, only feebly as a glittery pain sparkled in my hip. "No, I have to help, you have to get my dad, call my dad . . ."

"Charlie?" A long shadow drew across the dying buck and me as a woman crossed before the van's headlights. "Sheriff's on his way, and they're sending an ambulance . . . Oh my Lord, look at all that blood."

"He won't let me touch him." Charlie sounded both frustrated and scared. "All he cares about is the damn deer. Keeps saying he wants us to call his dad. Might be a good idea."

"*Hunh.* Probably drinking," said Cheryl, her concern giving way to disapproval. "They'll call from the hospital."

"Doesn't smell like he's been drinking," Charlie said, a new note of uncertainty in his voice.

"Well, then meth maybe. Who can smell anything with all that gas? We're lucky there's no fire. You just leave him alone, Charlie. Let him sit there."

They argued back and forth a while, but I'd stopped listening. I wouldn't let go of the deer either and, eventually, Cheryl stomped off, phone pressed to her ear, asking what was taking the sheriff so long. Charlie gave up trying to get me to let go of the buck. Instead, he shucked out of his jacket, then stripped off his shirt, which he balled against my bleeding forehead. He really was a nice man, and I never got to thank him properly.

So we waited: me, Charlie, the impatient Cheryl. The dying buck I wouldn't, couldn't let go. We all waited, then, for someone to take charge.

And me for my dad—for someone, for *anyone*—to take a gun to that poor dying animal and put it out of its misery.

OCTOBER 28

0030

TO ALL WHOM THIS MAY CONCERN:

Well. There you go. That's pretty much the whole story, right there. Just about. When I look back at all that, I hardly recognize myself.

Maybe two weeks after my wreck, I looked at Jimmy's picture, *Black Hoodie*, again. I still couldn't tell a damn thing. Girl, boy, me, Evie, Pastor John . . . shit. It could even have been Jimmy.

Like the evening Jimmy died, I wasn't sure now what I'd seen, other than flashes and glimpses from which I'd drawn a conclusion based on . . . what? A hope? An inclination? The mind is eager to make connections where none exist; psychiatrists say that the most common form the mind will devise out of random stimuli is the human face. Try it sometime. I dare you. Look hard at clouds or the stippled pattern of crushed limestone and see how many faces you find.

Of one thing I was certain. I was never going to figure out what really happened to Jimmy, what made him get in that Taurus, or why those men—boys, girls—killed him. Was Jimmy gay? Or had he crossed a line with *Black Hoodie* somehow? If that was Evie, that is?

Was either reason—or *any*—enough to justify his murder?

No. If I know nothing else, I know this: Jimmy had problems, and they weren't all his. But none were reason enough for him to have to die, just as there's no excuse for the rumors that might have led to his murder. Rumors kill. You have no idea how quickly. Trust me on this.

And why, oh why, is it so important for me to believe that Black Hoodie was—is—a girl? I don't know. I don't know.

Really, the only thing I know for sure is this: Jimmy was killed, right in front of my eyes—and I never lifted a finger to save him.

The rest was . . . *is* a fantasy, no more substantial than a face glimpsed in a shifting cloud.

Or the ghost of a face swirling in shadow.

———————

Why my parents never asked what I was doing out there, speeding in the dark, I don't know. They just didn't. I saw the questions in their faces, but the only thing I volunteered to the ER doc, who knew me, was I'd decided to go for a drive.

What were they going to say? Anyone can go for a drive, most kids speed and, contrary to Cheryl's prediction, I wasn't drunk. The worst I was guilty of was speeding, and that would just have to satisfy everyone. I decided that would have to be explanation enough.

———————

I never went back to Cuppa Joy. But the cards I kept muffled beneath a mountain of Kleenex. I can't tell you how many times I thought about feeding them to the toilet, but I didn't.

———————

The month rolled by, and then it was mid-December and THE DAY when Yale posted early action decisions online. My mom was working, and Mal had stayed after school for something, so only Dad was home, making sandwiches for third shift. We said hello, and then Dad gestured toward a hunk of leftover roast beef on the cutting board. "Want a sandwich?"

"In a couple minutes, maybe." I went to my room and shut the door. Booted up the computer, logged onto the Yale site, and then typed in my password. Sure enough, there was a message, and I read it over twice before logging off.

Then I went downstairs and had that sandwich. Extra thick. Dad didn't ask, and I didn't say. Knowing Dad, the date probably slipped his mind. At supper, of course, Mom asked if I'd heard anything.

I lied.

The whole next day it snowed, and Brooke said if I thought any harder, the top of my head would blow off.

"Yeah?" I asked. We were sitting on the couch in the senior hallway. It wasn't that kind of sitting together. Just friends. Outside, the snow was blowing sideways in billowing white curtains.

"Yeah. Did you hear?" When I nodded, she said, "You want to talk about it?"

"Not really." I gave a half-shrug and almost smiled. Agent Angela would've been pleased, I figured. If I'd been watching me, I'd have pounced on that gestural slip.

She was quiet a few seconds, and then she said, softly, "I'm sorry. I know you really wanted to get in."

"Yeah," I said—and that was no lie. I really had. I also reflected that people jump to a ton of conclusions with little to no data, even good people like Brooke. People grab a quicksilver hint and use that to convince themselves that nothing is really something.

"So, what do you do now?"

"Oh." As I looked at her, I tried to remember the feeling I'd had with her the night I drove her home; how I thought that maybe there could be something between us. What I hadn't known was that there *was* something there, just not the kind of *between* I'd imagined or wished for. Jimmy's murder was the something, and I thought that it might always be there, a permanent ghost image between me and other people.

"I don't exactly know." I wondered: if there'd been a mirror, would I have caught the way my mouth turned down? Agent

Angela would have, but I knew I wouldn't be seeing her again either. "Wait, I guess. There are always possibilities."

A few minutes later, the bell rang. As we walked down the hall together she said, "Did you ever figure it out?"

I was confused. "Figure out what?"

"What we talked about that night on the glider and then in your truck, after Cassidy Struthers. You said you'd lost your way and hadn't figured out what to do."

The thing was, I did have a nascent idea, but I wasn't exactly sure, so I said, "Not really. It's still pretty confused in my head, like a bad dream you only half-remember when you wake up. The more you try to grab at it, the more it frays."

"So maybe you should write about it," she said. "I keep this diary, and sometimes I don't write more than a sentence or two. Other times, I can go for pages. Just depends on how messed up I feel. So why not write things down? That way, maybe you'll see the connections and find your path."

I told her that was a good idea. I don't know if she believed me or not, but I meant it. Then she went right as I went left, and we returned to our separate lives.

That afternoon after school, the snow stopped. I went for a drive, uncertain where I was going until I actually arrived. Someone had put up an iron gate at the end of the drive, so I parked and slogged up the rest of the way in the fresh-fallen snow. The snow muffled all sound except the whoosh of the wind.

The Langes' house was locked up and dark. A shade

drooped askew in the kitchen window, but the curtains that Jimmy had nearly ruined were gone. The kitchen windows were black as the eyeless sockets of a skull on a bottle of poison.

The barn wasn't locked, and when I pulled open the side door, the smell of hay and old cow manure ballooned out. In the parlor, all the milking machinery was gone and the cement was covered with a fine layer of grit that took my footprints. Someone had emptied the loft, but I climbed up a creaking ladder to the top where Jimmy and I had rested and drunk Orange Crush on a summer's afternoon that was gone like a dream. The paper wasps had been busy since I'd last been up here, and the gray ball of their nest hung silent and sullen on its petiole in the chill. There were young queens hibernating in there, no threat to anyone. I sat and stared at the nest and listened to the silence close in as the queens slept their long dark sleep until I got cold and had to come down.

Dark came on early now, although the glare of town lights against the still-falling snow turned the sky a weird, alien orange. I waited in the truck, with my engine off. I guess I hadn't quite made up my mind until the second I saw the lights in his office go out. A few moments later, a giant in camouflage and heavy boots and parka trotted toward a snow-shrouded SUV.

His back was to me and he was brushing snow from the windshield when I came up. "Sergeant Pfeiffer?" I said.

My mom couldn't stop crying. She kept saying that she didn't understand and how could I throw away my future like this and what about Yale, and then she was tugging on my dad's arm: "If he doesn't show up, that makes the contract null and void, right? He can break it anytime before he's shipped out, isn't that so?"

I finally couldn't bear her tears anymore and went to my room. I was listening to Dad trying to comfort Mom when there was a soft rap at my door. "Come on in, Mal." At the look on my sister's face, I almost laughed. "It's okay, my head's not going to explode," I said. "Sit down."

Mallory perched gingerly on the edge of my bed. "I don't get it," she said, coming right to the point. "Why? What are you doing? Are you trying to get killed?"

Pfeiffer had asked the same thing. He'd been very nice, though completely perplexed. I'd gone to him because he was the only recruiter I knew, and I trusted him, but he wasn't sold on me not going to college. He actually tried talking me out of enlisting altogether: *We don't need people willing to get shot at for the wrong reasons.* Later, I would find out he'd spoken to the Navy people, trying to get my enlistment nullified.

"I just need to get away for a while," I said to Mal. "Figure out what *I* want versus what everyone thinks I should want."

"But the Navy? Why not just work for a couple years?" When I didn't respond, she said, "Is this . . . is this about the accident? Or are you trying to be macho so people will stop thinking you're like Jimmy?" She clapped her hand to her mouth. "I'm sorry. *I* don't think you're like that, and honestly, people aren't talking that much anymore . . ."

"We didn't know Jimmy," I said firmly. "We have no idea

what he was really like or how he felt. Those are all things we assumed about him, just like Mom's done all my assuming for me. Mal, I have to know who I am before I can figure out what I want to do. I can't do that in college right now. I know that sounds dumb."

"Maybe because it is. I don't see how you'll find out who you are if you get blown up." Her face crumpled and her eyes pooled. "I love you, you jerk. I don't want you to *die*."

"Believe me, I'm going to try very hard not to let that happen. Someone has to pony up, though. Someone has to be responsible."

"Why does that someone have to be you? Is this because you didn't get into Yale?"

"How do you know I didn't? I never said one way or the other."

"Well, of course, you couldn't have gotten in, if you're doing this because . . ." Her mouth dropped a smidge, and her eyes widened. "Oh my God. You got *in*?"

I said nothing.

"Well?"

I showed her a thin smile. "I can neither confirm nor deny."

"I can't believe it. You're throwing that away. *Why?*"

A good question, one I've been asking myself for a couple years now. Maybe this will sound completely lame to you, but I guess I came out here to see what I'm really made of. Getting myself exiled to the desert and plunked down in the middle of an endless war is about as elemental as you can get, all this life and death, violence and calm, blood and rock, and endless sky and a land so barren it's as if I've landed on an alien planet, a stranger in an even stranger land. I guess I came here to force myself to run *toward* something for a change. Before Afghanistan, I'd been running all my life: not just from Jimmy but my own thoughts and dreams, who I really was, what I wanted out of life.

So, is this all a delayed guilt trip? My way of atoning? Maybe. But let me tell you a story. Let me tell you what I've learned.

A month ago, I went on a medevac to a village maybe twenty miles from here where a bomb unit had been doing a sweep and got blown up instead. The bomb guys figure that the IED must've been hidden in the middle of the road and then paved over. Like, a while ago. So there was no pressure-trigger, someone had to be right there to trigger it, you understand? Someone hunkered down in a house and watched the Humvees going by and then actually picked out the one he wanted to blow up. Some coward waited and watched and then chose who he wanted to kill that day. There was no heat of battle. This was calculated, cold-blooded murder.

The other reason they suspect that's what happened is because everyone knows it's the lead truck in a convoy you want to avoid being on. The lead's always the most vulnerable position. But it was the third vehicle that went up, the one with the bomb-sniffing dogs. They weren't even going for *us*, for people. They were going for the dogs.

By the time I hopped off the chopper, the driver was already dead. The other guys had dragged two wounded men out of the ditch. Everyone was talking at once, the guys freaking out and saying that they lost one already. From the looks of things, they were about to lose another guy who was really bad, decaying right in front of my eyes, his blood pressure going down the toilet.

So it was chaos, an assault on the senses: the frantic shouts and screams and groans, the rusty stink of superheated blood that you never ever get out of your nose and this black oily smoke. The Humvee was a total loss, just a cratered chunk of smoldering, twisted metal. From the number of pieces, I figured there'd been maybe two dogs, but with a blast that powerful, everything gets vaporized pretty darned quick.

But that's when I noticed another dog, a big German shepherd maybe thirty, forty yards from the drainage ditch where he'd been thrown when the Humvee blew. Burned off some of the fur on his rump, and he had this big gash over his right shoulder that was bleeding like stink and it looked like his left back leg was broken. Yet, despite all that, this bloody, soot-covered dog was dragging itself along with all the strength it had—

But not toward us. The dog was trying to reach what was left of a fender, and that dog was going nuts, barking and whining and carrying on.

And then I saw this guy's hand sticking out from a scorched tangle of metal and flap of rubber tire.

That's when I realized: we'd missed one of the handlers. That dog just wouldn't give up, either—wasn't going anywhere without his handler. Every movement had to hurt that poor animal like hell, and yet it saved that man's life.

After something like that, you got to think: I can at least try to be as good and loyal and brave as that dog. I can try.

At the time all the stuff with Jimmy went down, I did the best I could and knew how. It wasn't near enough, and not remotely close to right. I know there's no going back, no way of making this turn out differently for Jimmy or me. What the truth was about Jimmy, about us, about *me* or *Black Hoodie* . . . whatever the truth *is* . . . I'm no longer certain.

I cared about Jimmy. I might even have loved him. Maybe what I felt was the same as for a brother or sister.

But maybe not. Maybe not.

Maybe those feelings are so gnarly and tangled with everything that happened in between, I can't get an objective read. And forget about figuring out Jimmy: he's dead and gone.

And the dead really are silent, even in memory.

———

Black Hoodie? Girl? Boy? A man? In the persistence of memory, I keep clinging to *girl*. Don't ask me why. I thought I recognized her in Evie. Maybe I had, but maybe not. Take it from someone who knows about ghosts and shadows. The mind's funny that way. The mind lets you see what you want and ignores the rest. I guess you could say I went a little crazy after Jimmy died. Or maybe a lot crazy.

I have no answers.

Which is hell, believe me. Remember: I'm the guy who can be eating breakfast with a buddy and scraping him up with a spatula by dinner, and so you tell me how that makes any kind of sense.

I know you want answers—and, brother, that makes two of us. If this were a book or a movie, you'd be like, *What, how can he not know?* You'd want your money back.

But I don't know. I can't. Maybe that's because I won't let myself. I have memories, but they're all in pieces and so mixed up with what the me I was *then* felt that asking the me I am *now* to put them together is impossible. It would be like trying to repair a Humvee, or a soldier's who been blown all to shit. The Humvee's scrap. The soldier might live, but he'll never look the same, be the same, not only because of the explosion, but also because that marked the moment when his future changed forever. He didn't ask for it, but he can't take his past back, and nothing from that second on will be like anything he could ever have imagined. When he can stand it—when he's gotten his courage up—he will look in the mirror in six months or a year, or ten, and try to square the face he sees with the ghost he was. What he was before will be so alien that trying to look for it—see his true self beneath all the scars—will hurt. It'll drive him crazy. He can't get his old face back, and there's no point in looking any deeper.

And yet . . . and yet Jimmy's murder is the explosion that, like an IED, is powerful and so horrible it generates its own kind of terrible awe. Like trying to stare at the face of God, I guess. You can't stand it. It will kill you. But you can't look away, either, even as looking steals your sight and leaves you, groping, in the dark.

I have looked at this for so long—and I am blind. I'm in the dark. Maybe I always have been. I have worked so hard to see things clearly, to put them in order, to understand how I felt, what I needed. Whether or not I really wanted Jimmy *that way.* Because not everything is fantasy, and what we desire is so much sweeter when we can't have it. Maybe the truth was in that picture of me, that shimmering sleeping boy Jimmy wanted so badly that the looking and the longing made me beautiful when I am anything but.

I know what I have to *do*, but I have no answers. I can't put this puzzle together for *me*, much less for you. I'm sorry, but I can't.

Anyway, my fingers are all cramped up, but I've gotten down what needed saying. The captain's Humvee pulled up about an hour ago, and I got stuff to do.

I said I don't have answers. I don't know what happened to Jimmy. That's true. But writing this all out has helped me see, more clearly, the patterns. Mine, mainly, how I've spent my life like a gerbil, spinning my wheel, following a prescribed path that leads nowhere. When I wasn't doing that, I was running. Even when I joined the military, I was laying down distance between me and what happened. I ran from Brooke—for good reasons; I really did want to protect her, didn't I? But you kind of wonder what would've happened if I hadn't stopped being her friend in the first place.

In school, we called them *decision trees*. Each point branches in a couple different directions, and then the next point after that and so on. Like that hallway in school: what would've happened if we'd gone down the same corridor together?

So, here's what I'm going to do. I'm going to put these in

an envelope and drop that in the mail. I wasn't going to. I was going to slip the envelope into my personal effects. That way, anyone going through my stuff before shipping it back stateside would send it, or my parents would.

But then I'd be off the hook, again, wouldn't I? Because sending this when I'm no longer around to take the heat . . . that's still running.

And I got to tell you: I'm pretty tired of that.

When I began, I wasn't sure to whom I'd address this. I was going to include a list of all the people who've sent things over the past couple years, but the more I've written, the more I've come to realize that these really ought to go to one of two people.

If I could only decide which is the right one.

These letters ought to go to you, Brooke. I'm sorry I didn't write back after the second letter. I told myself that our connection was formed in the transient stew that was high school, and fleeting at that. I ran from what you offered with the best of intentions, and I want you to know that. What I did with Jimmy—or didn't do—was like fresh blood on a crisp, clean, white shirt. After a while, the blood sets, and if you don't work fast, the stain can fade with time, but it will never vanish. That blood remains as a shadow, a ghost of pain and violence that will haunt you forever, like memory. And I couldn't do that to you, Brooke. Not to you.

These letters aren't meant to pull you back in, either. I had my chance. These are my diary, I guess, the one you told me to write to help me see patterns, get my head straight. You were right on that score.

What I wanted you to know is why I never kissed you that night. I hope you know now that it had nothing to do with you. Trust me on this. You care about pigs, for chrissake. You cared about me.

I figure that, now, you've got a pretty good life going. You must be, what, a sophomore in college? Are you going into medicine? I hope so. You'd be a great doctor. But take it from an expert: if the train feels like you're going to pull into the wrong station, get off. Find your own path. Don't let the adults tell you what to do. Well, except me. Okay, I'm not that much older. Still. I've seen a couple two-three things, and let me tell you something: it's a hell of a big world out there.

These letters are to let you go, Brooke. Or maybe they're about me allowing myself to watch you walk one way while I go the other. And that's okay. That's how things have to be.

Keep going, Brooke. Keep going, and don't look back.

———————

But here's the thing.

Agent Thorne? These letters could also go to you. You told me you already knew that I'd lied about something, but that doesn't mean I'm not sorry that I did so. I did what I thought I had to do, and I am more ashamed and sorrier than you can know.

Just . . . go easy on my parents, okay? They didn't know a thing. No need to wreck their lives—or Mal's . . . Jesus, leave her out of this. None of them deserve that.

Enclosed, you'll also find the memory cards. I don't know if they'll help you now. They might. You've probably got cool facial recognition software or something. I'm betting the Penitents are still around, if you think you might want to talk to them. Or Pastor John. But I'm not the special agent; don't let me tell you how to do your job. God knows, I had one chance to be Jimmy's friend—and I blew that. So I'm not one to talk about jobs well done.

I just never knew how to see what was right there in front of me all along, the same way I never took what Brooke offered, not completely, or understood that Jimmy was, in his own halting way, trying to make a human connection, maybe share the secret that so haunted him. Whatever that secret was.

In the end, connections are all we have. They are all the meaning we'll find in this frigging universe. Trust me on this. You know what the wounded need? The touch of your hand. The knowledge that there is someone holding on. They take your hand and they hang on, yes, for dear life, and in that moment, when their fingers close over yours, is the instant you come to life, too. Like that painting by Michelangelo on the Sistine Chapel, when God touches Adam and gives him life. Comforting the wounded and dying is like that. For that moment, you are the center of their universe and you are the *only* real, tangible thing.

The reason is blackness, chaos. Death.

So, everyone, hold on tight while you've got the chance. Hold on.

Anyway. Time to get off this merry-go-round and go volunteer.

Now, there are two ways this can go. Either I won't come back, but it won't matter because the cat'll be out of the bag, the train will have left the station, *hasta la vista, babeee.*

Or maybe a month, two at the most after I get back, my lieutenant will want to see me because he's gotten a very disturbing e-mail from my distraught parents because Brooke—being Brooke—knows what's right.

Or maybe that e-mail will come from a very special agent stateside and there are questions that need answering, ASAP.

What happens after either of those scenarios . . . I don't want to think about that because then I might lose my nerve. I don't think so. After all, I'm sending this to *someone*, right?

———————

Right?

ACKNOWLEDGMENTS

You hold the first YA novel I ever sold. Rediscovering Ben's story is like meeting your best college bud and picking up where you left off. Such a gift. I don't know how Ben's story began or where I got the idea, but it must be the shrinkly part of me, always interested in how we form our notions of who we are and what we're all about. I can't read this, even now, without choking up because I do think that Ben's struggle—his desperate attempts to figure out just who he is and what he believes—are ones every kid knows. Because, really, where does a person begin and his parents leave off? How do you know when you've had an original thought or feeling not predicated on where you came from, what you've been taught, or whom you love and wish to please? As for Ben's story, his town: you think you live in a world where these things can't happen? That adults don't act this way? That a kid can't lose sight of himself—if he even knew whom that person was to begin with?

Guess again. Blame all the years I spent mucking around as a shrink, but I know what I know.

I will never forget—it was a Wednesday in April—when Andrew Karre e-mailed that we really had to talk. As always, Andrew, I am blessed to have such a fearless champion. Here's to many risks, together, in the years to come.

To my agent, Jennifer Laughran, the woman who routinely talks me off the ledge and tolerates my babble: OMG, woman, I am so glad you have my back.

To the entire team at Carolrhoda Lab: thank you for your support and hard work.

To Dean Wesley Smith, whom I can never thank enough for a steady hand and level head.

And, lastly, to my stalwart husband, David, who has yet to eat a cat when I'm on deadline: thank you, darling. Dinner's on me.

ABOUT THE AUTHOR

Ilsa J. Bick is a child psychiatrist, as well as a film scholar, surgeon wannabe, former Air Force major, and award-winning author of dozens of short stories and novels, including the critically-acclaimed *Draw the Dark* and *Ashes*. Ilsa lives with her family and other furry creatures near a Hebrew cemetery in rural Wisconsin. One thing she loves about the neighbors: They are very quiet and only come around for sugar once in a blue moon. Visit her online at www.ilsajbick.com and @ilsajbick.